KILLING GODS

ALETHEA

CALYPSO

HERA

FATES

UNDERWORLD

ELYSIUM

THESE HALLOWED HILLS

TRICK OF FAE

TEST OF FAE

THORNS OF FAE

TWIST OF FAE

TRAITS OF FAE

~ 2 ~

CALYPSO

KILLING GODS II

Quick Quill Publishing

© 2019

This Book is a work of fiction.

All of the characters, organizations, and events portrayed in the novel are either products of the authors imagination or are used fictitiously. Its not about you.

DEDICATION

~ 5 ~

To Jude, Jack, and Gillian you are my dreams come true.

TABLE OF CONTENTS

PROLOGUE

The thrill of change can bring the trauma of evolution.

Pythia

CHAPTER 1

SYDNEY

It's been months, but for me, it happened yesterday.

I should get up and keep living.

The dried crust around my eyes scratch as my eyelids flutter open and close. All my attempts to rub them away, do nothing more than injure the delicate skin.

Smacking my lips together, I move my tongue around in an attempt to collect any moisture remaining in my mouth. If I didn't know better, I'd think people had been dancing on my tongue. The texture resembled the dry green shag carpet from my mother's living room. Every breath freed the odor of a thousand monkeys, poisoning the cabin air. A trail of salty drool has made its way down my chin to my neck. I rub it with the back of my hand, hoping to not scratch my face any further with eye crust.

Rolling into a sitting position, I throw in a big stretch. Boy, was that a mistake. Evidence of my personal neglect drifted up to my nose. Like a fool, I glanced down, getting a full blast of the rank stench created by bacteria from under my arms.

In a word, I was foul. Some homeless people smell better than me. They probably had less fur on their bodies too. I needed to get up but I couldn't.

I'm frozen here.

The thought of moving on without Gabriel caused my chest to clench. The ache radiated out along with blazing heat. My eyes burned as my throat dried again. The golf ball sized lump was always present. I choke on it, making speech impossible.

How do people do this?

This wasn't like it was when Adrian died. Back then, I was younger and had so much less to live for. This time there was no screaming. The numb silence wasn't there for me to drown in.

I missed Adrian and I always will. That ache will never go away, and now, it was only joined by the loss of Gabriel. The pain washed over me, filling and drowning me in despair.

I never saw Adrian's body. I knew he was gone, but still, in the back of my mind, I always hoped he might be alive, however feeble that wish might have been. But, Gabriel was gone and I couldn't even pretend he was alive. I saw him take his last breath, say his final words, smile his last smile for me.

My fist was at my mouth with my teeth sinking into the knuckles. The scream was coming, but the tears didn't. I was dry. The only moisture left was drops of blood from my bite marks. The flavor of warm copper slipped over my tongue and the weight of my pain was just as heavy today as it was yesterday.

The boat shifted. I needed to stop, breathe deeply in through the nose, out through the mouth and remove my hand from my mouth. The tears were long gone and dry eyes were all that was left.

Heavy feet shuffle across the floor of the salon above.

It must be Tristan.

He was shaking his head, causing further shifting of the boat.

< **This needs to stop.** >

< *Shut up voice! It's none of your business.* >

No reply.

The voice felt wrong. He hadn't spoken since Gabe got sick and died. But what was there to say? He couldn't make me feel better?

I should get up.

But instead, I rolled over, pulling my legs into my chest and began chewing on one of my fingernails.

< Get up now, beautiful girl… I mean it. Move! Isolde is in danger. She is about to make a terrible mistake. Stop her! >

< *Where is she?* > I replied, then yawned.

< Get your ass out of bed, Sydney! Your child is about to be... I can't let it happen. >

The force of the Voice's demand propelled me up in a flash. He was filled with terror. It poured into me, turning on like pressurized jet fuel. Without even thinking, I threw on a top and a pair of shorts, calling out.

"Tristan lock it down! We have to get your sister. Now!" I stomped across my side of the boat, shutting hatches.

< Sydney, she's with a guy. I can't get his name. They are 3/4 mile from you. Stop fucking around with your hair. Help our girl. Now! >

I snatch a hair clip and dashed to the back berth pulling and latching hatches in one swift motion as I went. The sounds of the boat closing drifted over from the other hull. I gained the companionway and snatched my purse from the galley shelf. Tristan met me across the salon two seconds later. Our eyes locked.

"Get a cab and tell me everything you know!" I ordered.

He didn't flinch, but instead bolted out the door, his deck shoes slapping on the dock as he ran to the local bar/hotel.

I moved around the salon latching every window and ended back at the door. My eyes swept the saloon. I grabbed the boat keys and stepped out onto the deck, sliding the doors closed, locking them in one swift motion.

The dingy was already up on the davits, but the motor wasn't locked down. I didn't have time to move it to the deck. Yanking the bike cable lock off the bikes, I looped it around the railing and the motor, then crimped the padlock closed. It was the best I could do. They could steal the bikes, I didn't care. But they could not take the motor!

< Sydney, move your ass! run if you have to. If I have to move you, I will! >

< *If you have to move me?* >

The terror was overwhelming and energizing at the same time. Adrenaline moved me at jet speed. I jumped off the boat, clearing the railing on to the dock a full 20 feet away. 200 yards away, Tristan was holding the door of a cab open, beckoning me. There was a click in my physiology and I shifted gears. In the blink of an eye, I was by his side.

The air displacement pushed Tristan's hair back. I expected to see a shock or fear, but instead, he greeted me with relief. Pushing emotions to the side, I stared deep into his baby blues.

"Talk! Where are we going? "

His eyes never left the road as the cab pulled out of the marina parking lot.

"She met him a month ago. His name is Jacques and he's 24. He's been hanging around, flirting ever since," he paused for a breath, drawing his brows together. "Take us to the old pizza place on Christiansted RD, by the pharmacy."

The driver pulled out on to the main street, moving at St Croix speed, 35mph.

< Move faster, Sydney! You only have minutes. >

A vision flashed in front of my eyes.

A sandy blond-haired man looms over Issy. Two other men hid in the back room, waiting for their turn. The man standing over her looks as if he hadn't bathed in a month. He has matted hair, watery brown eyes, sallow skin, and dingy clothing. I'm not sure what Issy saw in him. He must be a very smooth talker because he wasn't great looking.

Reality set in and I realized that I was staring at the back of the taxicab driver's seat, seeing every speck of grime that had ground itself into the headrest. The back seat had duct tape in some places used to cover the holes. We weren't moving fast enough. We weren't going to make it in time to stop them. I glanced over at Tristan. His jaw was clenched and the muscle was working itself over the bone.

<Sydney, you have to move faster! You're not moving fast enough. Our girl is in danger. He will hurt her. Move, damn it! >

< We are moving as fast as we can. I know our girl's in danger, but I can't make the driver go any faster. >

Glancing over at Tristan, I saw his eyes locked straight into the cab driver head. Tristan's fist clenched, making his knuckles white. He turned and glanced at me.

"Mom, she won't listen to me," he growled.

My head whipped over so I could stare at him with my heart hammering in my chest. "What do you mean she won't listen to you?" I whispered.

His brows pulled down, pressing his lips into a firm line.

"She won't listen, Mom. It doesn't matter what I say to her. She says she loves him. She will go through with it, no matter what we do," Tristan slammed his fist into the back of the front bucket seat.

Suddenly, everything slowed in my mind. I wondered how could she knew what we would do?

Tristan replied in a clipped tone. "Because, Mom, I can hear her and she can hear me. I can hear everyone," he finished his sentence scoffing and waving his hands around.

All the blood drained from my head. He could hear everyone. This meant he could hear me. It felt like the world was at a standstill. With my eyes boring into him, Tristan quirked a half smile on one side.

He was just like me, and so was his sister. A flush of relief and terror ran over me. I was not alone.

Re-shifting his focus back to the driver, Tristan's gaze became intent once again. The car jolted with additional force, pushing me back into the seat as we reached a new speed.

I was so focused on arriving, I rocked forward when the driver hit his brakes. We sat in front of an old pizza parlor. There were paper lined at all the windows. Everything around it was filthy and laced with abandonment.

I hopped out of the cab. The odor of urine emanating from the pots was combined with the ones from the dead plants. Tension coiled in my belly. In turn, the door and windows on the storefront rattled, the closer I got. I was not sure if I could control myself long enough to get Issy and not be noticed.

Tristan laid his hand on my shoulder, reassuring me. I turned to him. His face was a study of determination. Then he spoke in my mind.

< I'll hold the door. You do what you need to do and I'll make sure no one out here sees anything. >

I had no idea what Tristan was referring to, 'no one would see,' but I believed he was capable of anything. I didn't reply. I just gave him a nod.

The door swung open at my desire and I found that somewhat surprising. Tristan immediately shut the door behind me. Surveying the filth everywhere with my eyes, I finally land my sight on Issy. She sat on a dirty mattress on the floor. Beer bottles, cans and all kinds of trash littered the room. It reeked of stale cologne and unwashed body odor. Graffiti covered all the walls, including some paper on the windows inside. The interior walls had holes punched in various places, and someone had ripped anything of value out. Exposed electrical wires hung out of several of the outlets. It was a squat.

The fear lined Issy's posture. Her shirt lay on the bed torn. Her bra had been ripped and hung at an odd angle with the underwire stuck out on one side. Her left eye was red and swelling and the skin was covered in black and blue. She sniffled and glanced up at me with wide eyes filled with panic.

I pulled my eyes away from her broken face to stare down at her captors. "Get up and go outside to your brother and get in the taxi! I'll be there in a minute." I ordered Issy.

Jacques shook his hands out and rolled his shoulders, as his face curled up into a sneer. "Well, I don't believe either of you will be leaving. Not till I'm done having my fun with Issy. You look like you might be a good time yourself, Momma." He glanced over his shoulder. "Hey guys, why don't you come and show Momma how we like to have fun?"

Two 20 something Cruzans stepped out from the back. One of them popped his knuckles. I guess he thought it would make him look intimidating.

< Sydney, the knuckle-dragger has a knife in his back pocket. Watch out for him! >

< Don't worry about it. I've got this one under control. >

Amusement colored our connection, melting his worries and fears away.

I wanted to scare the shit out of them, but I wasn't sure if I could stop myself. I'd already seen from Jacques' mind that he had every intention of raping Issy, then sharing her with his friends. With his disgusting mind, he probably thought two-for-the-price-of-one would be a great time.

"Yeah, Momma looks juicy," one of the Cruzans chuckled.

I sneered back at the crowd. "Thank you very much, but I don't think anybody will be having a good time with me today, no matter how juicy I look." I stopped only for a second to make an impression and then continued "Jacques, I'm leaving, and I'm never going to see you three ever again, and neither is Issy. We call it a truce and let it be done."

As I spoke, Issy leaped up, and slipped out the door behind me. I angled my back toward the door to leave, but Jacques took a lame swipe at Issy across the bed.

The door swished shut behind me and I inched my way back to lock my fingers around the handle. Tension was building in my belly, fluttering and pulling to be released and I strained to hold it in check.

< Get in the cab! I'll be right there. > I ordered both kids.

Jacques moved first, twisting his torso to face me. Knuckles and Not-too-bright, his two Cruzan friends, followed as if on cue, in a rehearsed play.

All the tension that had been building in me was finally let loose. My mind heaved the mattress across the room, knocking Jacque and Knuckles against the half wall behind them. They both flopped head over tea kettle to the other side.

When he saw what happened to his friends, Not-too-bright hesitated for a moment, but locked his jaw and kept coming. I turned on him and flashed into his mind. He was filled with desperation. He wanted to prove himself a man. His only desire was to lose his cherry and was willing to rape anyone to do it. I pulled back from his mind, picking up the mattress and smashed his face with it. I didn't stop but kept pushing till I heard an oomph and the sound of flesh crashing into a wall.

They scrambled to move the bulky mattress. My opportunity appeared, and I dashed out the door into the cab.

I held the storefront closed as we went. The lurch of the car came from Tristan forcing the cab drivers' foot into the gas pedal.

I took a glanced at Issy. She had her brother's shirt on, but she couldn't meet my eyes. She carried a haunted and guilty demeanor. I couldn't decide if this was just her lousy judgment or my fault for not being there. Maybe it was both. I should have said more about boys or men, but I didn't know much about men either. I only knew about Gabriel and Adrian.

However, that was wrong because I knew about evil, and how people can and will hurt others for no reason whatsoever.

I'm a fool.

I should've paid more attention, instead of just wallowing in my pain. I'd left them unprotected. When they needed me, neither of them were capable of making the kind of adult decisions necessary at 16.

The cab ride back to the marina was more of the silent treatment, with serpentines every which way to avoid the potholes littering the road. The most annoying thing about St Croix was the roads. It still is the only place in the United

States of America where they drive on the left-hand side of the road. The potholes are so big you can lose a high school gym inside them.

The pounding in my chest didn't slow until we pulled up to the dock. All I could think was 'get on the boat and go'. I've been slacking for five months on autopilot, but now was time to take actions. I was wide awake now and nobody does survival mode better than me.

*****

Tristan was still staring. He was searching for an explanation of some kind, but any and all answers would have to wait till we're underway. My gut told me we shouldn't stay here not even five more minutes, so I turned on full captain mode.

"Tristan, check the diesel. We're leaving! Issy, come with me into the galley. We need to check our stores," I ordered while working the key into the lock and sliding the door open.

In the saloon, I wrapped my arms around Issy's shaking body and listened to her quivering breath, while still, warm tears moistened my shirt. Shuttering moved from her to me with the soft shifting of the boat rocking us as her arms continue to grasp at me until she finally broke away. I cupped her face with my hands checking her appearance. The ring around her pupils had darkened.

I rubbed my thumbs across her cheeks. "I know things have changed a lot in the last six months. Between daddy gone and you and your brother coming into your abilities, things are pretty scary."

She didn't answer, but both of us nodded our heads to each other and I continued, " I wish the two of you would have trusted me, or I had trusted you sooner. Whatever happened in that room before I got there, it has changed you. There's no going back from that. You can either choose to run away from it as I did, or you can embrace who and what you really are." I said trying to give her my most reassuring smile.

Issy broke eye contact with me to gaze at the floor. I knew I had to continue.

"Don't be like me. I've spent half of my life running away from myself and what I am and trust me. It doesn't work that way. I love you!" I pulled her back into my arms and kissed the top of her head. "Right now, we need to work together to keep each other safe. That man, Jacques, is evil. We need to get everything together and get out of here. Do you understand?" I implored, shifting my gaze from one eye to the other.

She bobbed her head again. Desperate urgency was pressing on me. No matter how fast we moved, we weren't moving fast enough.

I opened the freezer and pulled out a steak, covering it with a kitchen towel. I placed it in her hand and together we covered her swollen eye with it.

She sputtered. "I feel like such a fool. I didn't realize what he was until he kissed me. I saw every evil thing he'd ever done. It filled my mind. I will never get over the images." A sob broke from her mouth and she reached up with her hand to stifle it, swallowed and continued. "All those women he'd hurt. I can't get it out of my mind ever. Is that what you mean by ability?" She was sniffling and rubbing her hand over her nose.

I was taken aback. I didn't think what she was capable of. I certainly wasn't capable of that. To see the life of a person by merely touching them. How do you ever want to touch somebody again?

Swallowing back my own fears, I cleared my face and mind. "Yes, it is an ability. I know it doesn't feel special or even great, but it makes you special and different." I repeated the same words the voice said to me, the words Mary my biological mother used to describe herself.

I didn't know what else to say, so I started echoing the words, the voice had used on me many years ago. "People fear what they don't understand. Can you imagine how a government or a private individual might try to use you if they knew you had the ability to see everything someone had ever done simply by touching them?" Searching for answers, I glanced out the side windows and spied Tristan heading back our way. "Talk to your brother and me all you want, but don't ever tell even one other person ever."

I ensnared her eyes with my own and stared hard and deep. She bit her lip and bobbed her head in understanding.

"Did Daddy know about you?" she asked then pressed the frozen steak to hie face.

"No, I never told Daddy. He didn't need to know. It wasn't important to our relationship. It'll just be something you have to keep to yourself. Look at it this way, if your boyfriend ever cheats on you, you'll know," I put on a tight smile.

She wasn't all that amused. I didn't blame her. Touching someone who's a good, kind person and seeing their whole life isn't a terrible thing. But Jacques was one of the evil people. One of those people who've spent their entire lives doing terrible things to others with no remorse.

Rubbing my hands up and down her arms, I continued. "Right now, I need you to do a complete inventory of our food stores. We can't put to sea with nothing in our pantry. I don't want to dip into the emergency supplies for any reason. Don't worry about the fresh stuff. If we can at least get to St. Thomas tonight we can buy fresh in the morning and be on our way from there, okay?"

She shook her head in understanding, moved to open cupboards and pulled out the checklist.

I had to keep her mind busy. As long as she had something to do to distract her, it would make getting over of what just happened easier. Time heals all wounds or at least dulls the pain. Taking my own advice, I started checking the boat over, I opened every locker and gave the workshop a once over.

Tristan stuck his head in the workshop door with his face set in a grim line. "You will not like this, but we have maybe fifteen gallons of diesel. I don't even know if that's enough to get us out of the Marina."

God damn it! Well, I really screwed the pooch on this one, didn't I?

"Nope, that won't get us out of the Marina." I glanced down at the watch on my wrist. It read 4:30. The Marina pumps were closed for the day and they wouldn't reopen until 5 am.

"Grab a couple of our tanks and go around to see who's got diesel. See if they'll sell you a couple of gallons. We need at least 25. That'll get us out of the Marina and give us a little space for maneuverability. If we leave the boat on the hook in Saint Thomas, we can ferry the gas cans over for a refill there," I huffed then ran my hands over my hair.

Tristan grabbed two 5-gallon cans and left to walk the docks. I didn't really think he was going to get that much. Cruzans are usually pretty cool, but this Marina had a lot of long-term locals. I had not found St. Croix to be a friendly Island. Everyone was suspicious or shady.

My gut told me we wouldn't be leaving till morning.

*****

The vision of the map fascinated and haunted me. Even though I was desperate for Gabriel, I couldn't get that map out of my head. Laying here for months on end, I kept seeing it every time I closed my eyes. It was like a movie that kept replaying, stuck on a loop.

How do you find a map like that? I didn't know. I hadn't even looked on Google Maps. With the technology from today, I should have been able to find an island like that pretty quickly, I guess. Google Earth, maybe? I didn't have any latitude or longitude but finding an almost perfectly round Island couldn't be all that hard on planet Earth with all the satellites we have floating around in the sky.

Every time I thought about it, my body filled with anticipation. I had to, I needed to do it. I didn't believe in destiny, karma or fate. I didn't believe in God, but in the marrow of my bones, I knew every moment of my life had been leading up to this. It was something I had to do, find, see. I couldn't let it go. I couldn't turn away. No matter what I did, it was going to be there, and I had to do it. All I needed to do now was to figure out what "It" was and if "It" was real.

At least now, I know that I'm not crazy.

How could I be? Both of my children had the same strange abilities I did. If I was mad, would that be true?

Tristan and Isolde had abilities I didn't possess. How was that possible? Issy's ability was the most frightening one I had ever heard of. How do you live your whole life without touching another person? Or maybe it was like my abilities. You could choose. You could turn it on and off. I didn't know how it worked. I was a fooling bumbling around in the dark.

CHAPTER 2

SYDNEY

The dream had shifted. The blue of the sky moved through my mind on fast forward. When I examined the mountain, the distinctive edges that formed an outline of a pyramid were apparent.

As I pulled back into the sky for the overall view, everything turned into the map. I wasn't sure if it was made from vellum or parchment. The edges were ragged with age and were yellowish browns. The ancient paper had the dry, cracked look, like the skin of an old woman. The legend appeared to have been drawn with a ragged straight edge.

Everything was in Spanish with the scrolling loops and curls of the 1400s. In the bottom right-hand corner, there were words and numbers, but the focus of the dream shifted too fast for me to read it.

The island itself came sharply into view. It was round, unnaturally so. Rings of water channels encircled the pyramid and all of them were interconnected by bridges. Everything was in perfect balance and symmetrical in every way. Near the edge of the beach-circle was a fountain and above it, the cartographer had placed an infinity symbol. The Outer Circle appeared to have a portion that broke away, opening up like arms to welcome you into the various channels. The drawing showed what seemed to be some kind of hinging mechanism, or at least I guess. It was hard to see, and the vision was pulling me back again. The words were Juan Ponce de Leon, Isla Del Calypso with the date July 22nd, 1497. Everything about the map screamed age. There was more writing but I couldn't make it out because the dreams moved so fast. I could never catch up and look at anything.

*****

I was awake. There was shuffling on the deck along with whispering. It was Jacques and his two Cruzan friends. I'd locked the salon door, but we usually slept with our hatch windows open. I knew that I had left the one in my office open, but I didn't remember whether we closed the ones in the salon.

Jacques instructed his friends, "We should take out the boy first," as if he thought Tristan was the biggest threat. What a chauvinist pig. Only a stupid man wouldn't realize the mother is the more significant threat.

I slid out of my bunk, reached down, and took my socks off. The last thing I wanted to do was to slip and slide across the floor. I was grateful I had worn clothes to bed. I crept slowly down the gangway, keeping my eye on the office cabin. All the sound filtering through me said they were coming in through one of the windows in the salon.

< **Mom they're trying to get in. What do we do?** > Tristian asked.

< *Go to your sister! Stay with her and make sure your hatches are closed. Do it quietly.* > I replied.

Creeping to the gangway, I crouched to the side, trying to control my breathing. I felt the tension growing in my belly. I knew this feeling, and I needed to get control of it as soon as possible. I took a deep breath, inhaling through the mouth, exhaling through the nose.

Jacques was the first one inside. I was actually surprised that the bastard didn't send one of his lackeys. For all he knew, I could have had a gun and blow his head off. It was not like they really checked the boat when we pulled in. I could have had a weapon hidden anywhere. But I didn't have a gun. I never felt like I needed to have one. I had me.

He was heading towards Tristan and Isolde's companionway. I used my abilities to close all the other hatches, locking them down. Now, it was just Jacques on the inside with no way out. Then, I mentally tilted the boat to the side causing both his friends to fall overboard. All I heard where the screams and the splashing.

I turned at the corner and mounted the steps of my companionway, my eyes drilling into the back of Jacques' head. Tristan appeared out of thin air, right in front of Jacques. He yelped in surprise.

The saloon was suddenly awash in light. Issy was standing at the top of her companionway in her pajamas, holding a knife in one hand. She was staring intently at him as if she was hoping that he would die just from her glare.

Tristan filled with indignant anger and used his mind to push Jacques. He disappeared for a blink of an eye then he was back. Jacques slumped down to the floor.

"What should we do with him?" Tristan growled out wearing nothing more than a pair of shorts.

I was inclined to just throw him overboard with his friends, but I said: "Let's put him in the drink, then get the hell out of here."

That's when it dawned on me that Jacques wasn't talking or moving. I couldn't even hear him breathing.

"Tristan, can you hear him?" I whispered.

Oh, God! My hand flew to my mouth.

"No, Mom. I don't hear anything." Tristian's voice quivered.

I didn't want to go over and touch the body. I didn't want to see what had happened, but I was at Jacques side in two steps. He wasn't breathing. Crouching down I put my fingers to his neck. His body was freezing. His head sat there, rigid with the cold.

Awe fuck! He's dead.

My mind began to churn, as my plan formulated. I rubbed my hand across my forehead and down the side of my face. Then I moved. I struggled to pull the shirt off Jacques body and his shoes. I handed them to Tristan. He must have heard what I thought because he changed the look on his face. Jacques had a hat he always wore. I grabbed it off the floor and stuffed it on Tristan's head.

"Both of you, go on deck! Argue for a few minutes. Be loud. I want someone to hear and see you. In the early morning light, they shouldn't be able to tell who exactly it is but will assume it's Issy and Jacques. Tristan, after she pushes you in the water, I want you to thrash around and call her a bitch, whore, cunt, anything else you can think of. Swim to the dock and get out of the water. Walk down the roadways and keep yelling as you go." I instructed.

The adrenaline was really pumping in me now, and the tension in my belly was building. I needed to keep it under control. I continued to give instructions.

"I don't know how you got to the saloon so fast, but you need to get back here the same way, without being seen," I ordered.

He looked terrified and green. I put my hand gently on the side of his face "Tristan, I know it was a mistake, but if you don't focus now on what I am saying, it will get a whole lot worse."

He numbly nodded his head, took a couple of deep breaths, and stood up taller. I turned my focus on Issy.

"Issy, after you push him in the water, yell something about how sick he is and say his name. You need to be loud. I want everyone to think he got off this boat alive. Say his name as many times as you can. Then, I'll come up on deck, and we lash everything down. We're putting to sea as soon as your brother returns."

This could work. I was sure of it. There was just barely enough light and it was getting brighter. If the kids did their part quickly, the dark should cover them just enough for it to work, while we leave in the early morning dawn.

< You need to weigh the body down once you're out to sea. >

< *Not really. I just need to drop him in the right spot and the ocean will take care of him. Out in the open ocean, fish food doesn't last long. Dead men tell no tales.* >

I didn't know how Tristan has done whatever he did to Jacques. One minute he was standing here, then he was gone, and suddenly he was back again as cold as an ice packed meat locker. Whatever Tristan did, it appeared that he was able to move himself and other objects, not just through space, but also through time. Was it some kind of teleportation? Was it a beam me up, Scotty? I could move things from one side of the room to the other and I could shift objects around. I think they call it telekinesis. But what Tristan could do, that was a whole other level of crazy strange.

I heard Issy yelling, "How dare you come here like this, Jacques? This is my home. You can't just sneak in, and act like everything is ok." She was quite convincing.

Then, it was Tristan's turn to play his part, "You said, 'I wish you could come over sometime and be with me.' You're just a cock tease, you fucking bitch. You are just another dirty whore."

I bit my lip, I had no idea my kids even knew what a cock tease was.

"Fuck you, Jacques! I never said you could come over here and try to fuck me, you filthy bastard. I hate you! Get the fuck off my boat!" Issy screamed just before Tristan yelled out, followed by a splash.

He did some pretty good thrashing around in the water. I heard him holler, "You fucking crazy bitch."

I poked my head out of the saloon and came out onto the main deck. Issy was standing there laughing. "You stupid Cruzan. I don't know why you ever thought you could get into my panties. Get the fuck out of here, loser! Don't ever come back!"

She was really getting into it. I mean she was screaming so loud her voice sounded hoarse. I saw the lights pop on in several other boats.

He shouted something unintelligible, we could barely hear. I nudged Issy, I wanted her to say his name one more time. "Eat shit and die, Jacques!"

I whispered to her, "That's good. You don't need to say anymore. You can grumble a few times to me if you want."

She nodded her head in understanding. There were tears in her eyes. "It is all my fault," she whimpered.

Hearing her say that, cut me to the quick. I reached out to hug her, but she waved me away. I watched her retreat to the bow of the boat, to tie down kayaks.

I moved to the stern of the boat, and I called out rather loudly, "We're getting out of here. I'm not staying on this shit hole island one minute longer."

I hoisted the engine off of the dinghy, and onto the lockdown rail. I rechecked the lines on the dinghy davits. I didn't want to lose our only other boat. Also, I took all the folding bikes down below and put them in the storage room.

Looking around the deck, I noticed there were a ton of loose items lying all over the place. I got a mesh bag, and literally just started shoving shit in it. I didn't care what it was or where it belonged. None of that mattered at the time. We could figure that out wherever we landed or while we were at sea. We needed to go as soon as possible and I couldn't have it flying all over the place.

Issy gathered up all the cushions and lounging pads and shoved them into a watertight locker on deck, then we clipped the front transparent Bimini walls on because there was no sense getting wet on the passage if we didn't need to.

Tristan had managed to finagle eight additional gallons of diesel the night before. We had a total of 23. This was enough to maneuver out of the Marina and pass the reefs. Once we hit the open ocean, it was no big deal. Out there it would be smooth sailing. We just had to pick our course and decide how to get from point A to point B. Then, we only had to worry about maneuvering in St. Thomas. If need be, I could always send Tristan over with the dinghy just to be safe.

I turned the engines over and listened to how they rumbled. They both sounded good and clean.

"Isolde, cast off! We're out of here."

She opened her mouth as if she was going to say something but then froze. She kind of stared off into the distance for a minute, closed her mouth, and untied the line.

All the curtains in the saloon closed at once. I didn't want to run the risk of anybody seeing what was laying on the floor of the galley.

Issy informed me that we had enough food for about four days. It was a one-day passage to St. Thomas, and I wasn't going to eat anything for a while. At least not until the dead guy was off the galley floor.

< Don't worry, beautiful girl. It'll work out. > Voice reassured me.

< *What if someone catches us? What if someone saw it was Tristan and not Jacques?* >

I had to swing the boat around because we were facing the wrong direction. Green Key Marina was a tricky marina to get in and out of. The entrance had a narrow channel that was curved at the end. It was the best place to park a boat if there was a hurricane because it was so well protected. Once you were out of the channel, you were pretty much home free because the water was open and deep.

I got in. That means I can get us out as well.

We entered the channel, and Tristan appeared next to me. I screamed. It felt like I'd just jumped right out of my skin. He had a grave look on his face.

"What are we going to do with his body?" He asked and trailed his red eyes over the dead body in the saloon.

I couldn't tear my eyes away from the water and the rocks lining the channel.

"What do you think? We're going to send him to Davy Jones Locker. Let Davy sort him out. I'm sure all of Davy's little fish friends will find a use for him." I remarked in a sharper tone than I meant.

A puff of air blew over my head.

"I don't know what I did at that moment. I know, I wanted him dead. But I also wanted him to go away. What does that mean?" Tristian inquired in a tight voice.

How do you give someone answers when you don't have them yourself? "I think it means that you have the ability to send somebody somewhere where they die. I think if we want to figure out where that is, we might be better off making a video. We'll just have to find a sacrificial camera to do it with and I don't want to try it out on another living soul till then." I replied in a matter of fact way.

I needed to concentrate, and Tristan was just a distraction, but brushing him off wasn't what he needed. The boat shifted to the left. I could feel my power rising. If we drifted too much further, we were going to have a really bad day.

"Tristan, look, I don't have all the answers. I still haven't figured out how my abilities work. This is something we're all going to have to work on together. We're going to have to help each other. Right now, I need you to get up on the bow and make sure that I don't accidentally drift into a reef because until we're out of here, I need to focus on our safety. Priority number one is dumping that body where no one's ever going to find it." I turned and gave him a side glance.

He shook his head, lowered his eyes, slumped his shoulders, and went to watch our depth. Not that we didn't have the depth finder because we did, but sometimes relying on your eyes and not your technology is a better idea. I mean what if the boat gets struck by lightning and nothing works. What do you do then?

'Argg you be doing it the old-fashioned way, matey.

I used my mind to push the boat back into the center of the channel. As soon as we reached the open ocean and deep water, I raised the mainsail because we weren't going to drift into anything dangerous out here. We had a good 30 minutes of free sailing, so I focused my attention on Tristan.

"All right, Tristan. You need to figure out how it is that you move stuff. Don't get me wrong. If you want this body off the boat, I can do it because I've had more practice than you. But I want you to do it. All you've got to do is pick him up with your mind, then move him into the water outside the boat." I urged in a soft voice to ease his fears.

Issy had gone below as soon as we'd left the marina, but Tristan had just been sitting up on deck watching me. Maybe he was hoping it was going to be some magical, mystical answer that I was going to come up with that would solve everything.

"I'm not sure I can do it, Mom. I mean, I know how I put myself on the boat and how I put myself in the saloon. I just wanted to be there, and I was." He remarked and tossed a free line onto the deck table aimlessly.

He still had a childish look in his eyes and that exact look made me more aware of the role I was playing in his life. I was his and Issy's mother and I needed to teach them everything I could about life. And in our case, life was not normal.

"Okay, so there's your answer. You have to want it. It has to be intentional." I had never shown either of them what I could truly do but I guess now was the best time.

My eyes raked over Tristan and they settled on his wrist. I put my hand out, and his watch came right off his wrist and landed in my hand. He jumped about three feet out of his seat.

"Holy shit! You did that, Mom?" he rubbed the wrist where the watch had been.

"Yes, Tristan, I did that. I could probably move this whole boat if I wanted to. I can only move things through space. Like from one side of the room to the other but you see it move. You are shifting things through space and time instantaneously. You're saying you just wanted to be on the boat and suddenly you were. Why don't you do something in the reverse? You want Jacques in the water and suddenly he will be there. But keep in mind that you have to want it." I said. The logic of the mechanics made the most sense that way.

Tristan turned away from me, staring off into the horizon, sitting deathly still. He took a deep breath, closing his eyes. He straightened his shoulders and came to some kind of inner resolve. The surrounding electricity changed and the pressure in the air intensified. I felt a pop and looked at him. He slumped, shook his head and opened his eyes.

I leaned over in the captain's chair to get a look at the galley. The floor was empty and Jacques was gone. Tristan had done it. I wanted to jump up and run to him, but no matter how many hugs and kisses I gave him, it was never going to change the fact that we had just dumped a body. The child like look in his eyes died with his actions. He wasn't a baby anymore.

CHAPTER 3

HERA

Log entry

I have dispensed with my old name because I have no use for it anymore. Herathina was a Themian child. The shedding of my old self has freed me to make hard and necessary choices. If I followed my Themian education, my children would die. If I accepted this new paradigm they would live. As Herathina I was childless and part of the Themian collective. As Hera, I was a mother, a Goddess and a force for good, free to make my own way in the Universe. In truth, there was only one choice. Poseidon made it, and so shall I.

I vacillated whether to stay here and have my children or leave. Let none be the wiser. If I left the twins with Jorhan,

Zeus would be unaware of their existence. They would be hybrids, but none would know of it, but the risk was too significant. I was not sure what I should do. I feared for them. With every passing day, the danger grew along with my belly.

My decision changed from moment to moment. I would go to Jordan's village and give birth in secret there. I would leave both children with him, then return. In a few months, he would bring them to me, informing me that their mother was dead, and he had no woman to care for them. I would adopt them, taking them as my own.

It was a good plan. It could work. Only Jorhan needed to know the truth. I knew he would never betray me. His mind was locked. We would be safe.

CHAPTER 4

SYDNEY

After getting rid of Jacques, I had to take a few minutes in my cabin to get it together. I felt like I was going to lose whatever I had in my belly and what I had was just bile. I looked at my face in the mirror until I knew nothing was going to come out. However, I grabbed a hair clip and pulled my hair back anyway. No one wants to try and wash the puke out of the hair on a boat. When the feeling finally subsided. Issy was on the other side of the boat throwing up.

Poor baby.

I finally took a moment to look around, and everything outside was gray. The sky couldn't decide if it wanted to be clear or turn into a storm. The ocean had lost its turquoise hue. Instead, it sported slate with all the cold that goes with it. The wind didn't have its usual cooling kiss, it was hot and cutting. Everything surrounding us were a perfect reflection of our feeling.

We spent most of the passage in silence. I tried to speak to the kids, but they just weren't ready. As we pulled into the bay near Charlotte Amalie, St. Thomas, Issy opened the floodgates.

"Did Daddy know?" she demanded, standing with her hands on her hips. The only thing missing was a tapping toe.

"As I told you earlier, no. He never knew. I have never told anyone but you two." I let that hang in the air. They needed to understand how important this was.

She shot back: "What about that voice in your head? You never told him?"

Quirking an eyebrow, I leveled my gaze at her. "Now isn't that a silly question? I didn't need to tell Daddy this. Also, the voice advised me not to. He has his own abilities to hide." I said.

She sat down while leaning forward, eager for more information. "Who is he and why do you keep calling him Voice? That's stupid. You couldn't think of a better name?"

< It is the only name I need at this time.>

< *It is silly.* > I remarked.

"He says he doesn't need another name. Look, if I knew his name, I would use it, but I don't. What else do you want to know?"

Tristan poked his head out of the companionway. "Are we talking? Cause I had a few things, I want to say too." He came and flopped down in the nearest seat around the table.

Good, this is good. We can move forward from here.

Tristan was hunching and scowling. His clear blue eyes bore into mine with a painful force. I took the visual beating until he sat up straight and placed his hand in his lap.

"Are you going to tells us about the Island and the map?" He demanded then crossed his arms.

My mouth went dry.

Oh, God!

< Tell them everything you know. Don't hold back, beautiful girl. He will know if you do and they need answers.> Voice ordered.

< But I don't have all the answers! > I retorted.

< Give them everything you have.>

"It started right after I got my abilities. The dream of the island with the big blue sky. My father used to beat me, and after most of the beatings, I would have the dream and I could do things. Then, after your Daddy died, it changed. The dream ran through on fast forward to the map. I didn't think the island was real. But the map – that looks real." I finished with my hand spread out on the table.

They were both listening in earnest now. Issy's eyes grew to the size of saucers, and Tristan's forehead was pinched in concentration.

"I began to hear the voice at about the same time. It wasn't always clear, and mostly it scared the crap out of me. When he really began conversing with me, I was worried I'd lost my mind. He told me things that no one could know. Not even me. Over time I accepted that he was real and not in my head." I gulped to wet my tongue.

Tristan opened his mouth, snapped it shut and scratched his chin. "What are your abilities?"

"I can hear the voice and if you ask me a question, I will always know the truth. If you have lost something and ask me about it, I can find it. Also, I can move objects with my mind." My water bottle snapped into my hand, as a washcloth wiped the table off.

Issy was in awe. "Wow, you can clean house without moving. It's like that old show 'Bewitched', Tristan. The main character always used magic to clean her house."

I smiled and continued. "I get visions sometimes from people, like a movie playing in my mind. I can see what they see, feel what they feel, think about what they think. All I have to do is look in their eyes, and it happens. Now that I have control, it is easy to turn on and off, and I don't have to look into their eyes anymore." I was rambling a bit. I had never talked about it, so finding the right words was not easy. But they poured out faster and faster the longer I talked.

"Mom, you don't have to say anymore if you don't want to, but I want us to talk about the map," Tristan calmly stated.

The pressing feelings rose in my mind and with it an uncontrollable desire to go there, wherever there was.

Without even realizing I groaned: "We have to find that island. I think that map will lead us there. I can't get the picture out of my mind. Every time I close my eyes, it's there."

"I think we should look it up online when we get to St. Thomas," Tristan suggested.

Relief washed over me. They were on board. I didn't have to be the only one looking for it.

Issy smiled and added, "We are close to a place where it could be. Maybe Jamaica or Hispaniola? Juan Ponce De Leon was there and was Governor of Dominican Republic and Puerto Rico. He might have left something behind at a museum or something. You never know, and we have to go by it if we want to get to 'La Florida'".

Tristan and I were both floored. Issy had never been an academic. I didn't even know she could spout facts. That was usually my thing. "You are right. He discovered 'La Florida'. I had forgotten that."

Issy smiled, stretching her arms out to her knees and pointing her toes. It was her cutesy move. She did it whenever she was pleased with herself.

"So that's our plan. Hit the diesel station, load up on supplies, check the weather and head to Puerto Rico?"

"In a nutshell, Tristan, yes. Issy are we missing anything?" I asked.

She shook her head.

We had to drop anchor in the outer edges of the bay to Charlotte Amalie and I send Tristan to get fuel. I was on pins and needles over the diesel. We glided in on fumes. The idea of floating into a crowded bay with nothing but a sail and an anchor to stop was too crazy for me. I didn't want to use my ability to save us. It was too foolhardy for me.

Issy went with him to shop. Now, that we no longer needed cellphones, I didn't have to worry about keeping in touch. Tristan would inform me of any issues or changes of plans. I had given him all five diesel cans and three gas cans. The only problem could be the weight on the dingy.

< *Tristan, if it looks like you can't make it with all of the cans, move a few when you can. I'll lash them down as they arrive.* >

< **Right. Oh, Mom, I might move them anyway for the practice.**>

< Don't get cocky, kid! If you put them at the bottom of the ocean we will just have to buy a few more cans and start over. Savvy? >

There was a moment of silence and then Tristan responded.

< Yeah, I can do it. I'll just do one, k? >

Teenagers!

I took a deep breath and agreed with him. *< Okay. One wouldn't kill us, or so I think. >*

He had to have felt the joshing I was giving him through our connection loud and clear.

Sitting on the boat, I was finally alone with my thoughts. I still had an ear out for the kids, but for the most part, I was alone. I felt the desolation of Gabriel's lost threatening to sweep back in. I had to put this behind me somehow because I couldn't let the crushing feeling of my missing heart get us all killed. Gabriel wouldn't have wanted that. He wanted us to live and be happy, but I just couldn't stop thinking about how he spent all those years in pain, never telling us.

< Let it go, Sydney. He lived exactly the way he wanted to. He died that way too. He wanted to love and be loved, and

you gave him that. He wanted to be with his children, and you gave him that too. You found love before, you can do it again.>

< That's easy for you to say. All you have to do is sit and watch. You don't have to do the living. >

< That's ungracious of you. You're a better person than that, so don't lash out at me. I'm only here talking to you because I love you. I have always loved you, and I will always love you. You know you are never alone. >-

< I know, I'm sorry. I love you too. I just feel like everyone I love gets ripped away from me. At least with Gabe, we had a good long time. Just didn't seem like enough time and you're right, Gabriel did everything he wanted to do. >

I had to get a grip. Me having a breakdown or a pity party every time the kids weren't around was not going to help our situation or plans. I wasn't sure that any amount of time was ever going to be enough to stop grieving for Gabriel. At least this time I had a body. It was not like what happened with Adrian. When you can't see a body you just don't get any closure. Adrian still brought on a crippling pain in my heart. I loved him and that would never change.

It was different than Gabe. I was aware of the saying 'time heals all wounds', but I didn't think time heals anything. It just dulls the pain. If you keep yourself busy long enough, eventually there will be enough space between you and the initial pain. At this point, it didn't matter whether I was in pain or not. I couldn't shut down and I couldn't go on autopilot. Not anymore. Isolde and Tristan needed me too much.

I turned the computer on. Maybe somebody was bouncing some Wi-Fi around out there. Don't get me wrong, I could have turned on the SAT phone and pull in Wi-Fi that way, but it was expensive, and I didn't see a reason to spend that kind of money for this kind of research.

There were about 3 different weak signals running around out there, so I picked the best one and jumped on.

My first query was 'Juan Ponce de Leon Maps' and I soon realized it was a big waste of time. Most of what came up were Wikipedia crap and a couple of maps for the various suspected routes that he sailed to find central America.

I didn't expect to find the answer right away so I made my second query 'Juan Ponce de Leon June 22nd, 1497'. From first glance, it appeared to be a more successful search than the previous one. Apparently, from 1495 to 1500, there was really no record of where he was or what he was doing. Every source said that he got sick and lost a hand.

And after this mysterious period, he suddenly did a bunch of cool stuff. Starting with 1500 he became the governor of a couple of different places, built a couple of houses, found gold in Puerto Rico, and subjugated a bunch of the Carib Indian. After all these, the Spanish Crown financed his explorations with three ships and he managed to discover 'La Florida'. He then returned to Hispaniola, Puerto Rico, where everything was in chaos, but he took care of business there. After solving the problems, he went back to Florida where he was shot with an arrow and died of an infection, being buried in Havana, Cuba in 1559.

It appeared that the most interesting thing about Ponce de Leon is that he was supposed to been looking for the Fountain of Youth.

The map in my vision has a fountain on it.

I started to get excited so I did my third query that was 'Fountain of Youth'. This brought up a bunch of stuff about some Park in Florida which supposedly had the Fountain of Youth. Obviously, it wasn't the real deal, or everybody would be flocking to it regularly. It would be the most populated place on the planet and the most heavily guarded place on Earth, so I pretty much sifted through all of that pretty quick, moving on to more exciting stuff.

All of the Carib Indians claimed that the Fountain of Youth was in Bimini, so Ponce de Leon ran off to go look for Bimini. Now considering that Ponce de Leon murdered thousands of Caribs Indians in Hispaniola, Puerto Rico and the Dominican Republic, it could very well be that these people sent him on a wild goose chase, to stop him from killing them. But that begged the question if my dream was real.

His name was on the map I kept dreaming about, along with a date from the period there is no record about him. Maybe, he went looking for the Fountain of Youth while everybody else was off building the colony. I mean, I guess he did. I couldn't know if Columbus kept all his ships. The only thing that wasn't clear to me was why did he go looking for it again if he already knew where it was and had a map of it?

Come on, brain! Don't fail me now!

As I was struggling to find a good query, I Googled 'what's off the coast of Bimini', but didn't have any high expectations. Suddenly, all the hair on the back of my neck stood up as I read the search engine page. It talked about a lot of mineral deposits, limestone and diamonds. But one of the returns said something about the Bimini Road, claiming that a massive stone walkway under the water might have been one of the lost roads to Atlantis.

Atlantis supposed to be one of the possible locations for the Fountain of Youth. If the Carib Indians were telling the truth, then they were trying to send him not to Bimini but to Atlantis. Maybe the names got mixed up.

My heart was going insane. I could feel the shifting of the water underneath the boat. No matter how many times I smacked my lips together, I just couldn't seem to moisten the inside of my mouth. I had to pull myself up straight. Suddenly, I felt like the computer just didn't have enough screens for me to see everything I wanted to read. I must have had 20 different pages opened, and I couldn't read them fast enough. My eyes scratched against the inside of my lids. It was as if every drop of moisture in my body had suddenly been wicked away.

After reading as much as I could, I finally entered the query I knew was going to give me some answers - 'Atlantis Fountain of Youth'. The first thing that I saw on the page was an image an artist's rendition of what Atlantis was supposed to look like. It was based upon a description given by Socrates during a speech by Plato.

It's all about the he said, she said bullshit.

I shook my head again and I managed to concentrate on the important aspects. The Socrates - Plato part was not the one that I found to be most interesting. It was the circle within circles. At the center stood a pyramid and at the base of the pyramid, a Greek-style temple with a massive statue of Poseidon holding a trident aloft. There was a chariot being pulled by horses, water flowing from the base of the Temple into the circular channels surrounding the pyramid.

< Don't take the bait. It's a diversion. > the voice stated.

< What is? >

< Atlantis and the Fountain of Youth. Follow the map! That will give you what you are looking for.>

I could feel the wall in his mind. All the probing in the world wouldn't move it.

Why don't you tell me everything?

< You're holding back. >

< I have told you as much as I can. Follow the map! The rest is a fool's errand. >

If Atlantis was the diversion and I was supposed to follow the map, how the hell was I supposed to follow the map? I didn't even know if it was real.

Maybe I'm just sharing a mass delusion with my children. Excellent!

CHAPTER 5

HERA

Log entry

High up on the mountain it was cold and windy. Only Jorhan was aware of the location.

"You need someone here. No woman, not even you, should give birth alone." The crease between his eyes deepened.

I have tried to explain so many times, but Jorhan will not listen. "I do not need anyone to protect me. When my time comes, birth will be easy, as it is for all my people. Jorhan, you worry too much."

He took to his feet, pacing back and forth. "What if something goes wrong?" his brows shoot up. "What if an animal comes and decides to attack at that exact moment? What if you are killed? I would never forgive myself."

Reaching my hands out, he grasps them. "Jorhan, you have been a true brother and friend to me all your days. I tell you now. I can defend myself and you must believe me."

"Please, Hera, let me send a woman to help you. I will send one of the old women. Someone you birthed yourself and trained. Someone we can trust." He pleaded, his eyes held such worry.

"No, Jorhan. You know I cannot do that. No one must ever know. I cannot allow anyone to know of the existence of my children. Trust me! Every plan we've ever executed together always came out well. Have they not?" My eyes searched his face. One of the twins chose that moment to kick me and I rubbed the location with my hand to push the foot away from my rib.

He crossed his arms with exasperation.

"Yes, Hera, they have. I do not doubt your ability to properly execute any plan. I simply worry about your health."

He uncrossed his arms and ran his fingers through his long graying hair.

"If a demonstration is necessary, then so be it." I heaved a sigh.

He pulled back to his full height. "Yes, my lady. I do need to see for myself. If you can defend yourself even now, while you are heavy with child, I must see it."

Shaking my head, I pushed up, leaving the warmth of the hut behind. The twins in my belly shifted, always moving, intertwined. I was aware that I did not have much time before my children finally arrived. Perhaps a moon cycle or less.

"You must attack me, Jorhan. I will not lash out at you without provocation."

He stepped back, picking up a stone at the same time. Then turned and threw it at my swollen belly. His hand went to his mouth as his teeth clamped down.

I didn't move, letting my mind swat it away. The rock flew across the field to hit a tree on the far side, leaving a white scar. His mouth opened and closed seeking water like a fish fresh from the ocean.

The wind rose, pushing him onto his back. It lessened enough for him to gain his knees. I picked up every rock in the field, letting them circle over my head. The heavens opened, bringing down the liquid of life and death. It fell on him alone. My head filled with the glory of it.

A child in my belly kicked, pounding my flesh. Fire flashed from my hand. It lit the bramble on the ground and it blazed to life leaping for the sky.

I fought to pull it back. Finally, the rain came again washing the heat from the wood. I pushed back on my belly. The child quieted.

"I will have these children here alone. Make sure you have the wet-nurse ready for them." I ordered.

He nodded his head with searching eyes. "Of course, I will do all that you say. I would never go against your words." Jorhan had never shone me fear, but now I could see the seeds of it in his eyes. None of what I had done was directed at him. But humans fear what they cannot comprehend.

"Come and see me in seven days. I will be well. You've given me more than enough supplies to last a year on my own, let alone for a month."

"I know you are a Goddess and the likelihood of you dying from childbirth is non-existent, but I would never forgive myself if something bad happened to you. After all, you're my sister, and you've saved my people. The least I can do is make sure that you are well cared for in your time of need." He returned and bowed his head.

Jorhan embraced me and headed on his way, he was reluctant to go. His every step labored and faltering. At this point, I needed to be firm. I couldn't let loneliness or a desire for companionship rule me. My plans had to be followed, otherwise, my children would be endangered. I would not allow the same fate that befell Poseidon's to fall on mine.

*****

They came in the night. I had heard of mothers saying the birth of their child was the most amazing moment of their lives. I watched many human women give birth to children through pain and suffering.

There was no pain. Only two beautiful children emerged crying out while breathing in their first breath. My son was born first and I decided to name him Ares. After a short period, my daughter came and I named her Eris. Both of them were hollering. I knew that when Jorhan returned I would turn them over.

I kept telling myself that we won't be parted long. I swaddled them both tightly and left them in a basket. They were perfect in every way, but I needed something that would single them out from other children. Something only, I would know. I took a small knife and placed a pyramid shape, at the bottom of each of the right feet. This way I'd be sure the children were in fact mine.

I never knew that taking care of twins was so much work. My mother had said it was easy, but my mother also had thousands of people to potentially help her. With so few children, every person wants a moment to enjoy the magic.

Homeworlds aren't a dangerous place and children are safe. We're prized, treasured everyone wanting to educate you all at once. You never lack for companionship. You always have your twin or the other Themian parents to aggravate.

My children would stand out among humans in ways I couldn't even begin to imagine. I never even bothered to check into precisely what Poseidon's children could do or even how long they lived. I knew that at some point in time, I would be forced to tell them what they are. However, that will only happen if they start displaying abilities. Everyone will think they're adopted even then.

"They're here. How many days?" Jorhan faces the light with Ares cradled in his arms. If I didn't know better, I would think that he was the father.

"They came four days ago in the night. I named the boy Ares and the girl is Eris. Keep them safe and in a month or two's time, send them to me or bring them yourself." He changed babies for Eris, crooning and rocking her.

"As you say. All is prepared and I've already arranged the wet-nurse. She does not know, but I know she'll be ready. Her child is sickly, and she has more milk than the baby could possibly use. I don't know if the babe will survive."

His words scared me. The wet-nurse had a child? She would cling to my children and refuse to release them if her child died.

"If her child dies, when you bring my children, send her too. I'll not separate them." I couldn't spend my time worrying about petty issues.

"Is there nothing you can do for the child?" His face was pained. He hadn't told me her name, but I was sure it was someone I knew.

"Surely, you understand that I cannot meddle in every individual human life. I have already done enough for this entire region and I've managed to tame Zeus enough that he's no longer marauding around the countryside, killing everyone. What more would you ask of me?"

Jorhan's heart was so large I did not know how he carried it in his chest.

He released a breath. "Your wisdom is true. I'm sorry, but I feel for her. That is her only child. She is older and I know she will probably not have another. This is her last chance." He replied and patted Eris bottom to calm her.

"Send her and her child when you bring my children whether they are dead or alive. I will do what I can. However, you must not tell anyone whose children these really are. Simply turn them over to the stewardship of the Goddess—me."

He nodded tight-lipped.

"It will be as you say," Jorhan immediately picked up Ares holding him aloft laughing. He kissed him on his forehead and set him back in the basket, repeating the same in turn for his sister. Eris cried. Apparently, she did not like being disturbed in her nap.

Jordan took the basket and departed down the mountain. Watching him leave, I felt as if every hair on my body was being plucked out slowly one by one. It was taking all my self-control to keep me from running after them. I knew he would not harm them or allow any harm to come to them. Still, I felt the pressure in my chest as being away from them for more than 3 feet was almost more than I could bear.

As soon as I healed from my childbirth, I would return to Zeus' village. There was no reason to wait any longer. Zeus would be expecting me.

CHAPTER 6

HERA

Log entry

It took me only a week to travel from Jorhan's village down to Zeus. However, upon my return, I had not realized that I was actually gone that long. Time runs differently for humans than it does for Themians. I discovered that Zeus had aged several years. My homecoming was a warm one. There was an entire feast for my return. My handmaids both married in my absence, but neither had produced children, so they immediately gave up their marriages to come and serve me again.

It didn't matter how many times I informed then I didn't need to be served and that I was perfectly capable of taking care of myself. They didn't listen. They had their own ideas of what a Goddess should and shouldn't do. They absolutely would not allow me to bathe myself or make my own clothes, cook my own food or even make my own bed.

All had returned to normal. All, except me.

CHAPTER 7

SYDNEY

We were only a two-day passage outside Puerto Rico. I wanted to make land in San Juan. There are a lot of good places to Anchor in San Juan Bay, and we were going to be living on the hook for a long time. I only wanted to stop for a couple of days to get provisions, load up on diesel, to go and check out Ponce De Leon's home and then move on. I didn't want to spend one minute longer in Puerto Rico than necessary. Our main goal was to hit Mainland Florida and go to the University of Miami. The kids had to finish their education and the only way I was ever going to discover anything about the map was to start learning about how maps were made.

As I was thinking of all the next steps, I heard Isolde yelling, "Mom, we're loaded and ready to go."

I whipped my head around and looked at Isolde. She'd lost that youthful innocence smile. She'd become all seriousness and pinched eyebrows. I guess seeing into the heart of a devil changes a person. I was just glad I didn't have that ability. I was not sure that I could have handled my life if I'd seen the deep dark secrets of my father.

"Pull anchor and let's go," I ordered then worked my hair into a braid.

Tristan appeared in front of me, "Shouldn't we wait for the morning tide?" His eyes shifted to the Ipad and the predict wind app there.

"No. There's a storm coming. If we want to beat it, we need to leave now. That gives us 12 hours. We will sail straight through and we'll make anchor in Puerto Rico before the storm hits," I replied, but Tristan didn't look convinced that racing the storm to Puerto Rico was a good idea.

It was raining and there's nothing worse than being on a boat in the rain. During this kind of weather, you couldn't go out on the deck because it was too wet and yet you didn't really want to stay inside. This was especially true in the tropics because here, it got sticky and hot. There was no wind but wasn't a steady drip of the rain.

Rain in the tropics isn't like rain up North. In the North, those soft little drops fall gently down to Mother Earth, moistening the soil with the life-giving water. But in the South, these are massive drops. They look like they come out of a squirt gun and they splash everywhere. They fall fast and hard. One drop on your head will soak you to the core. One moment the sun is shining, the weather is perfect in every way and ten minutes later it's a torrential downpour with heavy wind pushing water into areas you thought were watertight. Here, the rain can go on for days or be over in 5 minutes.

Tristan and Isolde slept in their rooms. In the back of my mind, I could hear the two of them chatting with each other. I didn't want to intrude and find out what they were talking about. This trip to Florida was not exactly what they were looking for.

I told them both to study pretty intensely because when we got there they were going to take their GED and be done with the education part of childhood. I had a feeling that we needed to move on to bigger and better things. I was not worried because I knew they were ready for it. sixteen was not too young to have a GED.

My gut told me that being in Florida was the right place to be. Also, the Voice said the same thing, although how he would know, I couldn't imagine. As far as I knew, he was never even been to Florida. However, the University of Miami seemed like the best place to go. I just kept getting the feeling that there was something there I needed to know or find out.

Coral Gables has several excellent marinas. I didn't want to be on the hook out in the intercoastal because we were going to be doing too much back and forth, being in the Marina was better idea.

They put us on a dock close to the main Marina. Pulling in was a relief. It wasn't that long of a passage, but I think that the stress of everything was making it complicated.

Neither of the kids had been back to Florida in years. Not since we bought the boat. I was worried it would bring back memories, but apparently pulling up in a boat was a great deal different than flying on a plane because everything felt new and exciting.

Although I could still feel the sadness that drifted off of Isolde, this was the best place for all of us. There were no memories of Gabriel in Miami other than landing at its airport.

"Mom, we're a week late for the start of the semester. You still want to go and do this?" Tristan moaned and ran his finger through his hair back to front only to pull his bangs forward.

I cocked my eyebrow and replied, "Tristan at this point in time you, your sister and I aren't going to be able to take any classes. You don't have your GED yet. We're gonna need to get you signed up, and if they require some prep classes, you will have to take them. I'm going to go in and get whatever I can." I remarked. For a moment I got a glimpse of my attire through Tristian's eyes, and I looked like shit. Maybe I should clean up a bit before attempting UM.

The Geology department had everything I was looking for, cartography being one of the classes. If I wanted to see the old maps. I needed take the right classes or at least insinuate myself with the right professors. Maybe as a rich woman, they would think it was a hobby and be willing to satisfy my curiosity.

"Mommy, I don't think I want to do the college stuff right now," Isolde stated. Wining was Issy's go to, to get her way. But this felt different, she needed the space.

"Well, what are you going to do with your time once you take your GED?" I asked and leaned back in one of the deck chairs to keep the sun from blinding me as I stared at her.

She didn't look me in the eyes, but she didn't have to. "I thought, I might do some art courses. I think that could be helpful for our cause. After all, it was a lot of artistry that went into map making. Maybe, I could learn about ancient manuscripts. How to mix paints and stuff like that." She glanced up at me. Then quickly looked back down at her drawing pad.

My heart filled with pride. "That's an excellent idea, Issy. Is there an art school here or do you want to try some art courses at the university?" I leaned forward into her shadow to catch her sight.

"There are a couple of private art schools, but I was thinking maybe try at the University. However, not until next semester. I could just stop and kind of hang out. I need to try to figure out how to use my powers because right now, I feel kinda – lost." She replied without meeting my eyes.

The small sound of her voice struck me. She needed this. What could happen if she touched one of her fellow classmates? How would she react? It was a recipe for disaster.

"Isolde, I think that's a great idea. Growing into your abilities is probably going to be the smartest way to learn. Learning to control or block other people out could be important later on, so yeah. Although, I still expect you to do some daily reading and math to keep up. Maybe, an online course or two." I asked to test the water.

She sat up straight with a bounce. "You know, Mom, that actually doesn't sound like a bad idea. I can do all the research too. After all, I'm really good at it. You know, I can see all those little extra facts that most people don't pay attention to." The light returned to her eyes. Somehow, she had pushed the haunted look back.

I smiled to myself. Survival is all about the will to live. I had found it after Adrian and now Issy has find her will too.

"You know you surprise me." I moved to sit next to her and hug her to me. "Yeah, definitely do all of that. You're going to be more responsible for taking care of the boat, grocery shopping, and stuff." I rubbed her shoulder.

"Mom, I don't mind doing that. That's actually the easy part because it doesn't require any thought." She smiled and with that smile, I felt I'd got my daughter back.

CHAPTER 8

SYDNEY

The University of Miami was probably the most frightening place I'd ever been to. There were all these young people dressed in outlandish fashions, carrying signs and chanting. Some of the girls might as well held a sign that said 'I'm a hooker'.

A lot of the kids seemed insane. It was like they were speaking another language. Modern nomenclature was lost on me. I had no idea what they were talking about. I mean, I was aware that we've been at sea for a while, hopping around from island to island to get a broader view of the world, but I felt like I jumped into the book 1984. It was news speak or something, you know like the 'double plus negative'. I was half waiting for the 10 minutes of hate to arrive.

Tristan and Isolde's class for their GED was only one week long. It was a joke. Nonetheless, they took their test, and we had to wait for another week to find out if they passed. I really didn't have any doubts about this. Isolde was hands down my worst student, and even she said it was probably the easiest test she'd ever taken and that is was almost a joke.

"It was an 8th-grade exam being given to adults. There were only questions you should know the answers to immediately. They were so easy it was pathetic," Issy grumbled as if I'd wasted her time on purpose.

I wondered where exactly the educational standards had gone since my children claimed that a test that supposed to encompass everything they learned in the 12 years going to school was so easy they could pass it with little to no trouble. It frightened me severely.

The college agreed to let me join the University for late courses. They said one week wouldn't make that much of a difference. I convinced them to allow me to attend a cartography class just to get to know the professor. Also,

Professor Glover informed me that a lot of ancient map making was covered in medieval history and that it wouldn't be untoward for me to attend a couple of those.

"I'm not sure that I have time in my busy schedule. After all, I'm a single mother of two children." I said and shrugged.

He smiled and responded, "I'm sure you have plenty of time. I know for a fact both your children have applied for college here at 16."

Professor Glover. Some people called him 'The Hand', but I didn't get the reference until Tristan explained it. There was a TV show with a job titled 'The Hand'. He was continuously teasing me. I didn't think he had a crush on me or something like that, I just thought he was one of those naughty obnoxious guy types who's always giving you a hard time because it amuses them.

"You're clearly intelligent, so why are you taking this course? Actually, I think that you are much too smart for this class. You already know how to follow a map and my bet is that you could probably draw your own map quite nicely without any help from me," he stopped for a moment probably just to see if he made an impression on me. When I didn't respond he continued.

"Navigation is not an issue for you. This class is for kids that have hardly left their own home state. They only know about maps from there Geography classes in high school. Might I ask why are you taking this course?" He stopped speaking and held his breath.

"Professor Glover, I have to tell you a secret," my mind peddled around. "I'm taking this course because I'm obsessed with ancient map making. Specifically, the ones that are connected with the discovery of America and Conquistadors," I said and then smiled.

He quirked an eyebrow while wrinkling his forehead. "If that's what you're really interested in, Sydney, I'm not sure this class is correct for you. There isn't a course on that, here at this University. We do have some ancient maps if you want to get a look at them and I would be happy to show them to you. However, I think that what you're really looking for can be found at some of the other older universities," he said and his eyes clouded.

"Do you think there might be some at Florida State or in Gainesville?" I knew that I appeared as exuberant as a child, but this waiting around to figure everything out was making me crazy. The pressure to find the map grew in me every day. Whatever I needed to do was building to a head and I had to be out in front of it when it happened.

"I think you misunderstand me when I say older universities. You might need to go to somewhere like Columbia, Oxford, Cambridge, or maybe Princeton. Places like that," he replied.

I didn't want to sail up the East Coast. The further North you go, the harder it was to find a dock and also my gut told me that was the wrong way.

"There are a few in Italy or Spain. They would definitely be a good choice, especially if you're interested in Conquistadors. Spain would be your best choice. They have lots of ancient maps there, many of which survived World War II intact. Spanish explorers collected geographic information via field maps that found their way back to Spain and they were added to a master map. This master map was guarded with utmost secrecy by the Casa de Contratacion in Seville."

Professors Glover's passion for the subject was inspiring, but the underlying meaning wasn't lost on me. We weren't going to find what we wanted here. I wasn't in this to play Clue!

"I can't leave just yet. Tristan has courses and my daughter, Isolde, has decided to take a few art classes. I don't want to just abandon your classes either because I am enjoying everything I'm learning," I fidgeted under his intense scrutiny. My answer wasn't exactly untrue, but I wasn't being completely honest either.

"What I see is that you're extremely bored and not challenged," he reached out as if to lay his hand on top of mine, but then he thought better of it and pulled his hand back rubbing it on his slacks

"Maybe, you could take me on as a TA. We could go over finer points and have more philosophical discussions or something along those lines." I threw in my brightest smile.

His brown eyes filled with mirth as a chuckle escaped his lightly bearded face. "Sydney, somehow I think you're trying to insinuate yourself." He waved his index finger at me as if I was a naughty girl.

It put a twinkle into my eyes. I could be charming and I knew guys like him.

< Yes, you can. You don't need to try. You just are.>

< *I think your feelings blind you.* >

Desire blended through the connection along with amusement.

"Yes, Professor Glover, I am. I figure if you like me, maybe you'll let me look at your ancient maps," I smiled and bit my lip.

Yes, I was flirting, but it's a Machiavellian belief that says 'the ends justify the means'.

"We don't really have that many," he bemoaned and patted his jacket looking for something. I'd seen him do this before, it was a nervous habit.

I was swaying him, so I pressed my advantage, "But you do have some?" I replied before he could find whatever his was searching for.

"We do." He gripped his scruffy chin and nodded his head.

I pushed further "Do you have any 'La Florida' maps?"

His face carried a half smile that he tried to hold back by quirking his mouth to one side. "You mean maps by Ponce de Leon and Columbus?"

Screw it! I'm tired of pussy footing around.

"Yes." I breathed.

"We have a few. There's some after him too. Do you want to see them?" He asked.

Score.

"If you would let me, I would be most grateful."

His eyebrows rose and fell a few times as he worked his way to a decision.

"Stop coming to this class. You're wasting your time anyway and honestly, you're just distracting me. I feel like I'm not giving you your money's worth. Come to my office after school today. Let's say about three. I will take you to the library and I'll get you a special pass for it." He gave me a soft smile and patted my hand.

"Thank you!" I replied trying desperately to not jump up and down like a child.

There's a catch. There's always a catch.

Just I was thinking about what I would have to give in return for this favor, Tristan stepped in and said

< Mom, maybe he just wants to help you. >

And he was not the only one that had an opinion about this.

< Or he likes you. >

< Too many men in my head. Private convo people. >

< Every choice you make, affect us all. Even if you don't know it.>

I pushed both of them back.

"You're officially dropping out of my class. Where I'm taking you, you can't be just a student. You have to be a member of the Faculty or a grad student working on your PhD. I will take you there and I will sign you in as my assistant." He continued and made a note on his smart phone.

"Wow, really?"

"Yes." He didn't look up from the phone and hum and ha'd a couple of times.

"But what about the rest of my Geology courses?" I asked then pulled out my own phone to make it seem as if I was taking notes.

"You don't really need them. You've already said what you're looking for and it has nothing to do with studying rocks." He glanced up at me over the rims of his glasses, then went back to his phone.

I wanted to jump up and down with glee. I was finally moving forward.

"I'll withdraw." I stated.

"Make sure you drop before 3 p.m. otherwise I'm not going to be able to get your pass today, okay?" He replied.

"Thank you, Professor Glover!"

I smiled at him and then he patted me on the hand awkwardly.

I turned around and headed to the register's office. He was going to get me a pass to all the ancient maps at the University of Miami. Yes! there was no way I was going to be waiting around and get it done at the last minute.

I started talking to my clan of creepy listeners.

< You probably heard. >

The whoop within my mind was so loud.

The first response came from Isolde. < Congratulations! I'm so happy. Think of all the time we can save. I'm going to start looking at Universities in Europe. >

The next one who stepped in the conversation was the Voice.

< Sydney, yes, if you look at his maps today, that means that you could leave for Barcelona, Spain within a week. >

< Why did you choose Barcelona? Is there a university there? Wouldn't the one in Madrid be better? >

< Yes, and no. >

< Well, wouldn't the one from Madrid have more? >

< Perhaps. I don't know. It's whichever one you desire. >

< Okay, but I can't leave too soon. The kids have their various interests. I need to let them have a chance at normalcy. >

< You don't want to waste too much time looking for the map. I don't know how much time you have. Sooner is a better idea. >

< I'll talk to the kids.>

I had to balance what I wanted to do with what needed to be done. Every parents' problem.

*****

The entrance into the library was like walking into someone's inner sanctum. The holiest of holies. It was nothing you could ever dream to existed in Miami. It was filled with heavy wooden shelves and it was all climate controlled to preserve the ancient books and manuscripts. I practically had to put on a haze-mat suit just to enter it. I had cotton acid-free gloves and hair net. You know, the whole deal.

Professor Glover asked me if I had put lotion on, which I hadn't, but only because I had forgotten to do so. He led me over to the area where the maps were stored.

"Everything here is stored flat between cardboard like sheets. It's acid-free and specially preserved."

All of them were ancient manuscripts and some paperwork. I guess writing on Vellum and parchment was challenging to preserve, but I hadn't really looked too much into it. This was an avenue I was going to have to start researching.

"Over here, Sydney, this is the area you're interested in." Professor Glover took me down a long hallway.

"This is the table where you can bring the maps of interest to you. You must use two hands for everything, so do not attempt to take out anything with one hand, even if it is small. Everything is listed for the New World or the Americas. There is nothing that's going to be filed under a name or even a map maker's name. It will all be filed under the Geographic region that it's located in."

I listened like a first-grade student. He took a single breath and then continued.

"This is the computer you can type queries into. It will give you an alphanumeric code. The letters tell you the row and it's the number that gives you the shelf you're looking for. Pull them out one at a time. Do not allow them to touch anything. Touch them as little as possible. You're allowed to take pictures but only without a flash. Make sure you close them completely and put them back exactly the way you found them. Once you return them to their shelf, only then you may retrieve another one." He said. His instruction was precise.

I was flabbergasted, considering the security of this library. Only someone who is highly trained would be allowed to use this library. I had no training, and yet he was going to allow me access anyway, and he wasn't going to stay and oversee me. I smoothed my slacks and rolled my shoulders nervously.

"Professor Glover, I realize you're placing a great deal of trust in me. Why exactly are you going to let me go through all of these maps without any training in the handling of an ancient manuscript?" Why I had to asked I don't know.

"I did some research into you. You're a very wealthy woman who has been living on a boat for years. Apparently, you made a great deal of money in the early 2000s from the dot com bubble and you got out before the housing bubble burst. Currently, in the trading world, you're considered somewhat of a maverick and a mystery, but you're well respected. Several people have watched your trades and have made fortunes of their own based on yours." He replied in a matter of fact tone. The raised his hand to indicate where were headed next.

"Yes, but what does that have to do with ancient manuscripts and maps?"

"After looking into you one of the things everyone says about you, is you are meticulous, and very, very, driven. You also pay close attention to the details." Glover finished.

"That's funny. I would have never pictured myself with that kind of a description." I gave him a dry laugh.

"Whether you picture yourself with it or not, that is how you've been described. I know that if you were to actually damage something, financially you have the wear-with-all to pay for it. You might not be able to necessarily replace it, but you could pay for the repair to any damage. Considering how studious you were described as being, I highly doubt there will be any damage. Also, I have this feeling that if I don't help you, my future is in jeopardy." He replied.

Professors Glover's statement did not sit right with me. It was eerie.

*****

Some of the maps had beautiful, highlighted and heavily colored scroll work. The writing was flamboyant and artistic. But after 3 days of going through maps, there was nothing there. I couldn't find anything even remotely close to what I was looking for. I queried 'mysterious islands', 'Ponce de Leon', 'America, Bimini', 'New World', 'Atlantis', 'early American maps'. I searched every way you possibly could, including Isolde throwing in a few, but I didn't find anything.

I suppose I could have just started from the top of the stacks, and looked at every single map in the library, but that was really a waste of time. Frustration rolled through me every time I pulled out a new map. I knew that I had to make it look like I was really studying the map, so it was a waste of my time and infuriated me more than even the fact that I had to play this game. I was mentally bashing my head against a wall.

< Sydney, what you're doing is dangerous, but you have to do it. There is no other way for you to find me. >

< *What do you mean, find you? If I find this island, I'm going to find you?* > My heart rate jumped and the hammering in my chest beat into my mind.

< Yes. >

His emotions urged me on at every turn. There was fear in the background. He was afraid of being caught or found out. The necessity for secrecy was driving me insane. With him, it was a life and death issue. His loneliness came through. No words could describe it. The sheer aching of having nothing all the time. His mind was filled with resolved determination. To him, it was a project that was slowly coming to complete fruition.

"Have you found what you're looking for yet?" Professor Glover's voice cut through my mental musing.

I looked up. It was 1 o'clock. Professor Glover always came in to check on me at 1. Sitting up straight, I raised my arms over my head and stretched as a yawn escaped.

"No, I'm beginning to believe that it's not here." I realized that I shouldn't have said that only after I said it.

Damn it!

Prof. Glover quirked an eyebrow and asked, "What are you looking for?"

< Just move on Syd, maybe he'll let it go.>

"If I told you, you wouldn't believe me, Professor Glover," I gave him a smile and leaned back in my chair throwing my arms up to stretch.

Glover took his tweed jacket off and draped it over the back of his chair before sitting down next to me. "You know, Sydney, I could help you a lot more if I understood what you are really trying to do here."

"Well, I could tell you professor Glover, but then I have to kill you." I smiled at him then glanced back down at the worthless map before me.

A booming laugh issued. "I find it highly unlikely that you would kill anybody." He remarked.

The smile on my face immediately faded. He had no idea what I was capable of. The lives that had been lost in Panama City or that I would kill anyone for my children and I already had.

"You look thoughtful, Sydney. Did I strike a chord?" He inquired and raised his eyebrows.

My heart sped up. I needed to say something and fast to cover my tracks. "No, of course not. That would be ridiculous. Who runs around murdering people?" I followed it with a dry laugh.

< You didn't seem very convincing. >

< *I know, I wasn't very convincing.* >

< Change the subject. Talk about something funny and light. >

"Professor Glover, I think I've exhausted your supply of maps and it might be time for me to call it quits and move on to the next library of maps." I smiled again, but the joy in his voice fled with the weight of my words.

"If you could give me at least a few parameters, perhaps I can direct you better. I like you a lot. You're an excellent student and an extremely bright woman. You have treated everything here with a great deal of respect, including me, and I'd like to help you with your pet project," his voice was pleading, without sounding weak. Then he patted his shirt pockets looking for somethings. He truly wished to assist me.

I took a shot and tried my luck, "I'm really just looking for an old map. Obviously. It is from 1400, Ponce de Leon's time of the New World."

"You will need to go to Spain for this. That kind of map is not going to be here. We have a lot of New World maps, but as you've seen, most of ours are from the colonial days. If you had told me sooner your parameters, I might have been able to save you a lot of trouble. Are you trying to find a map, or identify an existing map?" His exacting question shook me.

"I can't answer that question one way or another." I replied keeping my face bland and under control.

"Secrets, secrets, Sydney. It's hard to help someone who doesn't let you help them," he shook his head and tsked me.

"You just told me I should go to Spain. That's a great deal of help."

At this point, I was just trying to make polite conversation because a thousand things ran through my mind. How long the crossing could take? We were at the wrong time of the year and we would have to wait. I calculated in my mind, 2, no 4 weeks before we could leave and that would put us in the middle of the pond for Christmas.

Glover's voice broke through my musing, "Only go to the universities. None of the museums are going to have what you are looking for. These sorts of things are going to be held at the universities and maybe a monastery or two. However, the church is terrible to work with on these matters. You may have to donate a large sum of money," he coughed.

"I see. So, you need to give a bribe to get in?" I was not sure if he actually said that or I just thought of it, but the Professor kept talking.

"Are you a Catholic? Most maps were held by the crown or rich businessmen/noblemen, which means that they would have gone into the keeping of the universities or various historical archives which are mostly kept by the Catholic church there." He continued.

My head spun with all the logistics of what we needed.

"How long can I expect you to still stay here in Miami?" He inquired.

I pulled out of my head, it took me a minute to answer. "My daughter has her classes and she'll want to complete them. Also, my son is taking a few courses, so we'll probably stay until the end of the semester. We only have 4 more weeks to wait for the end of hurricane season and it'll give me a chance to prep the boat and get it ready for the crossing."

"I was just wondering, if you're no longer going to be coming to the university, I wouldn't mind taking you out to dinner." He straightened his jacket sleeves.

I was taken aback. I didn't know what to say. I certainly hadn't seen that coming. Professor Glover was lovely, probably about my age, maybe a little older, but I didn't date.

"Why don't you call me Carl?" his cheeks curved up in a smile, adding a twinkle of amusement to his eyes. His green eyes had a slightly darker ring. Was he like us?

No, a dark ring doesn't mean anything. I'm reading too much into it.

"Carl, I don't date, but I would love to go to dinner with you as friends. Maybe bring the kids too if you were okay with that. I know my son would like to talk to you, and I'm sure my daughter would probably pepper you with questions. But I don't date. I'm sorry. My husband hasn't been dead – that long. I just – I can't." My halting was to cover the lump in my throat.

He shook his head and patted my hand, "You know, they say that dating is like a parking lot. All the best parking spots are taken, and the rest are crippled. So, I guess you're one of a crippled spots?" He was no longer patting my hand but held it gently.

Relief spread along with my smile, "I guess you could say I am. I loved Gabriel, and I know it takes time. I don't know if I can date someone or go out on a date with someone. I don't want to lead you on. You're a nice man and I would love to be friends."

"Sydney, I would be most honored to be your friend, and no, you shouldn't rush into dating or even pseudo dating too soon after your spouse dies. Why don't all four of us go to dinner and maybe we'll develop a beautiful friendship." His compromise came easy.

He thrust his hand out, and I shook it. "It's a deal!" My heart was pounding in my chest. I hadn't expected him to take it so well.

< You were very kind to him. He seems disappointed though. >

< *I know, but I can't date. I just can't. First Adrian and now Gabriel. I don't know if I'll ever want to date anybody again.* >

< Don't worry Sydney, you'll find love again. >

< It's easy for you to say. You've never found love. >

< This is not true. I did find love. >

< Then why are you so lonely all the time. It's painful? >

< You know why I'm lonely. >

< No, I don't... >

< Well, when you finally get here to this island, and we see each other, I swear to you that I won't be lonely anymore. >

< Why? >

< I've spent my entire life listening to your life. You and your children are my family. I'm only lonely because you aren't here. >

Tears welled up in my eyes. I didn't want professor Glover - Carl, to see them.

"Carl, when would you like to go to dinner?" I asked while clearing my throat to hide the emotions rolling at me.

He quickly moved on, "I was thinking if we're all going to go out together, we could go somewhere fun."

"Where would be fun?" I asked, my idea of fun was very different from most people I'd ever met.

"I don't know, but I'll think of something. Why don't we plan on meeting at the Marina? I'll pick you and the kids up at 3 o'clock on Saturday?"

"You'll probably have to text me and tell me what to wear because we don't want to be overdressed."

"Absolutely. I'll send you a message. How about that?" For a college professor, he was very hip.

I struggled every day with all the cell phone nonsense. "Excellent, I'll make sure the kids are free. I'm actually looking forward to doing something fun," a small smile played on my lips.

"I'm glad I could lighten your day and give you something fun and different to do."

"Thank you, Carl, for understanding."

"Sydney, life is too short to be sad for too long. Don't get lost in it." He advised.

< *It's nice to be admired.* >

< I admire you, very much. >

< You don't even know what I look like. >

< Yes, I do. >

< Yeah? And what is that? >

< Beautiful! >

His words made me blush to my toes.

CHAPTER 9

SYDNEY

There were clothes piled on the saloon table and dishes still sitting in the sink with flies walking over them.

I huffed, "Issy, you can't leave a mess like this on the boat. How many times do I have to tell you?" My words were met with silence and the light slapping sound of water on the hull. I started to panic.

< Issy, are you on the boat? >

< Yes, Mom. I'm in my cabin. I don't feel well.>

Her mind was weak. I charged to her cabin.

< What's wrong? >

< I started feeling everything. Every person in the Marina. Everything they're feeling. I'm going to be sick. >

The sound of retching filled the boat. Gagging sounds came through her door. Bursting into the room, she held a bucket up to her face as she dry heaved golden bile. Her face was covered in a fine sheen of sweat and contorted with pain. My hand slipped over her brow, looking for a fever.

"Issy, what's going on?" I demanded smoothing her hair back.

Between every gag and with her muscles tensing and body straining, she replied, "Mom, it's like having every emotion all at once. I can't handle it. We have to get out of here."

< You need to teach her how to lock her mind up. She's being overwhelmed by every persons emotions around you. Probably for miles. >

< *You mean she's an empath? She can feel what other people feel?* >

< She needs to lock her emotions and her abilities down. I told you about the room. Go into that place in your mind and shut the door. You need to teach her how to do it. >

< I'm not sure if I can do it. >

< You can do it, Sydney. You and Tristan. You all need to work together. Go look up books if you have to. Some of the books will refer to it as egging or shelling. You're going to have to get it at a metaphysical store.. >

"Issy, when did this start?"

She managed to gag out between dry heaves, "This morning after I fell."

Saliva filled my mouth. I swallowed hard to push the gag back. We didn't need two people yaking.

"Did you hurt yourself?" I moved my hands over her body searching for an injury.

She shook her head in assent before answering, "Yes, I hit my head and felt dizzy after, but I didn't black out or anything." Her scared eyes were pleading at me. She wanted me to tell her it was all going to be alright.

"So, you hurt yourself, and now you suddenly can feel everything." I asked holding her hair back from her face. I pulled the hair band from my ponytail and wrapped it around the thick mass on her head.

"Mom, the worry and loneliness pouring off of you is..." She was cut off by the gagging in the throat and the dry heaving into her bucket again.

< Sydney, you have to shut yourself off now. Shut me out too! >

< I– I'll try. >

I scrunched my eyes close and fell back into the white mist of my mind. Whenever I did this, it was always a shining white Palace, similar to the one in my dream. All the walls were reflective and filled with stars. I didn't realize how many doors and windows I had opened. It felt like they were millions. I had to focus my mind as tight as I could. I managed to turn the palace down to a small house. I walked around to close every window and door. Most weren't labeled, they were just representations, but I came to 3 doors. One marked as 'Voice', one as 'Tristan', and one as 'Isolde'. I closed all of them with one resounding smack.

Pulling out of my mind, I left a piece of myself back in that room. Everything was shut off. I was closed and alone. I haven't felt this ever, not since the moment the Voice started talking to me so long ago. I was taken away from my thoughts when Issy started talking.

"Mom, did you do something? I can't feel you anymore. Or Tristan."

"Yes, baby. I need you to do something, Issy. Go inside your mind. I want you to listen to my voice and follow my instructions. Close your eyes and visualize yourself in a room or a building. Imagine the exterior anyway you wish. The interior is what matters."

I stopped to see if she was following me and then continued.

"Inside there are many windows and doors. All of yours are open. You need to mentally walk around and purposely close every single one. Don't go too quickly. Take your time. You need to visualize that with the closing of every window and door, you are closing off an avenue for people to share their emotions with you. They call it shelling or blocking. You need to practice doing this. It will block out everything that's making you sick. Do you see the windows and doors?"

Her tear stained face bobbed up and down.

"That's good, Issy. Walk over to one and close it. Close all of them." I ordered.

"There's one that is marked as Tristan. I can't close it." She mourned.

"Yes, you can. Close it and if you see my name on one, close that too."

Beads of sweat formed on her forehead and around her upper lip. Finally, a decrease in the lines on her forehead came. Her eyes closed, and her face relaxed.

"They're gone, Mom. I don't feel them anymore." She slumped back on the bed exhausted.

"Good, Issy. You need to concentrate and keep focusing on that, but close them all. No one can come in unless you open a door for them. You need to practice blocking them out."

A few moments it later, a cell phone rang.

"Mom, is everything all right? I can't feel you or Issy. What's going on?" Tristian demanded.

"It's ok, Tristan. I'll explain when you get here. Just stop probing. Leave your sister alone. I'll see if I can open myself up to you, okay?"

"You scared me to death."

Not a second passed before I heard footsteps on the upper deck.

"Mom, Issy?"

"Stop yelling, Tristan." I didn't want to explain, I was exhausted.

< I told him it's covered. How is our girl? >

< *She is worn out and starving. I put her to bed. I'll feed her when she gets up.* >

"Tristan, we all need to work on blocking. Issy can't take the emotional onslaught. We're going to have to figure out how to communicate without sending any emotions through the connection."

His brows pulled together in frustration. "I can't be cut off from her. We need each other."

His words struck me. I didn't have a twin or that kind of connection but I understood it. The closest I could come was what I shared with the voice.

CHAPTER 10

HERA

It seemed that just being in contact with Zeus was enough for me to pregnant yet again. But that was impossible because pregnancies do not happen back to back in Themian.

Log Entry

I was once again impregnated. I expected Jorhan to come any day to bring the twins, yet I would have to leave again soon before my new pregnancy was noticeable.

I felt like such a fool. I could not put Zeus off because he would be suspicious. I've been gone for many months but in his mind, I've been gone for many years. He claimed to wait for me this entire time, but it was irrelevant whether he waited for me or not. Ours was not a true mating. I would have to leave with Jorhan and Zeus would not be able to go with me.

Zeus stood erect with both arms crossed. His blue eyes flashed his anger, "Why exactly are we accepting these strange children into our home? Why am I bringing a stranger's children to my hearth?" he demanded.

Jorhan looked at him and responded, "My sister told me if ever our village had a need, she would fulfill that need. I had but to ask. I found these children on the mountain path next to the body of a dead woman. They had no mother and they are marked by the sign of Mount Olympus. They have been chosen by the mountain, so they belong with the Goddess. We have a wet-nurse in our village willing to care for them, but we cannot care for parentless children. Our village cannot support them. They will die." Jorhan's argument was convincing, even I could have believed it.

It was like he wasn't even breathing. He just kept talking, "I know my sister has played her part as the Goddess of the Mountain, so I beg you, please accept these children into your home."

I never believed that the mark I had made would become a sign.

I did not even turn to look at Zeus. I was being treated like the Goddess of the Mountain, so I did not need his approval.

"The Goddess accepts the responsibility for these children. I will care for them as if they were my own. Leave them and their wet-nurse here. We shall take both into our village for care and keeping."

Zeus' eyes were on fire anger seething, "Hera, you take in a stranger's children, yet you birth none for me." His words burned my ears as they did the entire village. Many called out in rage against his accusations. I raised my hand to silence them.

"I will birth our own children in good time. Should I not be merciful to the weak? Are you not such a great king that you could absorb these ones? Should we not help children in their time of need? By raising them, we will ensure loyalty. Is loyalty, not prized?" I asked.

Hearing my words his face stained red with rage and shame. His grip on his throne had turned his knuckles white with lack of blood. I didn't turn my head to see his face.

There was no need. I was the Goddess, he was but my consort. Saying these words in my mind shocked my system.

"Your words are wise as always, Hera, but one day you will bite off more than you can chew. When that day comes, there will be a reckoning for all your high-handed ways." He hissed under his breath.

I didn't respond to Zeus, instead, I turned and gazed at Selene and in a passive manner, I instructed her. "Escort the wet-nurse into my private hut along with both babes."

Both my handmaidens prepared an area in the hut specifically for the children. I went to go lay down. After all three women left the hut to find food, Zeus barged in.

"If you think having some stranger's children in your hut saves you from my attention, or stop me taking my husband's rights, you are wrong." His eyes devoured me.

Wiping the sleep from my eyes, I rolled over, "Zeus no one denies you that. If you want me, take me." I replied.

"I swore to your brother that I would not take you by force, no matter how much I desire to do so." He growled and moved toward the bed.

"You can't force a willing participant. I willingly submit to your sexual machination." I smiled.

Hearing me say that, made his eyes to become hopeful, "Why are you sleeping in the middle of the day?" he asked his eyes moved to my belly.

"Perhaps I'm trying to entice you to my bed by laying down. Is it working?" I rolled on to my back with my legs open. I pulled my gown up to my thighs, letting him see my desire. I did want him. He was demanding, but I liked it.

"Is this your attempt to tame the beast?" He asked.

The lust in his eyes was contagious, so I threw my head back, exposing my neck to laugh, "Well I figured, I might have to work a little harder to tame a beast that is so wild."

He kissed me viciously on the lips, teeth tearing into mine. I wanted him to take me, but he stopped.

"I cannot. I have not the time. There are many matters that need my attention. I cannot waste time on bed play during the day. But I will be back in the evening for my husband's right."

I simply gave him a knowing smile because Zeus always insists on having the final word. He barged in here simply to exert his authority. Now, that he was feeling in control, he would leave and complete whatever important task was required.

Log entry

I've had several pregnancies. This was my fourth and final one. After this, I had to do something. I would have to find a way to alter my bracelet and keep a pregnancy from happening. I was a fool to let him have me so many times, but Zeus was suspicious. However, he has taken Ares to his breast. He publicly claimed him, but children look a great deal like Zeus with his black waves. All of my family are gold but not Ares. He has the domineering blue eyes of Zeus. The funny thing was that he didn't have a dark ring like all my people.

This was my final trip up the mountain. I had to travel farther this time because there was a family Jorhan felt it was too close. Jorhan wished to bring someone else in on my secret, the only answer was to stop having children.

I must confess, birth control was not something I ever thought I would need.

I loved my children and feeling the life growing inside of me was a blessing. Themian people live so long and some never experiencing the joy of children. That was such a shame.

I've already decided that this boy will be named Hercules to honor Poseidon's lost son and that my daughter would be Hebe, for youth.

CHAPTER 11

SYDNEY

Being at sea, you spend a lot of time watching the weather and the ocean. Otherwise, there is little to do. Before we left La Florida, I found some of Juan Ponce De Leon' writings. If I was going to find this map and figure out if it was a big joke or not, I had to get to know the players.

*****

Juan Ponce, 1493

Mother gave me this journal to keep my thoughts in order. I have fought in the Spanish army and together, we defeated the Moors. Just like all boys from noble families, I was trained to become a knight.

My memories of training under Don Pedro Nunez de Guzman bring a smile to my face. He taught me to read and write, use of a sword, how to ride and hunt. At age fifteen I ascended to be a squire. With Don Pedro Nunez de Guzman at my side, we fought fiercely against the Moors. In 1492 Spain succeeded in ejecting the Moors. After the war ended, Christopher Columbus offered me a position in his expedition to Asia, but I refused and chose instead to remain in Spain until 1493 Columbus offered again. This time I accepted his offer.

*****

I stared out over the gray water watching how the crested waves rise and fall and asked myself was this what travel into the unknown was like? Did Ponce de Leon feel the same thing as he crossed the ocean with Christopher Columbus?

I was aware that I was going to another continent and he was going to a new world, but what did he think he would find once he got there? That was the real question because Leon ended up finding natives who hated him and who he'd decimate with disease and slavery.

Me, on the other hand, I had to figure out how to navigate my way through the bureaucracy of Universities, Museums, and Governmental Agencies. They all demanded credentials I simply didn't have. Professor Glover had given me enough paperwork to offer me some credence without putting himself too far out on a limb. As long as he was the only contact, I would be fine, but if I needed to talk to anybody else at the University admissions I was fucked.

The ocean usually calmed and centered me. It helped me find that quiet place inside where I was at peace. But this wasn't the case today. Instead of the relaxing blue of Poseidon's seas, today it was an institutional gray water with a white sky. Green sea-foam was falling from every wave.

No, today I won't find any solace on the ocean.

Just I was standing there contemplating everything and nothing at the same time, Tristan reached out to me.

< **Mom, did you check the weather service before we left?** >

< *Yes, it said smooth sailing for at least four days. Why?* >

< **Looks like a squall.** >

< *Not from where I'm sitting.* >

< **Well, turn around and see for yourself.** >

There was a grouping of dark clouds off to our right. It wasn't directly in our path but we would have to change course, to avoid it. I didn't want to fight the wind or waves. I had enough to worry about.

*****

November 8, 1493

Queen Isabella and King Ferdinand of Spain have sent Christopher Columbus on a voyage to the West Indies and I have been given the great honor of accompanying him. Queen Isabella and King Ferdinand both consider Christopher Columbus the greatest explorer since Marco Polo.

New spices have been found on the islands that Columbus discovered, and Spain will become rich with trade from the New World.

On October 13th, we set out from the Canary Islands in search of the 40 men that Columbus left behind on his first voyage. I've learned many tricks about navigation and exploration. The older sailors were always teaching me new techniques, and I have been fortunate enough to be noticed by Columbus himself.

My eyes met shore again for the first time on November 3rd. The old sailors informed me how extraordinary the accomplishment of crossing an ocean in only 21 days was. The journey usually took much longer, but we reached the island of San Juan Bautista on November 19th, 1493.

Three days later, we arrived in Hispaniola and learned the Indians had killed all of Columbus's men.

November 28, 1493

Our journey has been long and strenuous, but I'm happy to still be alive on this sojourn into the abyss.

We have encountered many savages on the island named Hispaniola. They are the Arawak and Carib tribes, and they strike fear into many of the men. They fear our muskets more than our appearance. As long as I can maintain possession of my weapon, I believe I shall remain safe.

****

Crossing an ocean is all about timing. It's about knowing the weather and choosing the right time of year, inspecting your boat, making sure it's fully prepared, stocking your supplies, topping off all your diesel and gasoline canisters. Basically, you have to run a check on every system. You need to have backups for every major breakable part and have spares for those. You can't say 'but it worked yesterday'. Every part on your boat needs to work every day, every time, no matter what. It's a big ocean out there and you don't want to get lost on it.

I was again interrupted by one of my children. This time it was Issy and she was really excited yelling at me from the other side of the boat.

"Mom, we have dolphins riding our wake. That's a good sign, right." Her breathless question warmed my heart.

I smiled to myself. I didn't believe in fate or signs. I didn't care how superstitious sailors were, but dolphins were a good sign.

"Yes, baby, we have dolphins." I chuckled and turned my face to the wind to ride the wakes of the ocean, just like our ocean friends.

****

May 14th, 1511, Juan Ponce De Leon

San Juan de Boriquen or Puerto Rico as we call it. I am honored to have been bestowed the role of Governor of Spain's territory by King Ferdinand. As Governor, I named the island myself soon after discovering gold. I often miss my life as a conquistador and even the brutal ocean.

Diego Columbus, Christopher's son, will soon take over my position. There is nothing to be done for politics.

I intend to explore the New World further. The responsibilities of a conquistador are a better fit for me than the role of Governor. I miss commanding my sailors. I only wish to use my knowledge of navigation to discover new territories for Spain and Queen Isabella once again.

I long to hear the shouts of my crew again and long watches at sea. From the sweeping teak decks of my ship to keeping a lookout, the life of a sailor is not easy. However, the crew works hard and receives food and shelter along with their pay for their toils.

I write from my desk, under the title of Governor, but I will always be a conquistador in my heart, until the day I die, for my home is my ship and the sea, my true love.

April 11, 1512, Juan Ponce De Leon

My life is not on the way down. I have not suffered much pain or taken many personal losses until this day. King Ferdinand stripped my title due to some political mishaps, but was it reason enough? How am I to keep the peace or fully assimilate these people into our culture if we do not show them a reason to fear us? Whatever I do, I do it to convert them to our religion, doing a generous service to Spain and more importantly to God. I will have my glory. I shall reap the rewards from our Heavenly Father. I am already thinking of what I shall do to regain my honor.

I have heard whispers of an island with a fountain that bestows eternal youth on all who bathe in it. I intend on finding this fountain and gaining its use.

*****

When Ponce de Leon crossed the ocean he was with Columbus. They were on a giant wooden tall sailing vessel filled with hundreds of men. Yes, they carried water and foodstuffs. At the time the likelihood of finding somewhere to make land and stock up on fresh water and food was very low.

Don't get me wrong it took them months to cross the ocean and we only needed a few weeks. However, this was true only if we got a fair wind. If we were to hit a storm and lose our mast or end up having to motor through because the sea was dead calm, the situation would be different. There were 1001 different things that could go wrong while we were crossing the ocean.

Gabe and I had crossed the Atlantic before. It wasn't a big deal, but then there were only the two of us. We picked the ultimate weather window, crossed the Caribbean and hopped over into the Mediterranean.

This time was different. I was alone. We were leaving Florida and heading to the Caribbean. The children would take their watches, but it was all on me. Every course change, every weather report, I was responsible for everything. I had to digest and evaluate our best chances.

I hadn't decided if I wanted to take the Atlantic side or the Mediterranean side of Spain. I choose Gibraltar because it's in the middle. Gabe was the planner. He always knew exactly what route to take. He had a better feel for the ocean. I was not a planner like Gabe and I never would be, but I did have a plan.

*****

April 11th, 1513, Juan Ponce De Leon

I write this from the beautiful Santa María de la Consolación. The other two ships, Santiago and San Cristobal sail with us, in search of the fabled Island of Bimini. The Caribs whisper that it is the location of the Fountain of Youth. King Ferdinand himself commissioned me to search for Bimini and the Fountain of Youth. I learned from the Indians themselves that the spring on Bimini gives eternal youth to the person who drinks from it.

We left San German, Puerto Rico in March, in hopes of claiming Bimini in the name of Spain. I depend heavily on the navigation tools I possess, as well as the help given by the natives. My trusty compass amazingly always points me North. I do not understand how it works. However, the amazing astrolabe is invaluable to my life as a conquistador.

I claimed more land for Spain yet again. Although I have not yet discovered the fabled Bimini, I am satisfied with my explorations thus far. The land is now known as Pascua La Florida. This expedition is not wasted.

April 21, 1513, Juan Ponce De Leon

I have experienced many exciting adventures while prowling the ravenous seas surrounding La Florida, but none of the stories can match my experience to the East.

However, the various animals that I have encountered in La Florida interest me greatly. Alligators and crocodiles from there frighten me as much as they intrigue me. There are also various small critters scattered across the beautiful landscape. I've seen frogs, armadillos, and a majestic deer. The native tribes have not been so inviting. We were attacked by members of the Calusa and Timucua tribes on occasion. They are encamped by the resources necessary for us to populate the region. They will need to be disposed of.

May 21, 1514, Juan Ponce De Leon

Throughout all of my journeys so far, particularly when I was with Christopher Columbus, wealthy King Ferdinand took care of all of the vast expenses in the belief that at the end of the day, Spain and all Spaniards would benefit from the finding of new lands. I feel the Fountain of Youth's possibility, and I wish to find it. I am not sure I shall receive the funds necessary, which is why I will sacrifice my own personal wealth in the hopes to achieve greater wealth.

*****

Ever since Gabe died, I felt the water's movement. I experienced every wave as it crashed and as it held back. I was aware of every swale lifting the boat as it was rising and falling back into the ocean, but also of the feel of the slapping waves between the two hulls. I closed my eyes and feel the reefs filled with life. It was like something had awakened in me. The pattern was clear. Each trauma came with a new ability that was rearing its head and scaring the shit out of me.

*****

February 10, 1521, Juan Ponce De Leon

I have been at sea for 3 weeks now, searching for this 'Fountain of Youth'. The mere mention of such a powerful force feels like tempting the fates. The simple idea that I may never grow old, and live for all eternity in my present form, that I will never be subdued by morality, it is almost too much to bear. I may need a supernatural force to complete my work. All of the eternity may not be enough to fulfill my obligations. But, after this will be done, it will be worth it. I will retire from this straining business, choosing instead to spend the rest of my days with my loving family, whom I miss dearly. The King demands I continue my search and I cannot fail. If I can't locate the island again I fear for my place in the world.

*****

Reading different pages from Ponce de Leon's diary it appeared to me that he was a hard man, but then again, he lived in hard times. Similar to most men of that period, he was a misogynist. He hardly mentioned his wife at all, she was an afterthought. Also, his two daughters appeared to be pieces to maneuver on a chessboard. Political cannon fodder. That was what they really were.

The moment Ponce de Leon started to fall out of favor and he could feel all power slipping through his fingers he became a dangerous wounded animal.

I downloaded all of the various diary entries from the Prado in Madrid and I was sure they had more available directly at the Museum. Ponce de Leon himself was never even been in Madrid, so there was no guarantee the map was there. I had no information on it other than what I've already seen in my dreams.

****

July 5th, 1521, Juan Ponce De Leon

I lay on my deathbed in Havana, Cuba. I know my days are numbered, as I have been hit in the shoulder with a poisonous arrow. The Calusa Indians attacked and I was hit in the middle of the chaos. The physicians are using all their

God-given power, but the future is grim. Although I have experienced many dangers, I am afraid that this adventure was the most dangerous of them all. I, unfortunately, shall suffer the consequences. I have witnessed the many dangers of exploration. From the first moment, I have experienced many horrible nights on the sea. The Atlantic Ocean shows no mercy, and loss is a result. The life of an explorer is dangerous, but I accepted the challenge. Looking back, it seems that such a long time ago I was a young lad and hardened from my battle experiences fighting the Moors. I accompanied the esteemed Christopher Columbus on his journey to the West Indies. Some desire the freedom of sailors' life, but my only desire is that the world will leave me with one glory - to be remembered as the Governor of San Juan and great explorer of Spain. I feel the end coming and I am proud of my accomplishments. I shall die a happy man. Much has happened since my birth 61 years ago. I have learned and achieved much more than anybody imagined possible. My dreams of the shining temple and the clear warm waters cascading from it, haunts my every waking moment. Had I not seen it with my own eyes I might never be here. I regret nothing, the vision alone was worth it. Nevertheless, I plan on setting sail in a few weeks to continue my search, for a man with no goals, is no man at all.

*****

I had to know if it was real. If the map was real, if the island was real. What if Ponce de Leon was crazy at the end? What if I was the crazy one? What if I was looking for a map drawn by a crazy person? I was having dreams about a map drawn by a crazy person, who I never even gave two shits about or thought about before in my entire life.

But his final entry, the temple and cascading water? That sounded like my dream and the island.

< You overthinking everything, Sydney. Focus on the moment. All you need to do is to finish crossing the Atlantic. No need to solve the entire equation in one sitting. >

< Easy for you to say. You're wherever, waiting for me to magically find you. >

< Yes, I am but I don't want you to lose your mind on the road of finding me. I would prefer to meet you in person again whole and not crazy. >

< I'm not going to lose my mind over a stupid map. After all, I've been talking to you for years. If I was to be marked as crazy it would've happened already. I don't understand why you can't just tell me where you are. >

< As I don't know exactly where I am. That's my only clue. >

Fabulous!

I would've expected the man would at least know where he was. With all my abilities I couldn't find him with my mind.

I fell into a deep sleep. The slapping sound of water hitting the underside of the catamaran lulled me.

*****

Carnelian, Tiffany, Blue, Azul, the exact shades and the name is intangible. I grasp for it, but too soon it slips away before my lips and I can't form the word.

The dream comes in fast forward. I blast by the mountain pyramid and past the temple, hovering over the statue just long enough to feel as if something about it is familiar. The mist of the falls wet my lips and hair before I'm flying into the air over the island.

Her whispering words never come.

*****

I was awake. The water was angry and it filled me. My belly was tightened with fear. The boat was dancing with the waves.

< **Mom, I need help**.> Tristian called.

< *Coming!* >

I hit high gear to the deck. My hair whipped around my head, lashing my face. Rain pelted my clothes and skin and I was soaked to the bone in a moment.

"What the hell happened? We weren't supposed to hit any storms. I checked last night." I yelled.

Fear laced Issy's every move, "I can't get the sail down and the motors aren't working."

I grabbed the bimini for support and planted my foot on the deck. I pushed off only to find myself in the saloon.

"Lifeline, Mom," Tristan handed me my life vest. A moment later it was on me and I was back on deck next to the main mast.

The motor had seized up and the wind pushed me against the mast. My fingers sorted through the lines for the gray with pink striped line. It went to the mainsail. I needed to lower it.

I shivered as the wind blew every degree of heat away. The rain washed what little was left down my body on to the deck. I pushed my hair out of my eyes along with the rivers of rain that were running down my face and blurring my vision.

My hand curled around the pink and white stripe with every bit of strength I had and pulled, hand over hand until the sail nestled back in its sleeve. Straightening my arm I found the handhold on the top of the bimini. I repositioned my bare feet on the deck to grab the clips on the sail sleeve to secure the sail. I moved further out on top of the bimini, stretching my body, my fingers tickling for the last two clips on the sleeve.

The boat rose with the swell of the waves and slammed back down. I lost my grip on the handrail and my body slid across the smooth surface of the bimini. My heart was beating through my chest as my hand dragged over another handhold. My feet only found free air. I grabbed at the handhold again but missed. My skin streaked across the fiberglass. I was falling through open air.

< Sydney! > the Voice called after me.

I couldn't think about the Voice but I could taste his fear. I closed my eyes and slipped into the angry ocean waves. It wasn't as cold as I thought it would be. I was one with the liquid and it cradled me, muffling the roar of the wind.

Issy screamed in my mind

< Mom, where are you? Tristan, find her! > she cried.

Isolde's words came through in waves like the water around me. For a moment I thought of letting it take me, surrendering to the watery grave. There was a peacefulness here. The taste of the that ease was as tangy as the ocean itself.

< Beautiful girl, come back to us! Don't leave me! > He screamed in agony.

His words tore at my chest, the pounding that should have been there was slow and sluggish. I forced my eyes open letting the salt pour in but the burn never came with it. Pressure formed around my body lessening as I rose out of the water until I stood on the surface. My feet met the crest of a wave. We were one. Moving my hand, I reached for the sidelines on the starboard side of Calypso. The waves tilted her towards me as the water carried me forward. I slung one leg and then the other one over the side, planting my feet firmly on the deck.

The clamoring of the children's minds in the background grew to a crescendo.

< Silence, both of you. I'm okay. > I ordered.

They both groaned with relief.

I opened my mind and pushed the water flat. I felt the movement of every molecule of water from miles away. The massive storm covered 20 miles at least. I pulled every drop from the clouds in the sky, planting it back in the ocean, pushing the dust left behind into the distance. The boat stilled with the flat ocean. We were becalmed. I didn't know if I should be happy or relieved.

"Isolde, fire up the engines!" I barked as I took to the main deck checking all the lines.

I heard the engines sputter before the sweet sound of ignition roared them back to life. I stepped around to the wheel and looked at my daughter. She was exhausted.

"Go to bed, Issy. I'll stand watch till daybreak."

She sniffed her eyes downcast. I hugged and kissed her on the forehead. "It's not your fault. You did everything right."

"But you almost died. The storm came out of nowhere." She moaned.

It was me, but I didn't respond. Somehow, I had whipped the water into a fury. Tristan's eyes bored into me. I didn't want to say anything to him out loud, but I needed him to calm down.

< Go to bed! I'm fine. > I ordered and mentally pushed him at his berth.

He didn't take his eyes away from me as if he was the parent and I was the child. He didn't say much, he only gave me a swift response.

< You got lucky, Mom. >

CHAPTER 12

SYDNEY

Three days we motored before the wind picked up to carry us to land. I watched the horizon as Gibraltar peeked its rocky crag, only to grow to its full height. It didn't only mark the entrance to the Mediterranean, it marked a safe harbor. I looked forward to finishing the journey and having a full night sleep.

The song of the sea filled my ears, watering my dreams. Every night I dreamed not only of the island but the statue and the temple there. The glee filled visage from battles on the man's face followed me.

I wanted to get away from the ocean and its hypnotic song. For the first time in years, I wanted to get off the boat, to walk on dry land and not feel this siren call. I didn't care where we landed, I only wanted to end the pull.

But whatever relief I thought I would find on Gibraltar's soil, it wasn't there. Time and an ocean couldn't erase the pain of losing Adrian or Gabe. These new abilities never stopped at the ocean or land. I could move both or everything if that was what I really wanted.

Issy and Tristan watched me. They had been quiet since the storm and my display. The water answered to me. It was a power I never wanted, but I couldn't stop it. The waves pushed at the shore, demanding I return to them.

But the soil pulled at me too. The shifting of the dirt below my feet was so slight. I could close my eyes and pinpoint in my mind where the movement was coming from. My first desire was to run. It was what I was doing for years, moving from one place to another, one step ahead of myself and what could have been the truth.

My eyes followed how the craggy outline of the monolithic limestone rock was marking the divide between the Atlantic and the Mediterranean, but I didn't actually see it. Instead, it was the divide between me running away and me running to whoever and whatever I was.

The clanging of the anchor chain was the only noise that managed to rip me from my thoughts. Both kids moved swiftly to lock the boat down and head to shore. I turned my face back to the breeze and the scent of the sea.

I'm too old to run away anymore.

The monolith was my Rubicon, and I was about to cross it. There would be no turning back or running away.

CHAPTER 13

HERA

Log Entry

I returned and found Zeus was gone. None knew where he was. He went hunting in the mountains alone.

After checking all my children and seeing the worried atmosphere that was in the entire village, I went into my mind. I could hear a weak touch, but the distance was more than a three days journey. Running to my rooms, I slung my travel pack over my shoulder. I spied three warriors standing on the outskirts as I left the village.

"Gather enough supplies for three days travel and the ability to carry a man that is hurt," I told the soldiers, then I turned to Selena, "You are to care for my children in my absence." It didn't need to be said, but I said it anyway.

We left on our own hunt. We had to find Zeus.

The two-day journey into the hills didn't move with the speed I had hoped for. Zeus' mind grew weaker and weaker and I found it more difficult for me to pinpoint him, even though I was getting closer.

Finally, in the last day, I saw a crevasse in the earth. On one side, clearly the soil had recently fallen away and on the other side, had been clawed back, as if an attempt was made to jump over it but the person did not make it.

I turned to the two warriors standing beside me and instructed them, "You must climb down into the chasm. He's down there."

I knew that if they could just bring him to my line of sight, I could carry him up with my own powers.

Damn what anyone else thought!

The men anchored ropes on some of the rocks at the top of the crevasse, then slowly repelled their way down. Their muscles were flexing through the sweat and grime as the soil fell with every foothold.

A heavy voice reached me from below, "Goddess, he is down here, but he's barely alive and he has broken his leg. I think he'll die. Do you want us to bring him out?" The voice faltered as the words slipped out.

"Those were your instructions, were they not?" My throat cracked on my fears.

"Yes, Goddess" followed by the grunting of men lifting a heavy object.

"The sooner you bring him to me, the sooner I can save him." I barked.

I heard a groan and a bone-chilling scream issued from the earthen tear. My heart tore apart the rent in the earth before me with all the jagged edges.

"Worry not, Zeus! I shall save you. We shall nurse you back to health," I called.

The painful screaming continued as one of the warriors climbed out of the crevasse and immediately began pulling on the ropes, while the other one climbed out to help. Pulling slowly, they leveraged him out of the hole, dragging his body up the side. Every pull brought more agonizing screams.

When he crested the edge of the crevasse, his head lulled to one side. His face was bloated and thick with sweat and dirt, while his eyes rolled around in his head.

I had seen this before. He was in a deep blood sickness. His leg and most of his body was covered with vicious raised red lines and looked like someone had painted them on. His breath was shallow.

My heart clenched. A need deep inside of me didn't want him to die. Whatever was keeping him alive at the moment in time, he would never survive the fever and even if he did, he would never be able to use his leg.

Craning my neck back, I looked up at one of the warriors. "Go and fetch me a stout stick along with two long straight saplings! We need to build a travois to drag him back to the village."

"What if he does not make the trip?" The man inquired then hung his head in shame as I stared him down.

The wind picked up around us. It whip the hair on the man's head. He pulled back in fear as droplets of water pelted his face.

"You doubt your Goddess? He will make it to the village alive or neither of you will." I had never threatened someone before, but in every fiber of my being, I knew I would kill for Zeus.

Lashing the poles together created a sling for Zeus' body. They brought me two branches. I massaged the skin around the break in his leg through the moaning's. The bone protruded through the muscles just enough to poison his blood. The skin still covered his break but I could make out the ragged end of his tibia.

"Hold him down!" I ordered.

Both men moved into place. I grabbed his ankle bracing my left hand on his knee. I pulled and in slow motion, the bone popped back into place, accompanied by a blood-curdling scream. Zeus' body went limp as I strapped his leg between the branches, using parts of both my tunic and his to make sure he was bound tightly.

I was desperately worried he would wake up again. Reaching into my pack, I pulled out one of the vials of Primordium. He wouldn't need an entire vile. A few drops would be enough.

His body went into a deep and restful sleep and I didn't hear another sound for many hours, but his leg looked no better and his fever did not break. I was afraid that maybe the Primordial Waters only work on healthy humans. Maybe if the person wasn't healthy, they couldn't help.

Why did I not stay and find out what Poseidon had been doing? How did he make Cleito live so long?

Upon entering the village, all who saw Zeus whispered of his death. Despondency blanketed me along with their worry. Without their strong leader, their king, who they believed to be a God, they felt lost. They were all asking themselves what hope was there for them if even Gods could die?

"Take him to my hut!" I instructed the soldiers.

Once in our home, I closed all the curtains with the forces. Setting my pack on my sleeping platform, I took out the other two vials. One had a few drops missing. I set the other one on the table.

Two drops had eased his pain. He was in a deep sleep. Running my fingers over his brow, I snatched my hand away.

Heat, too much heat.

My hand reached for his, but scorching heat met my grasp. I lifted it up to my cheek and I rubbed my face across the scarred hand. My eyes closed and I released it. It fell limp at his side.

Burning filled my eyes and my heart seized. This could not happen. I had betrayed everything for him. My hand tightened on the vial I held there. Hot tears filled my eyes, running to meet the ground. I wiped my eyes with the back of my hand. As my hand passed over my eyes I fixed my gaze on the vial. I knew that with enough Primordial Water he will live.

Why hadn't I asked more questions? Poseidon had all the answers, but I couldn't ask him now. There wasn't enough time for a dreamwalk. I would have to find my own answers.

Tilling his head back, I poured the rest of the vial down his throat. Closing his mouth and holding his nose closed, I forced him to swallow it, he jolted in responce. Soon after, his thrashing quieted. There was nothing more to do but wait till morning.

I laid by his side through the night, praying to whatever God or Goddesses these people believed in, hoping he would recover. I hope that there was an actual God out there and I was not the only entity they were worshiping.

As the sun began to dawn, his state was unchanged. The two vials sitting on the table screamed at me. He did look younger already. Obviously, the Primordium had done something to him, but he wasn't awake and he wasn't going to be awake because his fever had not abated.

I reached out and ran my hand across his brow, hoping his eyes would flutter open. I took my thumb and my index finger and opened one of his eyes. His pupils were fixed and staring straight ahead.

I had no idea what I had done. I could very well have killed him. Poseidon's wife lived over a thousand years and he had clearly given her the Primordium. There was no other way she could have lived that long. Humans don't live that long.

Pulling the fabric aside from the window, I watched as the sky filled with golden pink shades, sunbeams racing across the clouds.

Will Zeus die today?

In the back of my mind, I knew there was only one answer. I turned to the only solution and squared my shoulders. Focusing down on the table, I picked up the second vial, slowly removing its cork, then poured it down between Zeus' lips and held his nose closed. I watched his larynx raise up and down with a gulp. Only then I released his nose so he could breathe.

His eyes fluttered open to reveal that the crystal clear blue I'd come to love was not present anymore. His retina was black with the clear blue, but a dark ring edged the clear blue. His body was no longer covered in vicious red veins and every muscle was honed to perfection. He blinked several times and curled his lips into a wide smile. His voice rang inside my mind.

< You have saved me. >

The muscles on my left brow raised. He reached out and caressed the side of my face.

< My beautiful, Hera. You have saved me from the drudgery of being a human. I am no longer stuck in a short human life span. >

A cruel smile met his lips as a big belly laugh shook his body. He sat up swinging his legs over the side. His leg had healed perfectly. At that moment I knew exactly what I'd done. He was now immortal.

His smile grew on his face.

< Am I not like you Hera? I am hard. As a human, you weakened me. You took my hardness from me. You cowed me.>

I immediately began shutting all the doorways to my mind. Clearly, he heard me. I was broadcasting far too loud, with too many secrets to keep for myself. His mind battered against mine. His eyebrows crunched together, creating wrinkles, while his eyes narrowed.

"Let me in Hera! Let me know everything I've ever wanted to know from you. Everything you've ever kept secret, you pernicious woman." He shouted.

My inclination was to step back, but I stood firm.

"I saved you out of love and now you turn on me like a rabid dog," anger and indignation welled up in me.

"You knew what I was when you took me to your breast. You knew I was a self-serving and power hungry, but still, you let me live. Did you think somehow over the years, just because I loved you a little and I allowed you to take strange children into our home, that I somehow had become a kinder Zeus? Do you think I ruled these people kindly for anything other than you and what you provided me?"

He reached over and picked up the other vial. "What is this? Ambrosia for Gods or water? It smells of nothing."

"Do not waste it! You may find one day you're in need of it," I warned him.

His eyes sparkled with power. "How do you know that you won't be the one in need of it, Hera?" He waved it in the air at me, then thrust it into the pouch at his waist.

"After everything I've ever done for you, Zeus," I him down, but he returned my love by spurning it and started to mock me with it.

"Oh no, I regret nothing in life, Hera. I have done everything to get here. And now, I shall go out into the world as the God I really am. My every whim will be obeyed. That includes you, Hera."

Pain gripped my chest. He hadn't said the words but there was no need.

"You're mistaken, Zeus. You're not my equal nor are you a God. Me, on the other hand, I'm a Goddess in my own right. I have no need to be ruled by such as you. If you wish to go on and rule humanity, then go ahead and try. I've just come from the very place where they will not allow you to rule the world and be king. There are a great many other Godlike people here, on this planet, all strong enough to control you." I schooled my face into a blank impassivity I did not feel and waited for his next move.

"That's funny. I've just heard from someone. He wishes to help me. He wants to become my brother." Zeus chuckled with his triumph. He opened his arms to embrace the world with the elation that comes with new found power.

I must have paled. There was only one person who would ally with Zeus.

"Who is this person that claims will be kin to you? And why would he do such a thing? So, you can rule together?" I demanded. My body trembled with the thought of the one person it could be.

"Oh, I'm sure you know him very well because he seems to know you. He calls himself God of the Sea and claims he will be my brother. He says I may have the mountain. He doesn't even care if I make myself God. He says he just wants to wrap his hands around your throat and squeeze the life away from you. Maybe, I should offer all of your adopted children to him as a gift of friendship." Zeus stepped in close to me to breath in my face. His size dominated the hut, but I didn't flinch back from him.

"Why would you do that? Why would you gift him our children?" I whispered. Pain in my breast leaked down to fill my belly and I moaned, "You cannot give our children to Poseidon."

"Why should I care what he does with other people's bastards?" Zeus whispered.

"They are your children. I have lied to you for years. I birth them in secret. Only Jorhan knows the truth. You cannot give our children to Poseidon. He will murder them all," the words were out of my mouth before I could stop myself.

Zeus' hand slapped me across my face and blood filled my mouth.

"Evil woman, you lied to me you kept them from me. You had me believing they were strangers," he shouted and the support polls of the hut rattled with his power.

"No, Zeus I kept them from everyone else. I brought them to our home so they could be with us but no one would think they were yours or mine. I was afraid of Poseidon. I'm afraid of them all. You do not understand. They killed every one of Poseidon's children that he bore with a human woman. They will do the same to ours," I cried, and fell to my knees.

"Do you really think now that I'm a God, I would allow anyone to kill my beloved children, Perseus being my favorite?" Zeus chuckled under his breath. He then stepped away from me and his narrow eyes scanned the room.

"I have no idea what you would do, Zeus, but there has never been a human that became an immortal. Poseidon never gave his wife the Primordial Waters, only a little bit at a time, I gave you a triple dose in a day. You are no longer a human. I can see that in you."

All around him, the air began to crackle, the room filled with energy. The crack of thunder echoed in the air. He grabbed me by my arm dragging me outside. The giant drops of rain splashdown on my head running down my face and into my tunic. The air filled with more electricity.

"I am the most powerful man ever and you will not live long," Zeus barked.

"My kind will kill you," I shivered with the thought.

In the exact moment, he raised his hand and the lightning seemed to hang in the air as he smashed it down into the earth. Throwing his mane of black hair back he let out a loud roaring laugh.

"You think that I'm really afraid of you? Your kind control you. You could have killed me. You should have killed me on our wedding night. Instead, you slept right next to me. I could kill you and take all your prestige for myself. Now, you are weak and rather than fight, you discussed your machinations. I shall take whatever I want, from whoever I want, because there is little to stop me," he thrust me away from him and into the mud.

Pulling my hands out of the muddy ground, I looked up into the heavens and encounter a giant rain cloud as it formed.

He simply wants to show his power.

I sunk in on myself. I have put all humanity at risk for my selfish desire.

"Zeus, you cannot keep going on. The more you display your abilities, the faster my kind finds you. They know what

Themian power looks like. Poseidon has managed to stay hidden because he hasn't used his abilities. We're all connected. I can feel you and that means that so can they," I cried over the agony in my chest.

I gazed around. The forms of our children surrounded us. Zeus used the forces to lift himself from the village. All the villagers came out to see what the lightning and thunder were about. They bowed down and there was nothing I could do. His former display with the lucky lightning strike was all it took for people to fear him. Now, as he floated up into the sky in front of his people, grasping a living lightning bolt, had no less impact.

I could not deny that he had a flair for the dramatic. This was something I have always lacked.

CHAPTER 14

SYDNEY

The steps down into the catacombs scared me more than the call of the sea. It led down into a deep dark pit. The void engulfed me because you never knew exactly which direction you were facing. The stairs turned around, twisting you and your mind with every turn.

The catacombs consisted of many levels, but I never recognized which floor I was on. My flashlight searched the walls for the marking Father Rizzo said denoted the various levels. Of course, everything was in Spanish, but it didn't matter much to me because I could read and speak Spanish. However, I realized that sometimes, when you're afraid and turned around, you revert back to your first language which for me was English.

Father Rizzo was a curator with the University of Barcelona. His job was to manage, control, catalog, and inventory all manuscripts, maps, codicils and artwork that entered the University Library System. I was informed that part of the University had once been a church.

"During World War II, the artwork and papers had been moved down into the catacombs. Many of them were never taken out. The church remained standing throughout the war along with its stained-glass windows and its beautiful frescos," Father Rizzo's deep tenor echoed down into the darkness and bounced back at us in a hollow tone.

"It was relatively undamaged. Although, there was some slight shaking. Some of the catacombs cave entrances collapsed but we were able to dig them out," he continued.

When I first submitted my request to view the collections, his immediate reaction was 'but you have no papers.' I was so fascinated by his cultured Italian accent, that I didn't even respond. I only realized what he said when I saw him smiling at me. When he didn't receive any feedback from my side he continued.

"You know, in Italy, if you wish to have papers, you can simply visit a friend." He was toying with me.

It was my time to smile. He had seen my last name and must have deduced its origins. The American version of 'visiting a friend' was 'I have a friend' or the New York version 'I know a guy'.

Apparently, the guy I needed to know was Father Rizzo's brother-in-law. For 1,000 euros, he drew up all the papers I needed in order to get access to any collection within the University system of Spain.

Father Rizzo's brother in law was a very talented artist. His specialty was mimic. He could mimic signatures, stamps or ink colors. Pick anywhere in the world that you wanted to have paperwork from and he could come up with the chemical compound necessary to reproduce perfect fakes. It was a true talent, one absolutely worthy of every euro I spent on him.

Speaking of talents, Father Rizzo was an excellent cook. His family was lovely and my children really liked his sister and her children.

When I told father Rizzo that I wasn't just looking for any map and that I was looking for a specific type of map, a map of the Americas from before the colonial era, from the time of the discovery, he replied shaking his head.

"All of those maps would have been categorized and kept under lock and key. They were guarded with utmost secrecy by the Casa de Contratacion in Seville."

"Is this a wasted trip?" I inquired and looked around.

He tsked at me, then closed all the doors and spoke in a low voice.

"Many of those maps were housed here during the war. They were kept in the catacombs. Not everything from the war has been brought up." Father Rizzo whispered conspiratorially.

I listened to him without moving a single muscle. He leaned in close with a stern face and almost whispered, "Most of the truly interesting items are on the third level. Anything lower down would be partially underwater or have been ruined by water. There would be no reason to look it over. Come to the University's side door on Monday. That's when the main museum and library are closed to the public. I will allow you private access." Rizzo touched his nose and winked at me.

I was waiting for him to ask for a bribe or a handout or the 'please donate to the leaky roof of our local church', but it never came. His kindly eyes just smiled at me, as he patted my hand.

It's not often that you meet someone that you feel is touched and special. Father Rizzo truly had a calling within the church. He was a kind man to everyone he knew. I never heard him say a sharp word to anyone. Being around him was like being in a room that had been filled with fire but the moment he came in, it was fresh and clean as a spring day after rain.

As I approached the side door of the University Library, Father Rizzo waited close by. He was standing slightly in the shadows and he stepped out the moment I got close to the door and immediately shooed us both in.

"Sydney, no one is here today. No one can know that I took you down into the catacombs." We moved quickly through the church.

"Is there something wrong? Am I breaking a rule?" I asked whipping my head left and right.

"No, but I know that sometimes people are watching. There is a great deal of information in the stacks here, so there is much to hide. Many people do not want everything that was lost during the war, to be found again," his brown cassock brushed the floor and rustled as we walked.

"There might be information down there that's dangerous?" I asked.

"Yes. Every day you must come to this door and only to this door. If you do not see me, walk by and come back later or don't return at all. I will let you in before the library opens. You must stay down in the catacombs for most of the day. Around about 3 o'clock the classes end, but the library does not fill right away. It is a very quiet time. I will let you out at that time. Wear a watch." He instructed.

He then led me to an alcove on one of the library's sides. Being that it used to be a church, there was a giant statue of the Virgin Mother gazing lovingly down upon her baby son in her arms. At the base of the statue, there was a ring forged into the stone with a rope attached to it. The rope was connected to a hand crank with a pulley.

Father Rizzo began to crank on the handle and, slowly but surely, the stone at the base of the statue behind the Virgin Mother lifted, revealing a set of steps.

"This is the only way into the catacombs. There is also another way out but I don't know where it is or how to find it. If you find it, you will tell me, yes?" He smiled, knowing I wouldn't look for it.

"If I have the need to find the exit of the catacombs without your help, Father Rizzo, I'm afraid I would be in a great deal of trouble. I'm not sure we would see each other again," I remarked dryly. Then brushed myself off in readiness.

"If you do find it, leave me a note where I'm sure to find it," he laughed and continued.

"There is a plaque on every level. Go down to the third. However, all the words are written in Spanish. The church was built during the Holy Inquisition and the tunnels are cut in the very stone of the ground. King Philip took over many of the churches in the name of the Holy Church. Back then, many died from diseases, others from their beliefs and were buried here. But the tunnels under the church are from a time earlier than the Inquisition. I was told they once led to a holy chamber where it was possible to speak to God. But those are just stories." He shook them away and urged me down into opening.

< One man's God is another's Devil. >

< *Shush! What if he says something important and I am focused on you?* >

Father Rizzo should have been recorded and presented on the internet or TV because his narrative could entrance even the strongest mind. I found myself hanging from his every word, waiting in anticipation for the next chapter of his story.

"There are no more bodies down there. They must have been cleared out or disintegrated long ago, so you won't find anything. But there are a lot of cubicles. Be careful and make sure that you find some way to keep track of everything. Take this rucksack. Everything you need will be in there. You can use your flash camera if you choose to take pictures of whatever you find. You just need to promise me that you will share them with me," he winked and continued, "I will do my best to try and categorize. Just make sure you let me know which floor and what cubicle you found it in and I will do my best to identify it from pictures. If needed, I'll have somebody retrieve anything of true interest. There's an email where I want you to send it to. It is also in the rucksack. Do not send it anywhere else. Do you understand?" He finished his monolog in a frightening deep voice with a hard stare.

His face darkened, as he furtively glanced around the empty space. I too looked around, but only encountered the sound of the wind. There was no one here but us. The Voice told me that what I was doing was dangerous but Father Rizzo demeanor truly scared me.

What had I gotten Isolde and Tristan into? They were teenagers. They should have been out having fun not worrying about the kind of trouble their mother was going to dig up. I don't think I managed to finish the thought when I heard Tristan speaking to me telepathically.

< **Mom, don't feel guilty about anything. We all decided to do this. I'm sure Issy and I would have found a way even without you**. >

And he was not the only one that had an opinion regarding this because Issy also joined our mental conversation.

< Don't worry, Mom. You didn't drive us into it. We came willingly. I don't know how you waited so long. >

I smiled and answered them both < *Like the Frog that was boiled to death in the water, slowly? I waited because I didn't believe.* >

The steps twisted in a circle and led me down, giving me a further feeling of a dread. Hundreds of people were buried down here ages ago. That was just creepy.

By the time I reached the third floor, I was all turned around and in desperate need of a light switch. The bare bulb light hung from an ancient black nylon cord, suspended from the ceiling which was nothing more than rock. All I could make out was the iron nail that was suspending the black cord above my head and the continuation of the black nylon cord flowing from the stairs down the hall. After I pulled the nickel chain the light swung in a circle. It threw an ominous shadow down the arched entrance that became a hallway.

Four roughed out archways laid beyond the only entrance to the cubicles and off the main path. Father Rizzo said he'd not been down here for at least 20 years and that he wasn't really sure of the condition it was in, so the first thing I did was to draw a small map of the hallway.

I approached the first cubicle on my right-hand side. There were manuscripts stacked on a table, and there were three tables. One had large sheets lying flat and one was covered with scrolls that were set up on all kinds of shelving. The last table looked as though someone had lunch and left it there for about a thousand years. The oily brown paper had chew marks. Something chewed the last bit of flavor from the leftovers. There was one chair, an unopened bottle of wine and next to it sat a chipped glass.

I slightly rearranged the room, putting the mostly empty table with the leftover lunch next to the table with the manuscripts. Then I brushed the leftovers into a waste bin hidden in a shadowy corner. I emptied out my rucksack onto the table. It contained 2 gallons of water in white milk jugs, 3 miners lights, a bunch of backup batteries and an emergency flashlight that turned on when you shook it. The LED light carried a note that said 'if you run out of light in a dark place shake me for good luck.' Father Rizzo's sense of humor had an interesting twist.

I strapped one of the miner's lights to a water jug and watched the room brighten with illumination. It created a warm glow over the stark light strapped to my forehead. It also revealed the damp walls and the black goo that covered cracks in the walls. I curled my nose in disgust and turned to face the stack of history waiting to be seen.

Working through the manuscripts on the first table was tedious. Some of them the writing was so faded that you couldn't make out what it was supposed to be. Most of them were not even maps. I simply moved them over to the other table. I wanted to make sure that I looked at every single one but after I got to 50, I just wanted to kill myself.

Gazing around the room at all the scrolls, I stopped for a minute to check the time. It was 11:30 am, so I took off my cotton gloves and set them neatly on the table in front of me.

Lunch in Spain or in Italy is pretty much the same as anywhere in Europe. It is not a big meal and most people just eat some bread and cheese with fruits such as grapes. At the end of the day, they have a large dinner. I had gotten used to the eating style on the boat where are you just kind of eat whenever you want, but on land it was different.

Several of the manuscripts were interesting with lots of scroll work and detailed illumination. Some were finished, some were unfinished, with the vivid colors that could only come from a medieval era or a scriptorium of a monastery. A few looked as if the person working on them had died just before finishing the work. They had a script trailing across the page.

One of the pages literally had a jagged line partially through it and I thought that maybe the monk died in the middle of finishing, although, the idea that someone would not have completed their work, I found to be unbelievable.

Monasteries and churches weren't known for their wastefulness.

I didn't want to spend my entire life down in the catacombs. Having no idea how big they were, I finished the table and checked the time. It was 1:30 p.m. That gave me an hour and a half to explore.

I needed to be a little more organized and thorough, so I went out into the main hallway and breathed out misty clouds into the frigid air. It was obviously getting later in the day and cooling off. I slipped back into the first cubicle and put my jacket back on.

Looking either way down the hall, I fixed my position with the stairs to the left and the other cubicles to the right. There were 10 cubicles in all and one was partially caved in room at the very end. The hallway ended in a newer stone filled archway, the color of the stones didn't match the rest of the stonework in the catacombs. Here, moisture wept from the cracks and the archway was a perfect geometric 180° half circle. The edges were smooth and precise and it appeared that this level of the stonework was relatively new, even though Father Rizzo had said that the catacombs were from a time before the Catholic church.

My thirst for knowledge had never found its fill but that was not the time to become distracted by a mystery in the stonework. Before turning back to my task, I reached out and ran my fingers along the smooth stone and trailed down the rocks used to fill the perfect archway. It was as if I'd touch a live electrical wire. Somewhere, not far on the other side of that rock, lay water and a great deal of it. The call of the sea reached me even down here. I turned my back on the wall and its watery secret.

I surveyed each and every one of the cubicles. One was predominantly filled with scrolls with the usual handwriting on them. I decided that I would save that one for the last. All of the rooms had three or four tables and, on each table, there were piles of manuscripts at least a foot thick per table.

I scratched the back of my neck and rubbed my temples. This was going to take forever, but I would just have to be methodical and go over every room. The front two rooms didn't seem to have much in them, so I took the empty table from one of them and placed it into the next room, moving the piles from the full table to the empty. Every day I managed to go through at least one stack per room.

After spending three weeks not getting anything but paper cuts and allergies from moldy dust bunnies, I wanted a break. The kids had hardly seen me and complained about this. But the moment my head touched the pillow or I closed my eyes it was there - the island and the map were shining in my mind accompanied by the need to find it and the urge to move earth and sea to get it.

A day later, Father Rizzo approached me in a furtive manner, "Sydney, I need to speak to you. It's very important."

"Of course. What can I do for you?" I said while smiling and smoothing my pant leg. These were my nicest slacks and we didn't own an iron.

"I've had several people come around asking me if I've spoken to you. I answered truthfully to their inquiries. You have been here on several occasions. But they wanted to know how often and what you did in the library," he glanced around to assure himself we were alone.

I swallowed back my fear. Was this what Voice meant?

"What did you say?" I murmured under my breath keeping a smile plastered to my face.

"I told them you come about once a week on Tuesdays." The lie rolled off Father Rizzo's lips so easily I could almost believe him. That a priest could lie with such ease worried me just the same.

"Okay!" I returned my guarded reply slowly.

"There was a lot of poking around and someone broke into the library last night. Nothing was taken but I did notice that the crank to the catacombs was in a different position. I cannot put my finger on it but I believe someone has been down there. I think we need to be more careful. You will need to come and spend time in the library on Tuesday mornings," he supplied with a satisfied smile. As if that was the solution to all him and my problems.

"Father, I don't know why you're so paranoid or what a big deal it is but if you say I need to do that so that I can keep going, I will absolutely do it!" I said and shook his hand as if we'd shared a lovely chat. For anyone who was watching.

"Also, I want you to stop emailing me the pictures that you take," he stopped and offered me a small box, "This is a thumb drive. Put everything on the thumb drive and we can just trade every day. Okay? The drive is encrypted so you won't be able to see anything else on it. You can only upload to it" He raised his right hand and crossed me with a blessing and I bowed my head in agreement.

He patted my arm, then led me to the entrance of the catacomb and pressed a key into my hand. "I can no longer meet you. You must let yourself in from now on."

"Okay, Father," I responded and I could swear I felt a million shivers run down my spine.

*****

We had rented a flat not far from the Marina. I couldn't be on the water. With my the desire to move with it, at this point the pull was too strong. At the flat, I went through all of the pictures. Some were just words written in Spanish, Italian or Latin. Some were drawings and others were maps. I slowly dated every single one of them and added them to the zip drive.

Everything worked smoothly until I got to the last one. There was something different, something wrong with the picture but I couldn't put my finger on it. The outline of the paper underneath was strange. It was a small square paper, not bigger than an 8.5 X 11 sheet, yet the next picture was a very large map. It was just a map of Sardinia so I didn't consider it to be very exciting. However, flipping back and forth between the two pictures, I saw that the real problem was the smaller page which had a different color and it wasn't parchment, but vellum. It carried that special yellow that only vellum can, discoloring the outline of the picture above and underneath.

The next morning, I returned to the catacombs and realized that I'd forgotten to ask about the security. When I turned the key in the lock, I fully expected the lights to turn on and a horn to blare, but the blinking display showed it was already off. I kept asking myself what if the stone was closed over the top of me?

"I will not let the stone be left on top of you. You will not be locked in the catacombs."

I jumped at the sound of Father Rizzo's voice, "Thank God, I…I, you scared me out of my skin," I heaved as I tried to regain my breath patting my chest to ease the pounding of my heart. When had I grown so nervous?

We both moved to the alcove. I went down into the catacombs and Father Rizzo closed the stone over my head. I went back to the cubicle I'd been working in the day before. The two pages that I discovered, were stuck almost like they were glued. It took me a while to peel it back, and I set the page off to the side.

< They're watching you. >

< Who's watching me? >

< They, them, someone. >

< How do you know someone is watching me? >

< Sydney, there's something on the wall. Some kind of a nail. They put a camera on it. Go hang your coat up over there. >

My heart began pounding again with fear. I wasn't alone, Voice's anxiety bled through.

< I've never hung my coat up before. > I replied and bit my lip.

< Go hang a hat up over there. Didn't you wear a hat today? >

< Yes. >

< Go hang your hat up! >

I stepped over to the damp wall and hung my hat up on the nail. I was just able to catch the reflection of something. It was small but it was there. I looked around the room and realized they could have put a thousand cameras in here and I would not know about it.

< Take pictures of everything. Don't spend any time on anything other than what you were just looking at, Sydney. If you can sneak it out that's probably your best bet. >

I needed to go through all the manuscripts and there was no way I was going to be able to finish. I figured they probably put a camera in every room.

I did the best I could to peel the two manuscripts apart and then suddenly the vellum just seemed to fall away almost as if whatever had been holding it suddenly let go. And there it was - a beautiful drawing that looked like a rough draft of the map I've been dreaming about. It didn't have any latitude or longitude on it, but it did have a legend key with the North, East, South, and West. However, it was incomplete.

I folded it in half as best I could and shoved it into my sweater. I went through the pile, taking pictures as quickly as possible. As soon as I finished the pile, I moved on to the next cubicle. There was only one table there and I noticed that the dust on the floor around it had been disturbed. Obviously, somebody had been in there and recently. My heart sped up filling the air around me with its beating.

I moved the empty table into the room and began working methodically as if nothing had happened. I did move my lunch sack and my lighting equipment along with my hat and coat on the one chair that I discovered. The walls were somehow lined with shelves but it didn't look like there was really much on them. There were a few scrolls here and there, so in an effort to try and see if there were any cameras, I looked on every shelf. I didn't want to miss anything.

Halfway through the manuscripts, there it was, the map in all its glory. I took three or four pictures of every manuscript in the pile, just in case. When it came to the map I took seven or eight, but I couldn't take it. If I took it out, they would know for a fact that was what I have been looking for, so I kept going until the whole pile was finished.

My heart pounded through my chest. I looked at the time and it was time to leave. I cleaned up all of my things like I normally did, putting everything back in order and went to the top of the stairs. The stone was already open just enough for me to squeeze through. And I heaved a sigh of relief.

I caught a glimpse of Father Rizzo from a distance, but I didn't want to talk to him. I simply left. I boarded the first bus that passed the University and took a seat facing the doors. A man in a red sweatshirt with a hood on it jumped on at the last moment. He carried the bulky outline of a gun in the center pocket. Most Europeans do not run around with guns.

He took up a seat near the back door. I ignored him and focused on the streets the bus followed.

Three stops later, I got off the bus and headed into a grocery. I wandered the lanes looking for nothing in particular. I passed the checkout counter and I dashed out the door. I jumped on the bus heading in the opposite direction of the flat. Mr. Red Hoodie rushed out and made it to the bus a moment after I took a seat by the back door. Whoever he was, he was trying to be inconspicuous but was not very good at it. By the time I reached the flat we'd rented, I knew that we had to get out of there quickly.

I always left the flat locked. I secured everything as if it was still the boat. However, I got that creepy feeling as someone had been here. Things were kind of in the wrong place or not exactly where I left them.

I wasn't completely sure that we were being watched until I looked out the window. Mr. Red Hoodie was now in a green hoodie. I rolled my eyes.

Inconspicuous—fail, where do these people learn these tricks?

You would think that if they were going to be watching someone they would switch out with a different person or something. Didn't these people watch spy movies? However, it was his body movements and the sense of danger that scared me most. I stared at him until the kids came home an hour later.

Tristan and Isolde came through the door, both talking loudly and giggling.

"Mom, how was your day? Find anything interesting?" Issy asked.

Tristan opened his mouth, but with my mind I shooed him.

< Tristan, be quiet. You too, Isolde. I was followed as soon as I left the museum. Also, the library was broken into last night. Somebody went through things and installed cameras down in the catacombs. They're clearly interested in what I'm doing. >

Tristan responded in a heartbeat.

< What do you want to do, Mom? >

< I think it's time to leave. I want you guys to pack up everything that's of value here in the flat. Tristan, shift it to the boat quietly. Tomorrow we're all going to leave like we normally do. Tristan, you're to shift your sister to the boat,

then come back to the University and get me. I'm going to go to the grocery store before I go to University, so I'm going to have groceries with me. I will meet you there but not in the library. >

< **Where then?** > Tristan asked.

< We will meet in the boys' bathroom by the library door. I'll pick up as many supplies as I can buy. They almost never open it to the public, so it should be empty. >

< **Ok, Mom, I will meet you there, but what if it's not empty? >**

< Well, Tristan, then we'll find out whether you can shift instantly. >

< **Matter cannot occupy the same space as other matter. >**

< Exactly. I'm counting on the Universe to automatically bounce you to the side of whoever it is there. Every life form has a natural instinct to survive. Maybe deja vu is part of that. >

I turned to Issy and her wide eyes, then I cupped her cheek.

< Issy, you prep the boat for us to leave. I found what we were looking for! Get as much diesel as you can. >

Issy's inner voice was trembling a little < What if they're watching the boat? >

< Just call the Marina's manager if something is off or you need help. >

I looked at both of them and added *< I've only got tonight to upload these pictures for Father Rizzo. >*

Issy winked at me and asked < You found it? >

< Yes, baby, I did. >

Surprisingly, it was Tristan who popped the next question with a smile on his face.

< Can we see it? >

I smiled at both of them and only added *< Yes, right after we clean house. >*

Most of the evening was painstaking. Issy did three loads of laundry, folded everything and then packed every bag she could lay her hands on. Tristan must have shifted at least seven loads. He moved every bit of our groceries, clothing and pretty much anything that was worth having. By the time we get to the boat, the salon would be filled to the ceiling with junk.

I pulled the map up on my computer and sat back for the kids to look at it. They were in awe of the aged image. They didn't ask many questions, I had expected more. They were tired and tomorrow promised to be a long day. I urged them off to bed.

I didn't linger over the map. We had it and that was enough. The only portion I needed was the latitude and longitude. They were written in Spanish, but the scrolling script was missing. I didn't care it me all I needed to know, not only we were in the wrong hemisphere, but we were on the wrong side of the planet.

Sleep eluded me, but I kept peeking out the windows. I'll sleep when we get the fuck out of Spain. The people watching us never wavered. They just changed shifts.

Survival, Sydney. That's what it's all about.

I breathed as dawn broke. We had to survive at all cost.

CHAPTER 15

SYDNEY

I watched the windows and the street. There were about four people and vehicles that didn't belong. I didn't know if they were all watching us, but Father Rizzo had said that the information stored in the catacombs was dangerous. I remembered him saying that 'Many people feel the longer it was ignored the better.' But what was the information he specifically referred to and how could a map be that dangerous? Regardless of what the answer was, we had to leave Spain immediately.

Tristan and Isolde got up as if everything was normal. We made breakfast and got dressed like nothing out of the normal was happening. Tristan shifted the last of our things to the boat, popping out of the apartment several times. He said everything on the boat looked completely normal and that nothing had been fiddled with. It didn't even look like they tried to break in. They either assumed we weren't there or they didn't know where the boat was. The last part was highly unlikely because they would most definitely be aware of where our boat was.

The kids left for classes. I was trying to keep the schedule normal. I looked around the apartment, moved a few items here and there, made sure all the curtains and windows were closed and locked the door. Every action that we took was perfectly normal.

I began walking toward the University. I was being shadowed by Mr. Green Hoodie. He was an average build man but it was the size of his hand and arms that worried me. I was sure I could defend myself, but at what cost? After a few streets, we were joined by Mr. Large Heather-Gray Shirt. He was well over 6'5". If one word could describe it, that was meat. Both of them hopscotched each other.

I wasn't sure if I should really approach the University's library at all. Also, I had promised Tristan and Isolde I would go to the grocery store, but now that felt like the wrong move. My colorful tails moved in closer and my choice was made.

As soon as I entered the University, I found the men's restroom and dodged inside. I contacted Tristan as soon as I closed the door.

< I'm in the first stall. >

He responded immediately. < **Gotcha, Mom. I just dropped Isolde at the boat. I'm back at the University. I'll be in the men's room, just hold on**. >

< Tristan, look out, please. There are two men here, one in a green hoodie and the other in a heather gray shirt. They followed me all the way here. >

< **Got it. Don't worry**. >

His easy confidence worried me. The young always believe they can win, until they can't. The five minutes it took for him to get to the stalls made my insides quiver. In the surrounding room, I listened to men urinate and fart. The scent of ammonia permeated the room making me gag.

< **Mom!** >

< I'm here. >

I stepped out of the stall and as soon as he touched my hand, the two of us disappeared to the boat. We landed in the middle of the deck. Isolde came out and hugged us both with trembling arms. I checked to see if the boat had been filled with diesel. It appeared that we were good enough for now.

"Where are we going?" Issy asked tears stained her face.

"Gibraltar. We check out of Spain, cross the border, check into Gibraltar and fill up with as much diesel as we can," I responded but Issy didn't agree with me.

Issy shook her head vehemently, "That's a terrible idea, Mom. I don't think we should check into Gibraltar at all," she was scared and her go-to was not much different from mine.

Just like me, she wanted to run, but in another direction. "We need supplies. I say we sail to the first Marina we can, check out of Spain and keep going."

Since both my kids had a mind of their own, Tristan had to throw his opinion too.

"We all agree that we have to check out of Spain, but before that, I think that a better idea is to pull in close enough to a Marina and get a service to come around and bring us diesel and supplies. Mom and I bounce back here and check all of us out of immigration. Then we sail around Gibraltar to the Atlantic side." Tristian pointed west, then north to emphasize his point. "If they don't think we're out of the Mediterranean, it can buy us time. If 'they', whoever they are, figure out we're on the other side of the rock, they're gonna think we either headed to the Canaries or are going over to North Africa, like Morocco." He raised his eyebrows and glanced from me to Issy hopefully.

Mulling it over in my mind, actually, Issy's idea was the best. We needed more supplies. I didn't think we had enough on board to make a crossing.

"We will do an amalgam of everybody's idea. We check out of Spain now. By the time whoever's following us realizes, they'll just think we've gone somewhere else. We leave the Med and go around to the Atlantic side of Gibraltar. We don't check in but we get supplies. Tristan, I think you should just shift into one of the stores nearby, buy as many supplies as you can and shift back."

With his eyebrows raised Tristan was a picture of astonishment. "Wow, Mom, I didn't even think about that."

I nodded my head and then continued, "Issy and I'll stay here on the boat. We pick a shifting spot and you move everything to that spot. You will have to take the diesel tanks with you. Also, I want you to get as much cash out as you can. That's really all we need to do. All right?" I looked from one to the other. They each, in turn, agreed so I said, "Lock it down, turn the motors over and let's get the hell out of here." I clapped my hands together as a signal to get to work. Moving this boat was work.

All hatches were already latched down. The motors turned over like a dream. Yanmar engines are the best. They never stop working.

We boated over to the Immigration Office. I got all our paperwork stamped and jumped back into the boat. It didn't take long for us to put to sea. We didn't have to motor out very far. I raised the sails and kept moving. I should have taken more time to check our boat over, but fear drives you to places you would never take yourself otherwise.

Tristan's voice broke into my world. "Mom, I really think that we should keep the sails down and just motor. I think we might go faster. We're not really making a great time. What if someone is following us? The faster we get wherever we're going, the better, right?" His eye carried the heavy weight of lack of sleep.

He grew up so fast. Once again, I felt he was the grown up and not me. I patted his shoulder and replied, "You might be right, but we need to conserve fuel until we're fully loaded."

Tristan didn't respond. He just nodded in agreement while Issy hugged me and joined the conversation.

"Mom's right. Yes, we need to outrun them, but right now, outrunning them that way will get us noticed. We need to sail as much as possible. It makes us less noticeable."

When had my children become so strategically smart?

As I was contemplating on them, feeling like a proud hen, Issy jumped up from where she'd been lounging, "Dammit I forgot to check the weather reports," she dodged for the nav table and took out the tablet, "I'll do it now."

She was all panicked and I wanted her to be calm. "Baby, it doesn't actually matter if a squall comes our way. We're not really prepared, so there is nothing we can do at this point. We haven't been on the boat in months and we really didn't check her over." I remarked, holding back the fact I might be able to flatten an storm that came at us.

We weren't far from Gibraltar. We had to sail around the coast side. That route got us soon within sight of Gibraltar. Tristan shifted out to get supplies. That just left Issy and me to maneuver the boat. Raising the main sails wasn't difficult and the water around Gibraltar was not treacherous. The British always loved it. Not just for its strategic position, but also for its portage.

The rock of Gibraltar always took my breath away. That monolithic rock has stood for tens of thousands of years and would probably continue to stand there for thousands more. However, this time I didn't feel the same as I had before. I stood there contemplating the view and also checking my mental list of things to do when the Voice contacted me.

< They know that you checked out of Spain. They think you're heading for Gibraltar and then the Canaries. >

< *Don't worry! I'm working on that. We're not even checking into Gibraltar. I just wanted to be close enough to get diesel and food.* >

Tristan popped back with bags of groceries. "Sorry, Mom, but I had to use the credit card. I just didn't have enough cash."

"It's okay. Take these gas cans and hop over to this Marina and get diesel," I pointed at a map on the saloon table. He looked at it and back at me so I continued, "You've been there before when we pulled in a couple of months ago." I supplied.

His shoulder eased and he smiled. "Will do. I'll be back in a jiffy."

I wished I could move as Tristan did. He had a talent I couldn't even begin to understand and it terrified me. Issy's capability, on the other hand, was even more terrifying. Experiencing everyone's emotions wasn't really a talent, but more of a torture. How you can go through life without touching another person ever again? What if you touched them just as they they died?

"Every day that goes by, reminds me that Daddy is dead and I will never see him again. If he was here, the tank would have been full," Issy's lower lip trembled as she said that.

"If Daddy was here, many things would be different. As long as you remember him, he never really dies. That's immortality sweetheart. It isn't about being alive forever, but being remembered. As long as someone still lives and remembers you, you will never really die," my words were meant to comfort her, but saying them out loud comforted me too.

Just then, the air pressure changed followed by a pop and Tristan appeared along with four bright yellow cans of diesel.

"I got all the cans filled. I told the harbormaster I'd like him to come out and have somebody fill the cans. He didn't ask any questions and I didn't offer any answers." He smiled in satisfaction.

"Good job, Tristan! When we are done emptying these into the tank, I'll let you know."

As soon as I finished the sentence, the air pressure in the salon changed, popping my ears, and with that Tristan was gone again.

Issy and I filled the main diesel tanks. Tristan popped back with five cans along with the ones we had, picked up the empty cans and disappeared again.

< Sydney, they know you were in Gibraltar due to the credit card payment. You need to get going. They don't know where you are, but in 20 minutes they will. You probably have 40-45 minutes tops. >

< Well, we need at least 30. >

< That doesn't give you a very large window, and you can't move the boat until Tristan's back. You have to make sure he knows where you are. >

< *Why would Tristan need to know where we are? Doesn't he already know?* >

< I'll explain later. Trust me! >

< *Thank you for the update. We will move as soon as we can.* >

< Beautiful girl, I just worry. >

Even though his voice sounded terrified, I moved my focus from him and contacted Tristan.

< *Tristan, we don't have a lot of time. The Voice says that they're going to be here in 45 minutes, so fill up what you can and get the fuck out of there.* >

His response was instant < **Right, Mom. Working on the third now.** >

< *And Tristan, skip the fourth.* >

There was no answer back, so I started to give Issy instructions.

"Isolde, we have 30 minutes to check the boat over. I want to check everything. How much water do we have?" I shook my head. We didn't even check to make sure we had enough water. I should have started the water maker as soon as I got on board.

Issy called from the nav-station. "Diesel tanks are full and the water is 3⁄4 of a tank but I think we should dump it and start over. It sat in that tank a long time." She called out to me.

"Dump it! Good call."

Issy pushed a button on the panel and the sound of falling water joined with the lapping of the waves. She then continued checking our status, "Our Solar is fully charged, but the wind turbine is not putting out. I think we might have a short." She rattled off.

I shook my head again. That was another mom fuck up.

"Yeah. I'll head up the mast when Tristan gets back and we're out to sea. He can then pop me up," I started hitting every cabin and began grabbing electronic devices. "We're reading 100% on the batteries. We can charge everything." I yelled up the gangway.

I moved power chords from the other rooms to the nav-station. In the end, the charging basket resembled a box with an octopus sticking out of it.

Tristan shifted back two minutes later and we lashed all 10 the cans down on the boat, then he moved to the bow and turned on the windlass. The clanking of chain along with the slapping of water and agitated air surrounded us.

"All right. Let's go!" I announced as I turned the engines over and maneuvered us away from the giant rock.

"Where are we going, Mom?" Tristan asked still puffing air. Then ran his fingers from the base of his neck to his bangs only to pull the hair there away from his scalp.

"Where they don't expect us to. They expect the Canaries to be our last stop before we jump the pond, but we're heading straight over with no stops. We are going to Cuba and then to Panama. We are going to need to stop somewhere for supplies. We had a chance yesterday, but now they will be watching all of the Caribbean," I said.

"Exactly. So where are we going?" Issy asked and pulled at her shirt seam.

"Bermuda. We'll stop there, load up on diesel and supplies, then hit Cuba. They cannot watch every mooring." I offered keeping my eyes on the water and our heading.

Tristan smiled, "Well that's a good plan, but I can add another point to it. I can shift from place to place, so why do we even need to show that we are there? We don't use a credit card and pay only cash."

"That's a great idea. But what if they see the boat, Tristan?" Issy demanded, then stuck her tongue out.

"That is something that I cannot control. It is what it is," I replied and let the wind push my hair out of my face as we motored out to the open sea.

Over the hum of our engines and the roar of the wind, a whoomphing sound began off in the distance.

"Mom," Issy pulled on my sleeve. "There's a black helicopter headed this way."

I whipped my head back to chance a glance at the black machine heading our way.

"Tristan, take the wheel!" I ordered. The water around us grew agitated as did I. "Issy go get everyone's life jackets and lines and clip us in." I ordered over the thumping of the blades.

I moved to the port side sugar-scoop and took a position at the top of the stairs.

< You don't need to kill them, beautiful girl. Just push them back. >

His words were meant to calm me, but I found they worked to the opposite in effect. The closer they grew, the angrier I became. Issy shoved my life vest at me with my lifeline already attached. I shrugged it on never taking my eyes from the low flying helo.

How dare they follow us over a map? A map I didn't even take.

My hands curled into a balled fist. Waves started to rise 20 feet above the rest of the ocean. The helo lifted sharply to avoid the wall of water.

They altered their course to come alongside our boat. As the helo turned, the light bled through the side opening, silhouetting a man hanging from the open door along with the mounted gun.

Fear flipped through my body. Unlike the fear I felt when my father was beating me, this didn't paralyze me. I was fucking filled with rage. They knew my kids were on the boat and they brought guns anyway.

I raised my hand and the wind picked up pushing the helicopter back. I opened the palm of my hand and the gun ripped from the side of the helo causing it to rock back and forth. The man in the opening fell out and hung by a cord, swinging back and forth. His body violently slammed against the landing pads folding him in half.

< Stop, Sydney, or you will kill him. >

< He was ready to kill us! > I snarled.

< But you're better than him. >

< Am I? I'm not the weak victim anymore. If they follow us, I want them to understand fear. >

< You'll just give them more reason to hunt you. >

I closed my eyes. The earth beneath all the water moved with my rage. I had to pull back because I didn't want to create a tsunami. Taking a deep breath, I reached out with my mind and tweaked the main rotor enough to cause them to lose power for a moment, then I batted the tail, forcing it to do a full turn and lose altitude. They regained altitude and rose higher before backing off.

"Open the mainsail, and let's get out of here!" I screamed over the wind as I watched the helo head back to Gibraltar.

"They'll be watching for us now, Mom," Tristan yelled, "We don't have anywhere we can go." His shoulders were set and I stared at the back of his head.

"Cuba doesn't listen to anyone. We will be okay there," I yelled over the wind.

CHAPTER 16

HERA

Log entry

Eris stepped forth holding her head up in defiance, "So it is true. He is our father."

The others gathered around. I could feel the collective leaning in. If there was an argument to be had, Eris would be at the heart of it. If she did not start it, she was the discord behind it. Yet, in this instance I could not blame her for it.

I released the breath I had been holding, "It is true. He is your father and I am your mother. Whatever is done, is done." I wanted to hide in shame for my subterfuge, but I held my head high waiting for the onslaught.

Eris continued, "Ares went down to the city, the one named for Athena. He says he wants to raise it to the ground." She tilted her head down and looked up at me through her eye brows.

None of my children had ever shown any signs of my abilities. Other than the time when I was pregnant with Ares and Eris, there wasn't even a whisper.

"What do you mean?" I could feel my chest tightening.

Eris turned her almond-shaped blue eyes to me and quirked an eyebrow, "Ares and I have heard each other in our minds for years now. We did not say anything, because we were afraid."

My heart seized with the notion.

Could they be like Poseidon's children, cruel and domineering?

"Be afraid no more, my children. We must organize. Perseus, gather your brothers and sisters. We must go on a journey to the ends of the Earth. All of you must tell me of your abilities, no matter how small they are. I have a feeling that we may need to fight and it will not be an easy battle. Zeus and Poseidon together are formidable enemies," my eyes burned with my words and the knowledge that they had heard everything Zeus said. The truth of my folly laid bare for all to see.

What I said hit me harder the G-force of a black hole. Zeus' thirst for power would never be quenched. My own words from so long ago echoed in my mind. I admonished myself. My feelings for him had brought this. Zeus was right from the beginning. I knew what he was and I took him to my breast anyway. The High Council was right. We should have not interfered. How could I have been so stupid? However, much I feel for my children, emotion had brought all this about. I've came too far to look back now, no matter how much my heart tore in my chest.

As always, Perseus was precise and to the point. "Who is Poseidon and why is he your enemy?" He crossed his arms and stood with legs wide.

I looked from one set of crystal-clear blue eyes to another. None of the five carried the dark Themian ring.

"He is a Themian, like I am. We are not of this world but come from the stars. We are scientists and explorers. Humans think Poseidon is a God. His control of the forces of earth and water is incredible. He also has a powerful mind. His specialty is mental domination." I was straightforward with the facts, hiding none of what I knew could save all of our lives. There was no need to candy coat it. Only Hercules and Hebe were too young to fight.

"And why does he hate you? Why is he your enemy?" Hephaestus stared up at me through his bushy eyebrows.

His giant form appeared hunched over, but it was only the overdeveloped muscles that gave him that appearance. Zeus had always referred to him as the 'Hair Weak Monster' or the 'Blacksmith of the Gods', so Hephaestus carried no love for Zeus before the knowledge of his parentage and I suspected he would carry none now.

I was dodging the question and giving only the pertinent information, "Human emotion is foreign to us. We shunned emotions many millennia ago, destroying all who exhibited them. We found them to be irrational. They entice you to make choices that do not make sense or are not always good for a Themian. Poseidon has succumbed to them. They rule his every move. He's quick to anger and easily offended. He's just as desperate for power as Zeus. They both hold a desire to not only be in control but have the absolute power that comes with it. Him offering to ally himself as a brother with Zeus is a mistake and it will cost your father his life," I stopped to move my tongue around the dry inside of my mouth.

Just speaking of Zeus and his death stole the very moisture from me, but the thought of water brought the vision of Poseidon to mind and I rushed on. "Poseidon is ancient and wise beyond Zeus' understanding. He hates me because I stood against him. I've always believed we were only here to be watchers. You only exist because I broke my oath. Now, I have more reason than ever to regret the breaking of it."

I stopped, took a deep breath, and looked to each of my children's faces and continued, "Still I look at all of you and the love I feel, springs from my breasts. It's like a summer sun flying everywhere, warming my soul and the universe is a more beautiful place with you in it." Tears pricked my eyes as my chest became tight. I hugged as many of them as I could. They had all grown up so fast.

The girls clung to me and my sons held us all loosely. There was so much I needed to teach them, and so little time to do it in, but first and most important, I needed to teach them to protect their minds. Walls weren't just for cities.

"I want you all to picture a white Citadel, and inside the door and windows represented every mind possibly. Now, close them all."

Their eyes grew wide, but each in turn seemed to find a new kind of peace. They were focused as I've not seen any of them before. The air around us grew wild, then settled before my son's voice broke it.

"I've returned. The city named after Athena still stands. Where's my father so I can kill him?" Ares voice rebounded across the stone edifice behind me.

"Now is not the time to rush into battle. First, each of you must train. Each in turn for his or her special talent."

I faced Ares down. Like his father, he had a thirst for blood. But unlike Zeus, he had a mind for tactics and restraint.

Hephaestus picked up his hammer with one hand and formed a fireball with the other. "We will need better weapons than what we have," he strode away towards the column of black smoke in the distance.

I watched in fascination as he threw the fireball into the forge and the flames leaped. Hephaestus loved to work metal.

If it created something for a man to use, it was in his preview. He turned back for just a moment to survey all of us before raising his hammer and bringing it down again on the red-hot rod he'd just pulled from the fire.

Eris, smiled and turned back to me, "I can sway people to follow my commands and I feel their feelings."

What I had always suspected about her slipped into place. She was an influencing empath, so she could move whole cities with her mind. This could work in our favor.

"This is good, Eris. Tell the people to find Zeus. Send word via bonfires or runners. If we find him first, perhaps we can subdue him."

Eileithyia stood to the side unsure if she should go to the forge and help her twin or wait upon me. I beckoned her to my side. She came willingly, taking my hand in her own. Before I could say a thing, she opened her other hand and a ball of fire formed. Just like Hephestus she too controlled fire.

"Is that your talent?" I inquired.

"No. I can ease pain and heal minor wounds with my fiery touch." She dipped her head, for Eileithyia had always been shy and unassuming like her twin. They both spoke little and chose to act instead.

"You must travel up the mountain, to Jorhan's village. There, you will find your newest siblings, Hercules and Hebe. Protect them, raise them, hide them for as long as you can. I don't know how long we will be searching and if or when my Themian counterparts will descend on all of us," I whispered the last bit, then bit my lip.

If Athena decided to move against us, there would be little I could do to stop her. Mica would shift us all before we could blink an eye.

Perseus and Eros both joined to speak at once then laughed before Eros nodded her head to her twin in the quiet signal that he may lead.

Perseus rose into the sky with his use of the force of wind then lowered himself back to the ground. "I can skillfully use any item you give over to me, weather it is a sword or a discus. I need not train. I have control of wind."

Eros smiled and said, "I too control the wind, but also the light. I can burn anything to the ground with the power of our sun and light the darkest night or cave."

I smirked to myself. Just seeing her smile, brought the light to our group. But she'd left out the men who flocked to her just to get a glimpse of her precious light.

"Go and search for your father!" I ordered and both took the air, Perseus on his winged feet and Eros in a chariot. I had no idea any of them harbored such power, but would it be enough?

CHAPTER 17

SYDNEY

The breeze sweeping off the land swept relief through me. No one would be looking for us in Cuba. We would be just a few more blond Gringos looking to experience the Socialist utopia. I glanced over and saw that both kids' faces were wrapped with anticipation. Being at sea for 3 weeks makes you long for the stability of the land. I, myself wanted to sleep.

"Where should we put in?" asked Tristan, always looking ahead for the next move. He liked to have everything planned. I was more of a reactionary person and Issy used to be a fly by the seat of her pants. Now, caution-filled her every move.

"There is a bay where cruisers like to lay anchor further down the coast. We will drop anchor and sleep there the night before going ashore," I said.

"Do you think anyone is watching for us?" Issy asked.

She just couldn't stop her eyes from shifting around the horizon, her willowy frame searching for our pursuers. She stood there rigid with dread. The amount of time that we had been out of touch they could have posted watchers at every port in the Caribbean. It was not like they didn't know where we were going. Or maybe, they didn't.

Issy muttered, "We should have gone to Florida. It's easier to hide there. There are so many boats." She fiddled with her sun bleached shirt.

Tristan quirked an eyebrow at her and made a sideways glance. "They know what we look like and the name of our boat. It wouldn't take the Coast Guard long to locate us. No, Issy. Mom is right. Cuba is the best place to be. It is low tech and corrupt. We should make a few changes."

I cut in, "I want both of you to go to sleep. I'll take first watch. Issy is right. They could have people watching, so we need to be ready to leave in a hurry if necessary." I slipped my shirt off and grabbed a fresh one from the lines. My bikini was two days old and needed a good wash too, but that would have to wait until later.

Issy rounded on me. "What are we going to do, if they do come for us?" The fear poured off her and her mind buffeted mine with worry.

"I'll push them back and propel us forward. Maybe Tristan can move a few things around for us." I said but it sounded feeble even to me. None of us were trained and that too was my fault.

If I hadn't spent all these years pushing it away...

Tristan's body waved from side to side. His shoulder ridged in the same pose as Issy's. His forehead wrinkled and his lips pinched while his eyes were darting around the boat.

"Issy, can you turn off the terror? I can't take it when you hit me with it." He growled out through his teeth.

Just like that, his shoulders slumped and his face relaxed and Isolde offered him a tight-lipped smile.

"Sorry, Trist, I have a hard time keeping it to myself."

My mind began working in overdrive. Between the three of us, we should be able to stop anyone that came our way.

*****

I jerked awake, the cushions in the saloon left a kink in my neck and my hip ached.

< They're coming, Sydney! There are three boats. Wake up the kids! >

< *There are three vessels coming only for us?*>

< They are coming to arrest you, but they'll use force if needed. >

I changed my focus to the children.

< *Tristan, Isolde, get up now! We don't have time. We need to make our plans.* >

The VHF squawked in the background and I shouted. Then rubbed my sweaty hands over my shorts and opened the saloon door.

"Issy, spread the fear. Spread it to them!"

"But not on us," Tristan chimed in.

"Thanks, Tristan. I'll make sure I try to spread it just to them," she shook her head to the side to get the sleep out of her eyes before picking up the cold coffee from the fridge.

"What do you want me to do, Mom?" Tristan inquired.

"I don't know," I rubbed my forehead to wake up. "Figure out who's on those boats. Listen to their minds and switch people around. Confusion is what we need. Invent as you go."

Pleasure filled his eyes. He liked the idea.

"What about you, Mom?" He asked and pulled his lips into a wicked grin.

"We're leaving, of course," I snapped.

I went out on deck barefoot as quiet as I could and I turned on the windlass to crank the anchor. I surveyed the lights from the adjacent boats in the anchorage. The last thing in the world I desired was to run into somebody else's anchor line or ram someone's boat. I had insisted that we park on the outskirts. If we had to make a quick getaway, we could. Also, we could see if someone was approaching. Now, I was glad I'd managed it.

"Mom, I'm not sure that my fear mongering is doing any good," Issy moaned.

Tristan spouted, "I moved two people around the boats. It created confusion, but they're still coming. There's someone on one bridge. I can't touch him. Something about him is different. Not like everyone else."

< Sydney, he's dangerous. Get out of there any way you can. Use your power over the forces. >

< *You're right. I can't expect the kids to do my job.* >

"Isolde, take over the helm. I have work to do."

I moved back to the bow of the boat and locked my hand on it for balance. Tristan contacted me.

< Mom, I don't think I'm causing enough confusion, but I can't do much more. >

I replied < *Don't worry about it, Tristan. I'm going to handle this.* >

Opening my mind, I pictured the entire area. I surveyed all the surrounding boats, situating them in my mind. It was like playing battleship, only this was real life and I played the game with extraordinary abilities. The three beacon lights streamed out into the darkness on the horizon.

"Isolde, shut off all our lights! We're going dark."

Issy didn't speak, but she answered nevertheless.

< Aye, aye, Captain! >

Using my ability to control water and air, I urged our boat forward, propelling it out of the bay, without endangering us. I turned and stared at the ships behind. They continued on an intercept course, so I lifted my hand and forced them back while Isolde gained traction with our engines and our sails. However, they were struggling against the magnitude of my mind.

That's when it struck me. I was such an idiot.

< *Tristan, break their engines. Still, their screws, drop their anchors. Do whatever you need to make them stop.* >

Tristan responded in a heartbeat. < **Brilliant, Mom! I can do that.** >

< *Tristan, I'm going inside for a minute but I'll be back on deck in a sec.* >

I went into the saloon. I wanted to hear what was coming over on the VHF Channel.

"Calypso, Calypso. Stop your engines, drop anchor and prepare to be boarded. Copy."

Fuck!

I needed to have some insights, so I contacted the only entity that could offer me one, the Voice.

< Are they really going to board us? >

< No, Sydney, they don't want to board you. They really don't want to stop you. They just want you to leave Cuba's waters. Whoever's with them is demanding that they say these things. They don't want to board you. They're not even going full bore. Tristan has stopped one of them. >

< Alright. I'll up my effort to pushing us out of Cuban waters. >

The squawking from the VHF continued, but they just kept repeating themselves, demanding we stop, turn off our engines and prepare to be boarded. It was the same nonsense.

Tristan did slow them down and was eager to let me know about his achievement.

< Mom, I dropped anchor on one of them and I pulled the propeller off the other. It sits at the bottom of the ocean by now. The third one is still coming but they won't be moving for an extended period of time >

I could feel him snickering through our connection.

He didn't need telepathic contact me because I found him with a smirk covering his face as I came out on the deck.

"Oh, and they're losing fuel at a rapid pace."

Isolde and I joined him in chuckling. I reached up and patted Tristan's shoulder, "Good boy. I like how your mind works."

CHAPTER 18

SYDNEY

After we reached international waters, the VHF stopped squawking and we needed a new plan. The trip to Panama was too long and we couldn't go much longer without provisions. No matter how fast I could move the boat without diesel, there was only so much I could do about food.

"Okay, we know they're looking for us and we need fuel and supplies. They, whoever 'they' are, know we need to make landfall. How do we hide a 56-foot Catamaran?" I voiced it out loud, putting the finger on the real problem.

Issy cocked her head to the side and squinted up at me. Tristan stretched his arm up reaching behind his head to rake his fingers through his hair. Crossing my arms over my chest, I looked from one to the other.

"Let's talk it out. Come on, people! I need ideas. I may not always be here and that trick in Cuba isn't going to work every time. Whoever we are dealing with, has to have an idea of what we can do. What if they send someone like us, huh?"

Tristan straightened his spine and crossed his arms before opening his mouth.

"Why don't we change the boat name?" he offered and ran his fingers through his hair.

The intense blue stare of his eyes reminded me of someone, but I couldn't say whom. I shook it off because I had more pressing issues.

"That's a great idea, Tristan, but when we check in our paperwork, will be the same. We can't change that at sea and hope for the best. The paperwork needs to match the name." I returned. Then took a seat at the cocktail table.

Issy leaned over and slumped onto the deck cushions. "Why can't we have Tristan pull his 'now you see me, now you don't' game at the next spot? He could pop into a register's office, pick up the paperwork and bring whatever supplies we need."

Her idea was a good one, but I wasn't comfortable with it.

"Issy, I can't hide us at sea. If we get stopped right now the gig is up. Can't we just change the boat's name and take our chances? We need help, we need a guy."

Isolde's face lit up. "Uncle Zack knows a guy. He's always saying he does."

I chuckled under my breath and responded, "Not the same, Issy. He doesn't know any forgers and that is what we need." The words slowly died on my tongue.

Tristan threw a piece of dry bread at her.

I didn't like us floating aimlessly in the big blue. We needed a heading and a safe harbor. Hurricane season was just around the corner and we couldn't be out in the open with our dicks in our hands.

"Father Rizzo. His brother-in-law. He is our guy. He did that paperwork for us in Spain. He would do it." I cried.

Both faces turned to me, filled with hope. We had been at sea for more than 30 days. But I knew that Lorenzo Fortunato would do anything for the right price. He also knew how to keep his mouth shut.

I darted into the saloon and I began digging through all my paperwork from Spain. The number had to be there somewhere.

"Issy, ask me where Lorenzo Fortunato's number is." I demanded pushing my hair out of my face.

"Where is it, Mom?" She cocked an eyebrow at me.

The image flashed. It was in my cabin under the stack of paper from my purse. I dashed down the companionway. On my way there, the Voice started talking.

< Call Zack after to make the money payment. >

< *I don't know how I'm going to get it here. That's my real problem. I can't use my name.* >

< It doesn't matter what name you use. Have Tristan retrieve it from the office for you. They'll never see you. >

< *They'll know we were there.* >

< Yes, but they won't know when. Open it and leave the package behind. Take only the paperwork. >

< *Leave the gun, take the cannolis.* >

< Yes. >

My cheeks went up as my smile broke. We could do this. I was sure about it. "Okay, guys, we need a name. I don't care what name you pick."

Issy shook her head. "I'm out, Trist. It's all on you."

He pinched the bridge of his nose. He straightened and closed his eyes.

"Mom, you know stuff right?"

I nodded my head. I didn't understand what he was going for. "Yeah, sometimes. What do you mean?"

He put a hand on either one of my shoulders and asked: "What is the most common boat name in the world?"

The name flashed before my eyes.

"Barefoot II. We could give it any number we want, but that's it." I put my hands on his and continued, "Tristan, that is brilliant. We have a name. All we need now is a port for the pick-up."

Issy jumped up and pulled out the tablet. She pointed to Jamaica. "Kingston is a great place. It's close and there's FedEx. We wouldn't have to check in either. We can get a boat side service. Plus, it's a wreak. No one in their right mind goes there."

I took my phone and dialed the number.

"Bongiorno!" the voice sang out.

I was happy that the talk was in Italian. Maybe it would throw them off.

"Ciao, Lorenzo. Signora Sydney. I need your artistic talents again."

A low chuckle emitted from the phone. I heard a garbled sound as if a hand had been placed over the receiver. The voice that came after wasn't Lorenzo's, but Father Rizzo's.

"Sydney, they came not long after you left and showed me an ID from the US. I don't think they were real. They wanted to know what you were doing in the Catacombs and how long you had been here. Demanded to see everything. I put them off as long as I could. I demanded they use the usual channels for viewing. But they came back with a representative from the church, Opus Dai," he groaned but didn't stop. "They rifled through everything. I don't know if they took anything. They said you were an international criminal wanted in 5 countries for theft. Your face is everywhere here. I don't know where you are and I don't want to."

I tried to break in a few times but he kept rattling on.

"Father Rizzo, whatever they say about me, I didn't do it. I need your brother-in-law to 'draw' for me. I need papers for a boat two sets. One named Barefoot III out of anywhere. I don't care. Plus, I need papers for the kids and me, three sets. The second boat can be anything. That doesn't matter either. I just need a cover. Make us Italian, Spanish, Canadian. It doesn't matter. Please, I will have the money sent to him," I caught my breath and bit my lip.

"Lorenzo will do more than that. He will get you everything you need. Go to the bay that was discovered by the Prince. There is a man named Jose. He will meet you. Don't go ashore. He will find your boat by its name. The new one. Do not contact us again. Lorenzo says to send 1 thousand euros per set. My sister and I will light candles to the Blessed Mother and pray for you and your children."

The phone went dead. I turned The SAT phone off.

"Where is the bay discovered by a Prince? What did he mean?" I asked the kids and no one at all.

Turning my head away from the kids, I stepped out on to the deck. I wanted to feel the wind blowing. It pushed my hair out of my face.

"As far as I know, no Prince ever came to the New World," Issy said.

"They didn't. But several here were named 'Prince' by the locals."

Think, think!

He would have chosen a conquistador, someone from that time period.

"Are you sure it's a person? We have to meet this guy somewhere. It needs to be close. So, what's close?" Tristan asked.

Tristan pulled out a chart and laid it across the saloon table. The edges curled from being rolled up for 6+ years, so Issy weighted the corners with books. Tristan trailed his finger across the chart.

"Okay. We are here off the East coast of Cuba. Jamaica is 387 Nautical Miles to the West. There's Kingston, and that was once called Port Royal." He replied in a hopeful tone.

I shook my head and stated: "That came later, not in the time of discovery. We need something older. Spanish, or French maybe."

Issy piped in, "What about Haiti? It is 238 nautical miles southwest. The largest city is..." Every index finger moved to Port Au Prince.

"Yes, Port Au Prince was named after the ship that found it, 'The Prince'. It makes sense. Yes, we have a heading and it's only a two-day pass." I finished and kissed Issy on her forehead.

Tristan ran his fingers through his hair and pulled on his bangs.

"We don't have any paint for the boat. I'll have to jump ashore to get some," he shook his head while Issy pulled in a quick breath covering her mouth with a hand.

"I don't have a landing spot. I need a picture of a place to jump to. That's how it works." Raising his head, his eyes bored into mine.

I answered, "We'll get you one. Don't worry. If you need to see it, we can use Google Earth." After that, I moved chisels into both kids' hands, tilting my head to the rear of the boat. "That name isn't going to scrap itself-off, so let's get it done."

I turned the boat to our new heading. The dip around the end of Cuba would take us two days. Then, it was a straight shot to Port Au Prince.

CHAPTER 19

SYDNEY

"Tristan, what is the farthest you've jumped?" I asked.

He ran his fingers through his hair, pulling the bangs in front, "I don't know. How far offshore were we in Gibraltar? 20-30 miles?"

I wasn't sure either. I just knew that we could see the rock and parts of the high rises.

"20 thereabouts. How did you jump there?"

A smile broke over his face, "When we pulled through back in November, we went to that restaurant with the Greek food. I used the bathroom there. It had a stain on the wall in one of the stalls. I jumped there, then I walked out." He winked at me and grabbed an olive out the open can on the table.

The wheels began turning. As I was trying to calculate all the possibilities, the Voice started talking.

< Do you think he can do it? >

< *Yes, Tristan is strong, It's the best way.* >

< If you think it's too far, have him go to Florida. >

< *No. This is the best idea. What would you do if you were here?* >

< The same thing. >

"Jump back to Gibraltar. Hit the ATM while your there. Use my credit cards, take the gas cans and fill up. Your landing zone for supplies is the saloon and for diesel is the back deck next to the railing."

His eyebrows shot up into the stratosphere. "But, Mom, I don't know if I can jump that far."

His eyes turned to Issy and she nodded. "Yes, you can, Tristan. Don't think about it. That's how you did it last time."

She got up and headed to her cabin, then she bounced back into the saloon.

"Put this on and I'll do up your face. Savvy?" She had a Captain Jack Sparrow hat with all the hair and a can of moose. She began shaking the can. "What about his facial hair?"

Tristan shook his head. "I don't want to wear eyeliner. Anyway, Jack Sparrow has a gold tooth."

Issy barked a laugh out. "Don't worry. We just need to make it look like you're a boat bum that thinks he's Captain Jack, not the real thing. There's no way they're going to think it's you. You always dress like a yuppie. Now you just need some dirty beach bum clothes."

< Brilliant! Our girl has some real brains. >

< *Yes, she does, but when did she become our girl? She's Gabe's daughter, not yours.* >

< I feel everything you do, beautiful girl, so she's mine too. >

< *Just because you feel everything, I feel doesn't make my life yours.* >

< Sydney, I'm sorry. I love your children with every fiber I'm capable of. I was hoping you… >

I crushed him, my chest clenched. His desolation filled me.

< I'm sorry, I love you too. Yes, I can share them with you. Please, Voice you are not alone. I don't want you to think just because you're not here, you don't matter to me. The kids, I can share. I know you need us just as much as we need you. Please! >

< Call me when you need me. I can't right now. >

As he pulled away, I slumped down to the table banquet. Apparently, Issy heard everything because she started talking.

"Mom, he's been with you most of your life. He watches over us. Without him, I would have been raped and God knows what else. He deserves more than you brushing him off. Uncle status at least."

I looked at her and replied, "That's not how he thinks of you. He feels like a father, not an Uncle."

Tristan and Issy locked eyes, then broke. Issy grabbed my hand.

"You can share with him, right?" She gave me a squeeze and her eyes widened with her pleading.

"Yes, I just… I share everything with him. I never thought about sharing you guys too." I felt like a heel. All he had ever done was help me, and comfort me. He is our family and families argue and forgive.

The space in my mind was vacant without him, so I just said a silent 'I'm sorry' and hoped that he received the message. The only response was from Issy standing right there with me.

"Mom, he'll be back. You hurt him, so he needs a little space." She rubbed her hand across my back.

The muscles around my heart seized. I didn't want to hurt him. I just… didn't think. Now wasn't the time to fight. We had to be a united front. There couldn't be any divisions. I was taken from my words when Tristan started talking.

"Mom, why don't you come with me? We could get it done twice as fast."

It was a great idea, but I had my doubts.

"I can't. Issy doesn't have any defensive abilities. We can't leave her alone on the boat. As long as you hit the ATM last, they won't know you were there until you're gone. Use the credit cards at small businesses that only run their machines once a day."

"How do you know which ones do that?" Tristian asked then scratched at the Captain Jack hat.

"Oh, the small places do it at closing most of the time when they close out the books for the day. Papa did it that way at the Restaurant. It's pretty standard. Only the next morning the bookkeeper would go over everything from the day before." I said and adjusted his hat.

"Okay, Mom. I'll move as fast as I can." He smiled and kissed my cheek.

"They aren't going to see you coming do the diesel first. We need that the most."

Biting my lower lip, I grabbed his shoulders and pulled him to me. Laying my hand on the side of his head I kissed his stubbled cheek. My baby had grown up and I couldn't protect him anymore. A hand landed on my arm pulling me back.

"Mom, the sooner he leaves, the sooner we can too." Issy supplied then kissed her brother.

Warm arms encircled me and I placed my hands over hers. Issy leaned her head on to the back of my neck. She didn't speak out loud, but she did talk to her brother.

< Go, Tristan and come back to us.>

< Yes, sis. It's like drinking a bottle of Rum, savy? >

A low nervous chuckle issued all around. His blue eyes twinkled and were gone.

We waited in silence for a few moments that felt like years, but we received word from Tristan.

< Fuck me, I made it! Hot dog, Mom. Do you know what this means? I can go anytime, anywhere I want. That's so fucking cool. >

I heaved a sigh of relief before answering < *Tristan, I'm thrilled that you made it, but this is a family show.* >

< Mom, you curse all the time, but I'll keep it down. > He humphed.

The gas cans arrived like clockwork, two at a time. Boxes with food arrived in the saloon. I was happy to see creamer for coffee.

< *Tristan?* >

He didn't answer, so I tried Isolde.

< Issy, can you hear him, feel him? >

The silence filled me like a rock in my belly.

"Issy?" I headed down to her cabin. Every step took an eternity. She laid on her bed with her eyes open. I leaped to her side. Running my hands over her, my heart throbbed.

"Wake up, Issy! Where is your brother?" I demanded.

I patted the side of her face. Her eyes stared up at the deck above unseeing. Placing my hand over her eyes, as I touched either side of her head, I started seeing through Tristan's eyes. Three men had him seated in a room. There was a two-way mirror on one wall. The men asked him where his passport was and how he had gotten into the country. He didn't respond. My mind took over his.

"I want the American Embassy. I want to speak with the American Consulate." The word came from me but out of his mouth. His mind was crowded and I could feel us all pressed together like tuna fish in a can.

Both men stood up and left the room.

< Tristan, can you hear anyone behind that mirror? >

< **No, Mom.** >

< *Then jump. Now!* >

I pulled back. Collapsing on Issy, I rolled to the side and she coughed

"Mom, I was there with him. You told him what to do. How did we get there?"

My head pulsed with the information filling it. I had not just been in his mind. Not just there but in control too. I could have made him say anything. This was more than weird. I didn't have time to think more about it because I heard Tristan speaking next to us.

"Mom, I'm back. They grabbed me at the ATM. I'm sorry. The card was rejected and I tried it again. That's how they caught me. I should have walked away."

I should have known. I started shaking my head and covering my eyes. The light pounded into my corneas.

If this keeps up we are going to be sunk in no time.

CHAPTER 20

SYDNEY

I was still not sure who the people following us were. Were they with the US government or a private entity? How did they even discover us?

But none of that changed the hardest problem I had to face - Zack. I had to call him and ask him to pay Lorenzo and I could not put it off any longer.

I dug the SAT phone out of the nav draw and flipped it on. I dialed the Cosimo's office number and waited for Maria to answer the phone. It rang three times before the pick-up.

"Ciao, Cosimo's how can I help you?" I bit back my tears, Nonna's voice sounded tired and distracted.

I had to reply. I gulped the lump in my throat down, forcing it into my belly and said: "Please ask Zack what is Veritas Rainmaker trading at."

A sharp intake of breath and a muffled voice later I heard Zack's voice, "Where are ya? How could you leave me like that? Are the kids okay? I'll come to you, it's not safe..."

I had to stop him from talking, so I shouted over him "I don't have a long time to talk. I'm in trouble. Check our old email for instructions."

Zack's voice came through muffled, "Is it them? Are they coming for Tristan too?"

I couldn't wait for Zack. I was too scared they would triangulate our position in the ocean, but then his words sank in.

"What do you mean 'too'? What the fuck, Zack?" My voice cracked.

"Email me. I'll get you what you need. Keep the kids safe and don't trust anyone," he sounded terrified.

The line went dead. I stood there shaking with the SAT phone held so tightly in my hand that Tristan had to pull it from my white-knuckled grip and shut it off. I wrapped both my arms around him and held on for a moment, shaking.

"It's okay, Mom. We are going to be okay. I promise." He pulled back and a déjà vu of Tom Shipman slammed back into me, but I pushed it away.

"I have to write uncle Zack," I pushed the tears out of my eyes and kissed Tristan's forehead. I looked into his eyes, he smiled and headed to his cabin.

Our old email was Veritas_Rainmaker and it was an encrypted email out of Georgia. Actually, a lot of traders have them, so this wasn't the only one. It was just the one Zack and I used. No emails were ever sent, only saved. Or sent to ourselves. It was one of the ways we tried to keep secrets, but with the NSA data collection, our attempts could be for nothing.

My father always said that the FBI had a file on everyone and knew how many sheets of toilet paper you wiped your ass with.

I logged in any way:

Zack,

I need you to deliver 15,000 euros to a Lorenzo Fortunado. The account number is below. Whatever you see, or hear, I didn't do it. I'm out of cash and can't access my accounts. I'm going to pull from Gabe's. I hope it still works. Then I'm heading out to the deep blue. They aren't after Tristan, 'they' are after me. I got myself into a lot of trouble. I can't explain and it's safer if I don't.

If the card doesn't work, I don't know what I'll do for cash. Sell my rings maybe.

Don't look for us. I love you, Zack. Also, Nonna, Maria and all the rest. Be safe! You didn't talk to me, you haven't heard from me.

I'll be back,

Syd

There were a bunch of old emails from after Gabe died. I clicked on one that was dated a year ago.

Dear Syd,

I know that you don't want to hear from me. By the way, thanks for the heads up that you were leaving, I figured you'd give me at least enough time to talk to you. But that's not what I'm emailing for. I'm not busting your balls. I promised Gabe I'd take care of you and the kids.

Great Uncle Federico died the same day as Gabe.

Zack

The next was a couple of weeks later and much of the same. Then I found one from three months ago.

Dear Syd,

I need to talk to you. It's important, really important. It can't happen over an email or a phone. Face to face only. I'll meet you anywhere. Something super important is happening and it affects all of us. I don't think you knew everything there was to know about Gabe and it's important you do. I could save yours and the kid's life. What I have to tell you is life changing and it will alter the course of mankind.

Every Sunday, I'll be at the coffee shop where we first met. If it ain't me, someone will be there. I don't care when but you must meet me.

Zack

Zack was not a drama queen, nor did he overstate anything, unless he wanted a trade. But this sounded bad, or he found God. I was not sure which.

It could be a trap, but if it was, why didn't he just say the name of the coffee shop? Zack was like that, always leaving little tidbits out of a story. He said you should always keep something for yourself. If you heard him tell how we met you'd think it was a bar, instead of cast-iron tables at a sidewalk café on Palm Beach. I always let him have his little secrets, it was part of his charm.

The computer pinged letting me know a new email arrived. Its origin was itself.

Syd,

I sent the money. I'm glad you and the kids are okay.

No, I don't want to know where you are. It is safer that way. Gabe's accounts are all still up and running. I'd send you money but then they could find you. Sell the rings if you must. I'll find them. Whatever you do, don't go to a church or trust a priest.

We love you.

I know you'll be back. Cosimo's are fighters.

Zack

It sounded sappy for Zack, but the church thing creeped me out. I didn't have time for Zack and his religious crusade. I logged out the turned off the wifi. Two mental groans followed the lost connection.

*****

Port-au-Prince was going to be sticky. We couldn't get off the boat and we couldn't let anybody see us change the name. Tristan was doing the best he could with what little we had on board, but I highly doubt that using electricians' tape to map out a name on the back end of a boat was going to convince anyone up close.

"You really sure the electrician's tape is all we have?" I mourned.

God, if I ever believed in you, please help us now.

"Ya, Mom. Got lots of marine grades white paint, and marine sparr. But we don't have any black paint of any kind," Tristan waved his hand over the contents of the workroom and the lockers we'd emptied.

"Dad always said 'if we don't have it, what we do have, will have to do,'" Issy inserted then giggled.

~ 263 ~

Both, me and Tristan, looked at her with exasperation, but he started talking first.

"Are you supposed to change the name in the middle of the ocean without anything to help?"

It was my time to intervene. "All right, use electrician's tape. Make it look as good as you can. Also, use a utility knife. Maybe trim it nicely or something?"

Yeah maybe if you trimmed it all nice and pretty no one will notice its tape. Or not.

Tristian examined the roll of black tape in his hand turning it over and looking at both sides. "Look, Mom, I'll make it as nice as I can with the utility knife. We're just block lettering anyway, okay?" His eyebrows reached his hairline with hope, so I had to give him something.

"I'm sure you'll make it great," I said as I forced the best fake smile a mother could churn out.

Father Rizzo had said that as long as we pull into the bay, someone would find us. I got off the phone without figuring out who that someone was. Jose, he said Jose.

We pulled into one of the bays. Issy lowered the windlass and set the anchor. We couldn't get off the boat, or we would have to check into immigration. Of course, we weren't going to get a marine ball because you had to check in for that too. We just had to hope we weren't in anyone's way.

Issy took the first watch. It was early in the morning and the sun was beginning to light the sky and reflect off the water and still no one had been around. I grew uncomfortable about staying much longer. In the distance, the sound of an engine broke the monotony of the water slapping between the hulls.

"Mom, I can feel him. He's anxious and scared," Issy said then shivered. The morning was cool, but not cold enough to warrant goosebumps yet the hair on my arms rose.

I immediately scanned the horizon; a small dinghy was heading our way. The gray panga blended in nicely with the surrounding terrain.

The closer he came, the more certain I was that he was our contact, but I grabbed the flare gun anyway. There was no way I was going to be caught by one man in a dinghy.

"Tristan, you stand at the windless. I want to pull the anchor immediately if necessary. Issy, I want you to sit at the bow ready to turn the engines and get us the hell out of here if this goes pear-shaped," I ordered and planted both feet on the deck facing the oncoming boat.

My family was becoming a well-oiled machine.

"Yes, Mom!" They both chimed.

The boat came alongside and the first thing the man yelled in Spanish, as I leveled flare gun on him was "Who discovered this bay?"

I replied, "The Prince." I wanted to make sure that both of us were talking about the same thing, so I added: "Who was the prince?"

"Why? She was a ship, of course." The man held his hand up as a sign of 'I give up'.

"Come aboard! We've been waiting for you." I waved him over.

He tied his dinghy up to one of the sugar scoops and stepped on board with grocery bags which he immediately set down on the table.

"My name is Jose. That is all you need to know. I do not need to know your names nor do I care. This is the package that was sent to me, that is yours." He laid a FedEx envelop on the table.

We didn't even blink. We didn't want to interrupt him.

"I will bring you more diesel and whatever foodstuffs you need. There are instructions in the package of what to do. The bags are filled with supplies, I was told to bring." Jose didn't smile, his shoulder were tight and he kept surveying the water between us and land.

Not once did he look at any of us.

"I will come back to this boat only once and then you must leave Port-au-Prince, or you will be noticed. Don't make your changes here. Find an atoll or a small island. I don't care, whatever you do, but don't it here." He was not unfriendly, just gruff. His eyes kept shifting left and the right scanning the horizon and he moved on his feet back and forth.

Jose was a short squat man with powerful shoulders and hands. He looked as if he'd been working the sea his entire life. I spied a glance into his boat. A machete laid next to the tiller. He clearly carried it in case of trouble.

"Port-au-Prince is a dangerous place?" He supplied.

"When you're being pursued, the world is a dangerous place." I returned.

With a sharp nod of his chin, he turned and loosen his boat line, climbed in and motored away.

I opened one of the bags while Issy opened the other bag, slowly stacking things on the table. It was an interesting mix of items. There was hair dye for three people. One black and two red.

I looked from Tristan to Isolde and asked: "Alright, who gets to be black?"

"There's no way I'll be a redhead with one of you two," Tristan stated then patted his hair snatched the box of black dye and shook it at us.

Issy and I laughed out loud.

"All right, Tristan. You get to have black hair, so Issy, I guess you and I are redheads."

"Mom, are you sure one bottle will I do it?" Issy asked while wrapping her hand around the mass of waving hair that crowned her head.

"Sweetheart, I guess that if we need more will have to make due," I replied.

I decided to dye Issy's first and us what was left to highlight my own. I kept searching among the rest of the supplies. There was a can of black paint and a large envelope with three sets of passports inside and three sets of boat papers. One of them said 'Barefoot III' as I asked. I pulled it out and set it off to the side. There was also a handwritten letter.

I heaved a sigh of relief. We wouldn't need to find a way to get the paperwork. I hugged the letter to my breast and thank Father Rizzo before starting to read the letter.

Dear Sydney,

I'm very sorry that you are having these problems. I don't believe all the lies they are spreading about you and your children. Go to Panama, into the Bocas De Toro area, 9.268812, -82.142601. There is a man there and he will help you. Don't raise your sails no matter what you do. I wish you the best of luck on all your journeys, wherever you go. I truly hope that you found what you were looking for down in the catacombs. Give the encrypted zip drive to the man on the boat when he comes back and he will get it back to me.

Thank you for all your help. May the Holy Mother Bless you and Godspeed!

Father Rizzo

"What's it say, Mom?" Tristan's voice cut the air and leaned over my shoulder to read the note.

"He wishes us well and good luck in all our journeys."

Issy went out to the back of the boat, looked at the name and came back in.

"I'm not really sure we need the paint, Mom. Believe it or not, the lettering looks pretty good. I think Tristan did a great job."

"Well, I don't how long we're going to have it. Just leave it and the next time we need to switch names, we will use the paint," I muttered as I stared down at the map I'd laid out on the table.

Even though our Bocas map was only a year and a half old, the area there changes so fast that you needed a new map every year. The entrance to the bay we were headed to was a narrow passage with a shallow draft. I bit my lip.

We can make it. We have to.

Deja Vu overtook me again when Tristan popped his head out of his cabin. For a moment I thought he looked like Tom, Adrian's father, but the boat shifted with my emotions and the spell was broken.

Isolde and I dyed her hair and it came out a deep auburn. It actually looked nice on her even with her tan. She didn't carry the freckles of a true redhead, so I was not really sure how it would stand up under closer scrutiny. Her disguise would hold out probably about as well as mine. Luckily, there was just enough dye to do my hair with pretty even coverage.

Seeing myself as a redhead was shocking, I'd never been anything but a blonde. A girl gotta do what she's gotta do to hide. I shrugged off my misgivings.

Every time I thought about where we were going, and how we were going to get there, I kept thinking to myself that there had to be some answers out there. After all the danger, and thousands of miles, there had to be some answers.

I'd heard people talk about premonitions, although they said it was the only one they'd ever had. Things like they decided not to drive the way they normally drive and turned out there was a giant accident. Or they decided at the last minute to make a turn just before a car exploded. My personal favorite was the woman who felt guilty about going home from work the day of the San Bernardino shooting. She said that she just felt like she had to go home because she left the coffee pot on. She didn't know why she had to leave work just knew she had, and survived.

That was what I felt like. There was no rhyme or reason why we had to find that island. I didn't know for sure if we would find anything there. All I did know was unequivocally, I had to go.

We swapped out all of our passports. The funny part was that they had pictures of both Issy and me with red hair and Tristan's hair black. I guess father Rizzo already knew exactly who was going to do what.

Father Rizzo said 'God knows all'. I didn't believe that to be true but you had to believe in God for that to work. A nice idea didn't make it real. Every time I thought about all the religion that they shoved down my throat as a child, got me angry. How could people hand themselves over to God without knowing if he was real? What if God was not real and this was just a giant mass hysteria to keep humanity under control?

As the sun finally went down, I heard a whirring sound of a small outboard motor approaching. Jose didn't come on board this time. He simply attached the diesel cans to our hoist rig and we lifted them over. Then we handed back empty ones. Last and not least we hoisted over groceries and I thanked him.

"Do not thank me, just go quickly. You never saw me. You don't know who I am. I will never see you again," he said without being unkind. He was just more scared about the fact that we had seen him than that he'd seen us.

"Do we stay or sail out tonight?" Tristan asked no one in particular, while he lashed the new cans to the deck.

Jose's quivering voice echoed in my mind 'leave as quickly as possible.' He was right.

"No, we leave now. What's the weather looking like, Issy?" I asked carrying bags into the salon to be sorted and stowed.

She gave me the thumbs up and she replied, "We have a weather window for three days."

"We sail out tonight. Tomorrow, in the morning, will see if we can find somewhere to lay anchor and get some rest." I ran my hand over my eyes to whip the sleep away. It didn't work.

I carried the bags of groceries into the salon and began pulling up the seat cushions and opening the storage compartments to put the canned goods away. Tristan washed his hands and added the fresh fruit and vegetables to our fruit hammock while Isolde rolled up the Panama Bocas Del Toro's map to reveal our main Caribbean map weighing it down at the corners with books. Something about her gait was uncomfortable. She moved quickly in an agitated manner.

"You find us a place to rest, Issy?" I inquired looked up long enough to see if she'd heard me.

"Yeah, Mom. We've been at sea too long and we need a rest. We're all getting tired. I too am starting to make mistakes," she barked then mouthed a 'sorry'.

Tristan nodded his head in agreement before talking. "She's right, Mom. I already feel exhausted. We didn't really get a lot of sleep last night. We constantly need to keep watch, we need to go somewhere where there are no people and we don't have to worry about being spotted."

I gave them both a tight-lipped smile.

"Find us an anchorage, Issy. We've got our new paperwork. They're not looking for the Barefoot III so it doesn't matter if our boat is spotted. As long as we don't raise our sails in front of anybody, there's no reason why anyone would recognize us."

Both of them nodded their heads. I was sure that they were having some kind of mental exchange because Tristan waited on Issy to glance through her eyebrows me.

"We were thinking that this would be a good spot." She pointed to an atoll on the map and continued, "It is a relatively deserted grouping and is the only landing place between here and Panama. We could probably park out there for a couple of days, get some rest, clean up the boat and maybe make a few changes here and there."

Issy shrugged and rubbed her eyes. This was taking a toll on all of us.

"That'll do nicely. Lock it, stow it, and let's head out. That's a two-day passage, with me maybe less," I rubbed Issy's back.

She pulled a bag of coffee out of the last bag and we all smiled.

"There is a God," Tristan announced while looking at the ceiling his hands held in supplication.

Issy shoved him and I went and raised the anchor.

CHAPTER 21

HERA

Log entry

Searching for Zeus proved to be more difficult than finding a single grain of rice in a field.

"Somehow we have to find Zeus. I heard a rumor about a village where a young girl was abducted and violated. When she returned, she committed suicide. They said the man who took her had black glossy hair and claimed to be the King of the Gods."

Every report about the evil that started appearing everywhere in Greece filled me with shame.

"That sounds more like Zeus." I held back the Poseidon reference.

I still couldn't understand the lack of restraint. Both Zeus and Poseidon were scavenging in the countryside. They were trying to draw me out away from my children.

"I heard a rumor." Perseus began, "Not far from where we are, many buildings collapsed from the earth shifting and people died. Perhaps if the Goddess of the Mountain had come down to help them, they might still be here."

Perseus words cut me. He knew I wasn't strong enough to save them. Not on my own. Earth was not my specialty.

"Perseus, I cannot confront both of them. I don't know if it was Poseidon or Zeus, but one of the two is trying to entrap me. I barely drove Poseidon off the first time he attacked me. If Zeus is with him, I can never win." I shook my head to drive out the fear that gripped me over a confrontation.

My fear was that I could not drive Poseidon off this time. My worry had nothing to do with Zeus. Poseidon was the greater threat.

Ares crossed his arms with a tall stance, "Mother, there are many people that are hurting. It could easily have been my sister because Eris loves to create chaos and trouble. I'm surprised she's even still on our side and hasn't joined our father."

I had to get all my children in hand. We had to move as one force. The years were flying by at a rapid pace. Hercules and Hebe would soon develop their full abilities. They will join our search for Zeus. By then there will be no excuses.

Because I didn't answer, he continued. "She likes to terrorize people, Mother. She's not maliciously cruel. She doesn't pull the wings off flies, but if you are Gods and we are your children, then we must be Demigods. She sees our differences and forgets herself."

"Toying with humans is like pulling the wings off flies. Don't you see that meddling with any life form that cannot defend itself from you is wrong?" I shot back in irritation, running my hands down my tunic to smooth out the folds.

Hercules approached, "And yet, our sister seems so enticed by all the wings of the male flies."

I felt the air move over my tongue as it dried. My mouth hung open in shock.

"You too, Hercules, have found most human women quite interesting," Perseus replied.

"Yes, I will admit the flies are sweet. Especially on the back side where they are so ample and close." He chuckled.

The boys snickered. I knew that my sons loved to play with all who they desire and that every woman wished to carry a child from a son of Zeus and Hera.

"Can you not help us find whoever is committing these atrocities, Hercules, or are you too busy playing with the flies?" Perseus loved to bait his younger brother. At sixteen Hercules resembled a man more than a boy. He was already larger than most men would ever be. He carried the strength of three bulls and a lion all rolled into one.

I watched their male-by-play long enough, with Perseus poking fun at Hercules. Hercules tossing his long hair back and bellowing in mirth and irritation. But now was the time to intervene.

"Your playful lust filled bantering has no place now. You shall have to find other times to do this. Now is the time we need to sway as many people as possible to help our cause. We must put a stop to their evil machinations anyway we can." I instructed and tilted my head to the side.

It didn't matter how many times I used the forces to move myself around Greece looking for any news of Zeus. All I came across was always old news and every time it came with a long line of dead bodies, widowed women, fatherless children and women who desperately wished to never see Zeus again. With every passing day, month, year I despaired of ever catching him and always playing catch up.

"Mother, a strange man appeared in the village asking for you. He looked at me strangely." Hercules resembled me greatly, but all in the region knew I had adopted children.

My belly clenched. "Did he give his name?"

"No, he only said that he was an old friend and you would know who he was." The boy belted his sword on and quickly added daggers to his arsenal. I placed a hand over his to still him. There was no need to ready for a fight.

I did not have friends old or new with the exception of Jorhan.

"Did he say what village he was sent from?" I asked still hoping it could be from Jorhan's village.

"He said he was from Alethea. I've heard you mention Atlantis before, they sound similar." Hercules leaned in holding his breath and waiting for my answer.

"What color is his hair?" I asked and swallowed back the churning in my belly.

Oh, please let it not be Apollo.

"It's black and his eyes green like moss."

Micah. It must be Micah. He appeared alone?

I stood up and gazed at my image in the reflection of the metal shield. Brushing my hair lightly my fingers, I ran my hands down my tunic hoping to smooth out whatever wrinkles may be present and I lifted my head.

"Yes, you may open the door now."

It swung wide and standing in the middle of the main thoroughfare was Micah. Many of the villagers were bowing to him. He had a staff in his hand with two snakes twisted around the end. It was the staff of the High Council.

I stood in the doorway with the sun at my back. He would be blinded by the dazzling light. I didn't want him to be comfortable seeking me out and demanding information from me. I walked to the center of my dais, taking my golden colored throne. My head was 5 feet above his.

"Herathina, I've come at Athena's request to seek out any information you have on this new 'God', Zeus." Micah squinted up at me.

"He is not a God. None of us are. I simply rule here and nothing more." I answered without giving any information away.

"Don't play semantics with her. Athena is enraged." Micah chided and glanced around at the gathering crowd of men.

"My name is no longer Herathina. It's Hera and you may call me that. Herathina died when Poseidon took over Alethea and you stood by and did nothing. As for Zeus, he is my husband. I gave him the Primordium and now he is immortal. I know it was wrong and he must die." The iron grip on my emotions barely held.

Micah's shoulders sag as he shook his head slightly from side to side.

"You know what this will mean for you?"

I did. "I will be punished as I deserve to be. I have broken my oaths and no one likes an oath breaker. I have shamed my people and myself. I will be punished as I deserve to be. Before the High Council rules, I will use all my power to help eliminate this scourge from humanity. Our ancestors were correct. Emotions are vile, they are like an illness that infects you. They affect your very thinking, making you so sick that you will take the very things that you hold most dear and turn your back on them. All for the sake of an emotional feeling, a chemical reaction from your mind." I had to calm myself, for the wind was picking up.

"Hera, they intend to exile Poseidon as soon as they can find him. Do you know where he is?" Micah's short tunic kicked up with the wind.

I knew all of that. There was no need to repeat Hermes words. I had been in the citadel along with him.

"Poseidon offered Zeus a deal. He agreed to be his brother and his ally. They are both playing a scourge on humanity. They've been attacking the humans all along the Greek countryside, mostly close to the ocean. They are trying to lure me out." I supplied holding my head high and my face blank.

He knew all of this. I could see it in his eyes. I was waiting to find out what Athena's plan really was.

"Then, you must agree to lure them to us and we will take them both." Micah moved closer to the dais.

Bait, it made sense. I was what they wanted and if I was Athena, I would use me too. If I were to die I would have paid for my mistakes.

"How can you take them? Poseidon is strong, arrogant and bloodthirsty. You have no idea what he's capable of. On the other hand, Zeus does not know restraint. He will use any and all means at his disposal to kill all of us, all the while, killing as many humans around him as pleases him. I will help you, but what is the plan?"

"Do not leave the village. I will return tomorrow. Zeus marauding around the countryside and killing humans is not really that great of a crime in Themian world. He's only killing his own kind. Poseidon, on the other hand, is the true criminal."

Still focusing on the wrong objective. How do they keep missing the mark?

"Have you ever known a human that could use the forces, Micah? He is not human anymore. He is something else and I already tried to poison him. It does not work." The desire to bite my lip or cover my face was strong but I held my body in check.

"Athena is the best battle tactician. Trust your fellow Themian's. I'll return to you as soon as possible. Be ready!"

He must have been joking. They left me here for thousands of years and now I had to trust them?

"I will be here," I demurred.

Micah glanced over at Eris again and a couple of times at Hercules. Micah shifted out and the surrounding crowd squeaked in shock at his disappearance. I was not sure exactly why he was giving them the once over.

There was only one thing that I could really do and that was to dream walk Zeus. However, he pushed me out.

< I don't want to hear the evil machinations of an old woman.> Zeus spat.

I was such a fool. The Themian's were right. You should only have children with a true mating. It was foolish to believe being with a normal human would be all right.

A few hours later, Micah knocked on my door.

"Athena has a plan. You are to be transported with me to the Straits of Herakles. After I'm done shifting you there, you are to send for Poseidon and Zeus. Lure them as close as possible to Alethea. I will check in on you every now and again. We will not allow them to harm you. I will shift you out if I must."

I didn't for a minute believe that he would save me. I was an oath breaker and expendable.

"Why does it have to be the Straits of Herakles? It's a highly populated area with many human settlements there. Aren't you worried about the death toll?" I asked while trying not to release myself.

"Hera, they don't just want to kill you. They both want to kill humanity down to a more manageable size, so they're easier to control. You know this is about power and in order to rule over the human race, they have to get rid of the first Goddess." Micah stared me down.

That is not all they want.

"What about Athena? She has an entire city, a temple built to her. Is she not a Goddess?"

"It is not the same. In their minds, you are the problem, not her." He shook his head.

My shoulders slumped. I was the target, I and my children.

"I will go there, but when it seems they are close I want you to shift me to the other end of the continent, further away from the human settlements. I want to be just out of their reach. It will further enrage them. This way they are more likely to follow me wherever I am. Shift me to where there are no human settlements. From there we can take them. We will still be close to Alethea."

With that being said, I contacted my children, sending them an image of the battlefield.

< Come, my children! It is time to fight. Gather all the humans and move them as far from the straits as possible. Use whatever means necessary. >

Their voices were a choir of assent.

Micah never touched me as the air pressure changed.

The giant statue of Herakles spanning the Straits was truly amazing. Humans felt enough for a God to be willing to construct this. Who was I fooling? It was built for a hybrid that believed he was a God and forced them. He wasn't a God at all. The stories they were telling even now of myself and Poseidon were unbelievable.

When the dust falls what would they say then?

The sky filled with electricity and every hair rose on my body. Zeus was coming. The air filled with the tang of the sea salt and the clouds bloomed in the sky, dark and ominous.

< Micah, let them see me! >

I saw Zeus. If I didn't know he was a human, I would have believed he was a God. He had all the attributes of one. He appeared bare-chested with his toga partially slung over one shoulder and his black mane pushed back from his brow by the wind. All of it capped off with a devilish smile scraped across his face. He carried lightning in one hand, and the winds blew himself up so he could float. Expending that amount of power must have been tiresome.

My heart leaped. Was I capable of doing this? This was the first time I'd seen Zeus in almost two decades. Clearly, he was not just surviving on Earth, he thrived and he had found a bracelet. The crystal light shot sparkled from it.

I looked out over the water as a giant wave rose from the sea bed and saw Poseidon riding atop it. He too was clothed in a tunic to the waist slung over the opposite shoulder, while his golden hair was whipping around his head with the wind. Every muscle in his body wound tight ready for the pounce. He was riding in a giant half clamshell fashioned into a form of a chariot drawn by a horse-like creature.

They were giant sea creatures that looked like horses, but they couldn't be. The creatures pulling his shell had halters made of crystalline beads. Bile rose in my throat when I realized that they were Themian's. He forced them by dominating their minds, using them as slaves and making them take whatever shape he desired.

I wanted to allow my body to expel whatever food remained in my belly but swallowed it back instead. I would need the strength, more than the emotional release. I was not sure that the emotions weren't, in fact, a disease of the mind.

Every muscle in my body trembled with anticipation. Lightning strikes and thunder rumbled in the background. The wind became more remote and with every moment I waited there and the tang of ozone thickened.

< Micah, he's very close. All Zeus has to do is hit me with one bolt and I will be dead. Is that part of your plan? > I demanded.

< No, just a little closer. Taunt them. Say something to enrage the both of them. > Micah urged me.

< Enrage them? Can't you feel their rage already? > I retorted.

Inside I was quaking with fear, but outside I had to put on a demeanor of cool indifference. These two men together certainly behaved like brothers.

"So, Poseidon, I see you finally found your King to rule over you. Do you find him to be a benevolent or a malevolent ruler?" I needled.

Poseidon's lips curled into a sneer, "Zeus rules not over me. We are allies, brothers in our fight against you. You are the one who has done all of this." He hissed.

The waves behind him rose up and crashed back down with his anger.

"Are you so sure he doesn't see himself as your ruler? See how he lords over the top of you, holding onto a lightning bolt? You know electricity will kill everything in the water around you, including your enslaved witless Themian's that you're using like beasts of burden. Do I know who it is that you enslaved into these forms? Anyone important? Anyone I know?"

He laughed, shaking the shell and causing the ocean to heave.

"No one who is noteworthy, Hera. That is what you want to be called these days, isn't it? Hera, Zeus' whore?" He whipped the water horses and they screamed in pain.

"Yes, everyone seems to be changing their names, so I changed mine."

"Hera, did you like the presents I left all over the Greek countryside for you? All those little girls, all those dead people?" Zeus asked with a smile.

Zeus' glut for death filled my mind. I could feel every conquest and his delight in them. The lust disgusted me.

"Your mind is filled with sickness, Zeus. You see yourself as a God, but you are nothing more than a deranged human who has taken up a partnership with a deranged Themian. Both of you are out of your mind with insanity. You don't belong here. You weren't meant to rule humanity.

Humans won't allow you to rule them. Too many Greeks know exactly what you are, Zeus, and that is nothing more than a man gone insane. You think they're not going to listen to their Goddess?" I pose, putting out a hand under my lovely face as if displaying my innocence, knowing it would enrage him.

There have been many statues carved with me in that very pose and only a few statues carved with him. Most of them did not make him look very good.

"Your pretty face does nothing more than hide the evil black heart inside your chest. When I am done here, I will take all my children, the ones left alive that I care about. Then, we will rule the world. The rest I will give to Poseidon to kill, because I don't care about them." He chuckled.

"So, you'll give Poseidon his Hercules back?" I asked innocently.

Poseidon's voice boomed as he dove towards me. "Herakles is dead. You cannot give him back to me. It is because of you he's dead." He bellowed.

A flash of wave washed over me. I shook the water from my hair and allowed the heavy tunic to fall to the ground leaving me in only my old Themian under clothing.

"You're right, Poseidon. Herakles is dead and I cannot give him back to you, but I did not betray my oath to you. Neither did I dreamwalk the High Council, or entice anyone else to do so. If you want to know who your true betrayer is, you should ask Athena. She will give you answers and you may find the answer most surprising. As for Hercules, my son is alive now. I cannot give your son back to you but I didn't name my son after yours out of honor, even if your son had none."

He roared, "So, you feel some guilts for the part you played in having my children butchered. They slaughtered every one of them. Not one stood a chance against Apollo and Artemis. As a team, they are a perfect killing machine." The ground beneath me rumbled with his anger.

It was true. Apollo and Artemis were killers, no matter what the humans believed of them. Apollo could burn a body to the ground with only the light of the sun and Artemis was the perfect hunter, her control of sight was capable of shooting the dust off a grain of sand.

"I did not play a part in your fall, Poseidon. That was all your doing. I was too busy in a village ensnaring Zeus in my evil womanly machinations to be bothered with you and the barbarous children you begot on the temptress that enchanted you, Cleito. Or are you too stupid to have seen it."

< Now! > I called to Micah

With a blink of an eye, I was alone. The wind was gone, the static electricity that had built up in the air dissipated and all around me was nothing but the green pastured land and the smell of the ocean breeze. I could feel Poseidon's mind searching for me with Zeus' weaker one participating.

< They are coming. We are already in place. Simply stand there and continue mocking them if you wish. > Micah's words did not reassure me.

The sea rose and I was watching it without any idea about what was going to happen. I turned and lightning flashed off in the distance. I spotted a giant wave coming toward me. It was unnaturally large and parted in the center. The sky turned gray as did the ocean. Birds flew away in fear. I could feel the departing of all animals in the area. Terror was thick in the air, as was the electricity building, crackling and zapping. The hair rose on my body and all around my head.

The waters parted and there standing on the seabed was Poseidon. All manner of sea creatures laid on the bottom of the ocean on the path between him and I. He carried a staff that had three prongs on it, known as a trident.

"Now, Hera, you will never get away and I will have my revenge."

He raised the Triton into the air and slammed it down onto the seabed. The earth around me quaked with the force of impact almost as if a comet fought its way into this planet's gravity well.

Earth, sand, coral, rocks and all manner of seabed flew into the air and massive amounts of it blacked out the sun. I quaked with fear. Every hair my body stood up. Zeus closed in and lightning struck the ground not far from where I hovered. I pushed the earthy debris away with the wind, but I had to fight for control of it. Zeus exerted great power.

If I could hold on just a few seconds longer.

CHAPTER 22

SYDNEY

The count was now 50 days straight at sea. To say I felt ragged was an understatement. My body never seemed to stop moving. The call of the ocean dragged me down in every draft and pulled me up with every wave. Tristan and Isolde carried dark shadows under their eyes. I needed the rest but that was not to be. We needed to find Miguel's Bay before sun up. Without the local maps, I had no idea what was under that dark water. I used my ability to push some of the rocky bottoms to the side buying us inches in depth at best.

"Tristan, you stay on that depth finder. Issy, I want you out on the deck at the bow."

The slapping of the waves fell the further we went into the Bocas Del Toro area, until they did nothing more than lap at the sides of the boat.

< You think we're going to run aground? > Issy asked.

< *No. Getting caught on a mangrove would suck worse than that.* > I responded.

The dark stain of the sky transitioned to pink and then blue. Visibility was just enough to maneuver into the small inlet. There was a house with turquoise window shades. However, saying it was a house was too generous in my opinion. It looked more like a fishing shack built over the water. The dog on the dock went crazy barking. A small dark man jumped into a cayuco to row over. The closer he came, the clearer I could make out his hand in the air waving me off.

"Signora, you must go back out to sea. Change the name on your boat. They are still looking for you. Throw the kayaks over the side. I'll give you new ones. But they are looking for your green ones. Don't raise your sail for any reason."

"Why?" Issy called.

"They know what the sails look like. Take it down and set it aside for me." Miguel grabbed the line on one of the kayaks and rowed toward the other. "I'll collect the sail later in the afternoon with a bigger boat. Don't come ashore. Anything you need, I will fetch for you."

"Thank you, Miguel, for all of your efforts and for helping perfect strangers," I yelled.

"Señora, I am always ready to pay back a favor. Now my debt is paid. I'm happy to help you and your children. A woman alone in the world should never be preyed upon by the strong." He shrugged and smiled.

As he rowed away in his cayuco, it struck me. He was not well-dressed. His house was not lavish, but more of a shack. It could have been built with pallets. His dog didn't look well fed. Yet he had a worldly knowledge about him. Miguel carried himself with a military air. He was too tall to be one of the local indigenous people. His eyes had been sharp, darting back and forth. He had said he didn't want to identify us. Maybe he was hiding out here. Maybe he was the one who didn't want to be recognized.

I glanced around the bay. If I hadn't known where to look, I was not sure I would have found this little spot. It was out of the way and difficult to see through the mangroves from a distance. It didn't even look like this bay was here. The view from afar was just more mangroves. You had to approach from the North and swing around another row of mangroves to pass the bay entrance.

With blurry eyes, I turned the boat around and head out of the secluded bay. The water levels around us rose up with my irritation, giving us better maneuverability. We motored for 35 minutes into the open waters of the Bocas area and as far from the mangroves as possible. Then, Tristan and Issy pulled our old name off the boat and began painting the new.

I shivered to think what Capitan Ron would say about all the name changing. I pulled out two pieces of foil and wrote the old boat names on them then tossed both overboard, grabbed the last of the cooking wine and poured that in. It would have to do. If Poseidon wasn't happy, he could sink us, if the other guys didn't do it first.

We slowly took the mainsail down folded then rolled it up and set it near the stern for a quick offload.

I went into the main salon to the navigation desk. Reaching behind the table cushions, I pulled the file out of the cushions I'd shoved it into. There were three new sets of passports and two sets of new boat paperwork. I took our old paperwork Barefoot III and I put it to rest. Then pulled out the new one. Welcome to Reel Genius!

< What's the new name of our girl? > Issy asked. She came through with warm affection.

< *Reel Genius.* > I supplied.

Tristan chuckled and entered the conversation.

< So real genius it is? >

< *Yes. Just make sure you spell 'R E E L' and not 'R E A L'.* > I chided.

Issy mentally snickered. < Will do, Mom. >

We sailed back into the private bay and waited all day, but Miguel never came back. Finally, as the sun was going down, a mid-sized boat approached. The name on the side was 'Just Ray's'. It was Miguel and he had two men with him. Before he pulled up, he yelled, "Go below deck! We don't want to see your faces." The sound was echoing across the water. "Take your children with you".

I waved Tristan and Issy into the saloon and I closed every curtain at once. The last thing in the world I wanted was for them to identify our faces. Even Miguel hadn't seen us up close and with this red hair, I wasn't sure that anybody would recognize us anyway. I mean, they were all looking for three blondes.

A few moments later, the other boat engines revved up, creating a wake that rocked our boat as they departed. I came out on deck to watch them leave. The sky was aflame and the sun slowly kissed the top of the mountains. A moment later it was gone. It was a gorgeous sunset.

Bocas Del Toro's gorgeous all the time.

"Hey, Mom! Let me take first watch and you and Isolde get some rest. I don't know how long we'll be in Bocas, but we got a chance to get some good sleep. You guys sleep and I'll wake you up in the morning," Tristan's hollowed eyes urged us on.

"No, I can't have you sleepless. Wake me up in six hours. I'll take over and you can get a couple of hours of sleep. We do need to be rested. One person will sleep all night and that will be Issy, but tomorrow it'll be you. We keep doing it hopscotch style like this and everybody should be pretty rested in a couple of days." I gave them both a tight smile, then threw myself on my bunk to embrace the oblivion of rest, but even in my tired state my mind never shut off.

Miguel returned two days later with a new sail and one two-man kayak. He also brought a few pieces of vinyl fishing reels to through on the back of the boat.

I had never named my dingy. I thought that naming it makes it too easy to see who wasn't home on a boat, making it easier for the thieves to rob you. However, he put a few on the dingy too.

He ferried boxes of groceries to our boat, diesel and even coffee. Most items arrived on the deck with no sound and he was gone before we could say a word. We took the time to rest and I took a complete shower. We washed down the boat and went over the systems.

"We need a new light at the top of the main mast," Tristan moaned.

"That we can live without. How about the leaking hatch in my cabin?" Issy chimed in.

All of our clothes had taken on the worn salt stained look of pirates. We needed a new membrane for the water-maker and a filter to replace the one I'd just put on the diesel pump.

The list got bigger, the longer we stayed and we were running low on cash.

The ring around my finger for the first time felt heavy, I moved it around just to feel it twist. I grew queasy thinking of selling it. In this country, I'd never get what it's worth, a fraction at best.

I could take the two rings apart and sell Gabe's, but that only brought the burning threat of tears. I stopped fiddling with them and climbed down into the engine compartment on the starboard side and took inventory. The storeroom Gabe had built down here could carry three-plus months of food, but now it was more empty than full. I'd insisted on keeping three months' worth of freeze-dried food on the board. It was a good thing because half that supply was now gone.

Gabe never understood my obsession with being able to control our supplies. But if food and water are life, I wanted as much as I could get. I dug into the last bucket of rice down to the bottom and pulled out the ziplock bag of cash.

There were probably a thousand dollars left at best in the bag. I screwed the gamma lid back down and opened the bean bucket. The scent wafting out of it told me we should eat more beans, and there was only enough left to cover the money bag at the bottom. I pushed the beans back and grabbed the bag and pulled it out. It was full, maybe three thousand. Enough to get us a few supplies for the boat repairs and five hundred in food. The other three thousand would be for the canal. However, then we'd be broke and really fucked. I rubbed my hand across my forehead.

What have I done?

< You only need enough to get here. > The voice said.

< *That's easy for you to say. You know where you are and there isn't an entire canal system and thousands of miles of ocean to cross. Plus I have to pay immigration on the other side.* >

< With your ability, you'll cross the Pacific in record time. > He chuckled.

< *Easy for you to say, again. You're already there. How'd you crossed it?* >

His chuckled disappeared. < I swam. >

I laughed out loud. < *Impossible! You must be joking.* >

< I'm not. >

Then he was gone.

CHAPTER 23

SYDNEY

I didn't think that being in the queue for the Panama Canal would take so long. Father Rizzo's connection said we'd be next in line and that all we had to do was check in. It all sounded so simple, too simple.

We were next in line but not for today or next week. It was for two weeks. It was a two-week wait to get through the canal. That doesn't count for the big boats. They go through rather quickly, but little boats have to wait their turn. However, even the big boats have a backlog of 72 hours at this point We were lucky it was only two weeks. In the height of the season, it can take three. We couldn't afford to sit in Cologne for three weeks. They, whoever they were, knew we had to go through the canal system. It was just a matter of time before they could figure out which boat was ours.

The easiest way to keep them from noticing us was to change our group makeup. I checked into immigration with only one child. Issy would stay on the boat and keep out of sight. We both had red hair. From a distance, she could pass for me. Tristan had the ability to have her join us wherever we were. It didn't matter if we left and went out to a restaurant or grocery store, he would retrieve her. Having a human transporter in the family did have its perks.

It also meant that if we wanted to stay on the boat for a week straight, we could. I didn't want to go stir crazy. The closer I got to Panama City, the more emotions churned up. We were closer to square one. Where all of this started. I didn't want to go back to the scene of Gabriel's death. I never wanted to set foot in that city again. None of us did.

I had to keep telling myself 'It's a pass through. Once we're on the other side of the locks it's free sailing to the Galapagos. From there we jump off for the Marquess'. Short of sending out the US Navy. It will be us and the water and thirty full days at sea. Unless I push us.'

Cologne at one time was considered a jewel in the crown of Panama and Central America, the main resting place for the beginning of the canal and a city built for trade. Most of the buildings here were old Spanish colonial style stucco. There were beautiful Cathedrals and defensive forts. The Panamanian people were friendly and welcoming. From the ocean, Cologne looked beautiful. The closer you got, the more you could see the age and decay of the crumbling of old buildings, hitting you in full force. The lack of recycling and trash pickup was apparent in every waterway and Marina. Everything here was just a little bit filthy, just a little bit decrepit, and a little bit neglected. It felt like meeting an old whore at a bar. You could see she was once a great beauty, but time and wear have taken it from her and all that was left were shabby clothes and poor makeup.

The canal office immediately put our boat in the queue. I gave them our burner cell phone number along with a $2,600.00, half was the canal fee, the other half was to be returned to you at the end. You had to pay it to cover damages if any. I prayed there wouldn't be any because we needed the cash.

We were just 'Turistas' waiting to take our boat through the canal. Nothing unusual about a mother and her child sailing around the world. I was not sure if I was able to pull off the most uninteresting people ever. The fact that we were headed for an island that didn't exist on the maps, that shouldn't bother anyone. It wasn't bothering us. I walked out into the hard Panamanian sun.

God, I hope this works.

"Do you think they'll move us up in the queue?" Tristan whispered just outside the canal offices.

"If Father Rizzo and Lorenzo have any connections within the canal system and they have strings to pull, I'm sure we'll get moved up. They know the name of our boat. They chose it but really doesn't matter. We just need to lay low. Nothing to see here so move on," I shook Tristan's inquiries off by pulling my best Jedi mind trick. Then I waved my hand in front of us.

"What if they spot us?" He continued his probing.

"There's nowhere to go once we're in the canal system. If they spot us, we can kiss the boat goodbye."

"Well, we can always head off-road." He remarked.

"That's not gonna work, Tristan. Where we're going we need a boat. If they spot us on our boat, we have to simply go and take a bus to Panama City. From there steal a boat and hope it's seaworthy enough to get us there."

I hated the idea of stealing, but there were thousands of boats here for sale for years. I could have Zack make it right later.

< We can have uncle Zack buy us a new boat. > Issy piped in.

< *Issy that is a great idea and if I had the cash I would buy it. The truth is, that kind of transaction will be noticed and tracked.* > I remarked, shaking my head again.

Tristan moved us both back to the boat in a dark corner of an alleyway.

"Mom, is there anybody we can trust to buy the boat for us?" Issy pleaded as soon as her green eyes landed on us.

I hated dashing it but wishful thinking wasn't going to keep us safe and off the radar.

"I can't think of anybody. We can't contact Father Rizzo again. Other than Zack and Maria can you think of anybody you would trust with several hundred thousand dollars?" I inquired.

She shook her head and turned to look back out at the ocean. "No, not really, Mom." Defeat didn't sit well on her, me either.

"Well, there's your answer." I muttered.

The world is a cold place. I didn't want my children thinking that it was ever going to be easy. Everything has to be fought for with blood. You have to be three to ten steps ahead of whoever you're trying to outsmart or run. We simply needed to keep our heads down.

Tristan left again and picked up our boat parts. We wiled away our time checking lines and making repairs. We cleaned out every locker and chucked all dead weight. You can't carry a lot of extra crap, but it does build up. By the time our turn came to enter the lock system, there couldn't have been a speck of dust anywhere. We were ship shape.

Going through the Panama Canal sounds romantic, exciting and it really is. I had never gone through before but truthfully, I was terrified. Someone was watching our boat 24/7 until we make it to the Miraflores locks.

We pulled out of the Marina and up onto the flats with our canal advisor. His only job was to tell us where to go, then when we get there, he kept in contact with the canal workers. He was actually kind of shabby.

Most Panamanians were relatively thin short and had light chocolate colored skin. His name was Ricardo, he was 67 years old, he had five children, 15 grandchildren and he had been married since he was 15. All he talked about was his family and food. I was shocked by the food part. Tristan offered to make him some Italian food, but I wasn't really sure how.

Then he asked me if there was another person on the boat. Suddenly his mind went blank and his smile fell away. I put on my best smile and responded staring into his vacant eyes, "There's no one else on this boat."

His entire mind laid out before me like a suit on a bed. I could pick and choose what to take away or add. For a moment I was terrified. His humanity sat before me so fragile and weak. My first reaction was to pull away to retreat, but my fear for Issy took over…so, I did what I do best, fight. I edited his mind, adding where I needed, he'd seen Issy's passport and she was in the country legally. Not to tell anyone and we were unremarkable. I made him believe it.

When I released his mind, he smiled at me and said how nice it was to see such a good family going through the canal. Guilt flooded my chest because I took away his free will, bending him to mine.

"Mom, what did you do?" Tristan whispered.

"I don't know. One minute he was standing there asking me if there was anyone else on the boat and the next minute, I had complete control over his mind. I made him believe he'd seen everything he needed to see." I replied.

"Shit, Mom! You mind controlled him. That's like crazy science-fiction stuff," Tristan breathed and ran his fingers through his hair pulling on the bangs.

"And everything else we do isn't crazy science-fiction stuff?" I retorted.

"Yeah, a bit, I mean you like own him or something. I could feel his mind like lay down. You could have wiped him, given him a blank slate, reprogrammed him any way you wanted." Tristan was in awe, but I was disgusted.

"I know. I just don't know what to do about it. I had to protect Issy. She's more important than the free will of one person. Would you risk your sister just because you didn't want to implant an idea in some stranger's mind? It's not hurting him," I glanced back at him to assure myself. "He won't lose his job. We simply told him that she was legal and that's all. He won't talk about her to anybody. It's everything we need and harms no one."

Right? I had to tell myself that.

"I guess. I mean I can't believe you could do it." Tristan swallowed and rubbed his hands on his board shorts.

"I don't know, Tristan. I'm not even sure I could do it again." I whispered then bit my lip. Did I even want to do it again?

He shook his head, squeezed my arm gently and went about his business.

"Signora, we need to move the boat in proper alignment to enter the canal. Your sister ship boats will be pulling up alongside you any moment now. You will tie your boats together and they will be your canal companion along with me for the rest of the trip. You can untie when we get to Gatun lake if you wish or the two of you can work in tandem to move through the lake faster, but it is up to you. I do not know if you wish to stay the night in the lake or simply move on as quickly as possible through the canal zone. You shall have to make your choice once we get through this set of locks. Is Bien?"

"Si, Ricardo, is bien."

The doors to the first lock looked like a massive steel wall about five stories high. The closer we were, the more intimidating they became. Off to the right, a giant brick red cargo ship covered in shipping containers dwarfed us. Sitting in the bay you see all of the backlog, big boy boats, but you're not right next to one. The ocean is big and gives you the feeling of insignificance. Next, to one of these bad boys, it was a wonder that my boat ever made it from one side of the Atlantic to the other.

A ringing sound filled the air as the double set of the door swung open. I glanced over at our buddy boat Dreamer and her Capitan. He touched his index finger to his brow. I returned a thumbs up as we pulled the two boat forward into place in the lock. Panamanians walk the walls of the lock each one with a weighted line. Dreamer's Captain and first mate caught their lines as the workers tossed them over. Tristan took two tries.

The first throw was well short of the boat landing in the murky water. The Panamanian lineman pulled the line back up the high slimy cement walls. The second toss hit a side stanchion rebounding into the water. Three was a charm. It hit the deck and I wrapped our line around it. When he'd had the line in hand I wrapped my end around a cleat. The lines help keep you into place while they raise and lower you in locks. They also use the lines to move you where they want you.

We had entered the lock first. We had to move to the other end to allow for another catamaran and a tug boat.

The canal never sleeps. They always have boats moving from one side to the other. We were traveling through this set with two other boats. It was just like a carnival ride. They try to fill every spot before they turn it on.

Our boat was tied up to the 40-foot Irwin named Dreamer. The couple on Dreamer were friendly. Their names were Craig and KC.

Young lovers are often blind to the world around them. They don't have eyes for anyone but each other.

"Where are you headed?" KC called to us from the bow of her boat.

KC was a beautiful blonde with dark eyes. She looked like she liked to eat good food, but she wasn't fat, comfortable.

I smiled back at her. "Cancun, Mexico. The kid wants to check out the beaches." I half covered my mouth. "I think it's girls. I just want to get a look at some of the Hammerheads that like to hang out in the Sea of Cortez."

It was a perfect cruiser story. One I hoped to pass without anyone asking too many questions and forget just as quickly. She nodded her head hearing but not caring about the answer.

Why do people feel the need to make small talk? They don't care what I have to say and I don't want to tell the truth. So why ask? It's a big waste of time. Here I am decades later and I'm still surprised about the niceties of polite society.

In a dreamy voice, she replied. "We're heading to Hawaii for our honeymoon." Her face shone with joy.

"Congratulations!" I exclaimed.

I actually was happy for them. New love and adventure. For a moment I daydreamed of the early days with Gabe.

"Oh, no! We've been married for two years, we just didn't get a honeymoon. We worked too much, but now that we're cruising, we can finally take it," she kept talking.

I let her but I only half listened to what she was saying. I didn't want to talk about myself, or the kids. She was sweet and fresh. It was relaxing to hear her mental and verbal hum.

Just as quickly as she had started, she moved into position on Dreamer's bow with her line. The great doors swung shut and I heard the rushing of water from a massive sump pump.

Looking over the side of our boat I saw blooms of water and gunk broke the surface forcing water into the lock. I could feel the rise of the boats. Both boats shifted in the water as the underwater jets pushed us this way and that in the lock.

"Mom, your line!" Tristan broke me out of my trance as I took up the slack in my line. We rose faster than I could imagine. When the doors shut we were sitting at the bottom of a very large box. Five minutes later we were at the top and ready to move into the next lock and nine meters above sea level in five minutes, unbelievable. They walked us into the next lock and repeated the process.

Having made it through the first set of canals locks, we were sitting in the great Lake Gatun.

I had no idea how long we were going to be stuck in this portion of the canal system. The sooner we got through the locks at Miraflores and past the bridge of the Americas, the happier I would be. I couldn't shake the constant feeling of being watched. I couldn't seem to sleep and being in the canal system we were nothing more than sitting ducks.

Looking around the leafy beauty of Panama it is easy for one to be lulled by the humidity and the variegated green jungle.

"We're out of milk again, Mom." Issy hadn't been off the boat in a week and cabin fever was making her crazy.

"Sorry! I'll send Tristan out to get more. I know this sucks. You're a teenager. Nobody wants to be stuck at home all the time. Being home can't be all that exciting. Just keep in mind that once we leave here, we'll be at sea for another month." I wanted to comfort her, but the harsh reality was better medicine.

"Look, Mom, I know that once we make it through the final locks we will be at sea for 30 days to cross the Pacific. Can't we stop somewhere along the coast and I'll just run around and have some fun for a couple of hours?" Issy wined.

She paced the pontoons all day and her mental chatter kept me up most of the night. I wanted to set her free. Girls are not meant to be kept in a cage.

"I promise you that when we get somewhere safe you can run around and have fun for a few days." I pulled her to me giving her a hug. She returned it, then simply turned her head away and went back to reading a book. I just wished there was some way to make her understand.

Approaching the outer doors of the next set of locks must've been how ancient peoples felt approach the city of Jerusalem. All those walled cities with their massive entryways. The lock system for the canal is truly amazing engineering work. Everything is based on steam engines that pump water in then out. The pressure allows them to raise you up and lower you down. From the Cologne side where we went to the Panama City side. Miraflores is the last lock. Until we pass the bridge of the Americas we were not out of the woods.

We pulled out of the locks and dropped anchor on the Panama City side. I couldn't go ashore. I couldn't look at this city again.

I left the boat long enough to get our deposit back. I turned on the WiFi just long enough to shoot Zack an email with one sentence 'I'm sorry and I forgive you.' Then, I sent the kids around the city gathering supplies together.

"Meet me back at the boat. It should give you a half a day off the boat," I cupped Issy's chin and a smile broke over her face pushing back all the dark clouds.

"Thanks, Mom! Thanks for letting me get off the boat. I'm already going stir crazy. Can you imagine 30 days from now?" She rushed on then ran down to her cabin and shrieked with joy. The sound of clothes hitting the floor reached me and I smiled.

"Yeah, I can imagine," I remembered when I was stuck at home all the time and how unhappy I was.

CHAPTER 24

SYDNEY

I stared out at the raising and lowering of the horizon. The blue was deep and mysterious, but we had been at sea for so long I was tired of it. The ocean was a big blue-gray void and the clouds flew into the horizon, disappearing with the curvature of the earth. It was all the same. It didn't matter where I looked: the bow, the stern, leeward, starboard. It didn't change. Water in every direction as far as the eye could see.

The children, they weren't children anymore. I had to stop calling them that. In my mind, they would always be my babies. The two people I brought into this world. Was I doing the right thing taking them with me?

All this water and the nothing surrounding us made me question myself. Was the island real? Could I really find it? Should I leave the kids in the Marquesa Islands? Did we have enough diesel? What if something breaks?

I knew second-guessing was not helping me. It just fed my insecurity and anxiety, but sailing across the largest body of water on the planet leaves you with too much time to think. The days are dully filled with repetitive motion. You're on watch alone. You eat, sometimes with the kids and sometimes alone. You go to sleep for a few hours. You wake to eat and have some downtime, then you're on watch again. Rinse, repeat.

"Mom, can we play cards or something? Anything. The monotony is killing me," Issy rolled her head from one shoulder to the other, while she was standing on the deck staring out at the big same.

"I don't feel like it. But I will if you want," I replied and heaved a sigh.

She bobbed over to the table. We had a card deck box. It was plastic with suction cups on the bottom to keep the cards from sliding off the table in a swell. She cracked it open.

"Poker, One Eyed Jacks and Suicide Kings are wild," she said while she happily dealt out the cards.

I despised Poker, but the kids loved to gamble. Why couldn't she choose a nice game of Gin Rummy?

"Mom, if you wanted to play Gin why didn't you say so?" She leaned over the table sliding the fourth card at me.

I lifted my middle finger letting the card settle under it before I lowered it and I cocked an eyebrow at her.

"What have I told you about trolling people's private thoughts?" I demanded.

"Not to top skim, but it's hard when you're so loud. Can you tune me out?" She shot back.

I curled the corner of my lips up into a half smile. "Touché. I'll put a damper on it."

She smiled and plopped down her card waiting for my play. I didn't know why I played. I always lose and this hand was no different.

Shit.

"Ten cents and I'll take three cards." She threw her money in the cup passing me my cards, taking two for herself.

Great, she doesn't have shit either.

"What's your bet?" She was too eager.

"You need a nickel to ride this train, Issy." I snapped.

She laughed. She liked it when I got sassy. "I see your nickel train ride and raise you a dime for the subway." She was cocky. She knew I didn't have shit.

"Okay, I see your dime and call. Show me why the subway is better than the train." I snapped.

Her face faded to a bland smile as she played her cards on the table.

"A pair of deuces. Really that's all you had?" I remarked.

She snickered at me and I shared my cards with a little pride.

"You, Mom! You had three of a kind the whole time? It felt like you had crap. You faked me out." She huffed and then chuckled.

I raised my eyebrow and lowered my eyes with my small smile. "If you're going to cheat, Issy, you need to be 2% smarter than the person you're cheating. I've been playing Poker a lot longer than you. You learn a few tricks in time. Don't top skim people's thoughts and you won't get played." I chuckled dumping the poker cup into my change cup.

She huffed and shook her head.

I got up and put the fishing lines out. We hadn't caught a thing in days. We were approaching the dull-drums. We were at that space at the Equator where the oceans don't flow and there's no wind. We'd been barely drifting along for the last 12 hours. It's the in-between of the world where everything feels dead. No birds or fish and no waves. I could wish for a storm but we were too far for help.

"Tristan, can you give me a position? I want to know how close we are." I called to him in the salon. I give us a push, but how would that motion affect the tides elsewhere? Better to play it safe and motor through like everyone else.

He gave me a curt nod and ducked into the salon.

"Issy, I want you to get one too but you need to use the sextant." I ordered and took some of our cloths off the side lines on the boat. They were clean even if they were sunstained.

"Mom, I hate that. I'm not very good at Math." Her lower lip puffed up and out and if Gabe had been here it would have worked, but girly crap didn't work on me. I didn't buy it.

"I don't care. Only one way to get better." I smiled and tossed a tangtop at her.

She huffed and left for the Nav station.

"By my calculations, we will be in the Doldrums like any minute. That's why there's nothing. Everything's died down. I think we're already there. Can I check the GPS?" Tristian asked and leaned out the sliding door gripping the frame.

"I'll check the GPS but I think you're right." I didn't want to check the GPS. The ping could be enough for them to find us. Whoever they were? I still didn't understand who these faceless pursuers were.

Tristan was correct. We absolutely were in the doldrums and probably had been for about an hour. I could feel the change in the water slapping against the bottom of the Catamaran, in the way the waves moved. Even the air felt different. It was like it lost its electrical charge or something.

We didn't have a lot of cans on the boat but we did have a few cans of root beer. It was mine and the kids' little evil pleasure. Every now and again I pulled one out and the three of us would share it. There's so much sugar in one, I couldn't drink it by myself, so we just shared. This time Tristan got the last gulp. It was usually me but this time for some reason it just ended up to be Tristan's turn. Instead of crushing the can and putting it in with our recyclables, Tristan tossed it to the floorboard alcove of the boat. It was a small subset in the deck where water could leak away before flooding the salon.

The swell of the waves rocked us from side to side with little excitement. Tristan's pop can rolled from side to side with us and it was the most entertainment we'd had for the last few days. For the last week or so, we watched this aluminum pop can roll around. It was actually quite entertaining.

In an infinite universe, there was an infinite number of ways for the can to get from one side to the other. Forced confinement changes your perception of entertainment.

For 19 days we watched the can for at least ten hours, but on the 19th day of our Pacific crossing, using my power and our diesel engines, we motored through the Doldrums. Three days later we pushed free and into the South Pacific. If I hadn't been pushing the boat myself, we might not have gotten through as quickly as we did.

"Feel that? Oh my God, it's a breeze, and it's cool too," Issy exclaimed then sprayed her body down with water so the breeze could cool her skin. Her boat dress stuck to her and goosebumps rose on her arms.

"Yes, is heavenly," I replied and spritzed my face and neck.

"I feel as though we've been sitting in a sauna for the last two weeks," Issy smiled.

"We have been sitting in a sauna for the last two weeks," Tristan called from the saloon, then joined us in watering down his clothes and opened his arms to the gentle breeze.

"Yeah, doesn't the cool breeze mean we should be near land or something? Please let us be near land. I'm tired of looking at the ocean. I never thought I'd get tired of looking at it, Mom, but I honestly I just want a piece of dry land. I want to stand still," Issy moaned and then hopped up to the side deck holding on to the bimini and leaned in to meet my eyes.

"I know what you mean, Issy. I would like a piece of dryland too, only because it means that we're just closer to our destination." I stared off into the distance, in the direction my mind told me the island should be in.

I wanted to stop the boat and let all of us take a quick swim, but that place in my mind wouldn't let go. It pushed me harder every day, to move faster, to get closer. It invaded even my sleep. I couldn't even close my eyes without the image of the island before me pushing me on.

"What's the first thing you want to do when you get on dry land, Tristan?" Issy asked spraying more water on her hair and letting it run down her face. Then blowing drops at her brother.

"Look at someone else's face other than you two. No offense, Mom, Issy, you are both beautiful but you're my mother and my sister. I'd like to see the face of another woman, a child, another guy, anybody. I love you I just don't want to stare at you for the rest of the year." He laughed and Issy snaked the hose and sprayed him in the face, getting me at the same time.

I screeched at her and waved my fist. The truth was that I loved my children but I wouldn't mind seeing a new face myself.

"Nice, Tristan, I love you. You know what I want to do the first thing when we reach dry land?" We shook our heads so she continued, "I want to take a complete long shower. One where I can wash everything and then just let the water trickle down my body for an hour," Issy giggled, then ran to the front of the boat to set the spinnaker.

"What about you, Mom? What do you want to do when we hit dry land?" Tristan asked while pulling the starboard line and tying it down to a cleat.

"Truthfully, I hadn't really thought that much about it. My mind is focused on our final destination. I don't want to be in the Marquesa's long. I'm not sure we can afford to be there. I mostly want to make sure we have enough supplies and go find the island. Every fiber of my being says we are where we're meant to be and that if we don't get there, something will happen." I stared off in the islands' direction.

The air filled the spinnaker and it snapped into shape, the light breeze filling it and pulling us along. I took the air in and continued.

"It feels like my whole life is to get there. My entire life I've been wandering around aimlessly like I'd never had a real direction or focus, I mean other than making money and being happy. I think that's what everybody in America has ingrained in them - make money, be happy. And I did all those things with Daddy and with you guys. But I almost feel as though I'm missing my higher purpose. Now, I know where to go, but I don't know why that's what I want to do." I rolled my shoulders.

Tristan and Issy sat at the table behind me. I looked down at the display screen, checking our wind and speed. It was 3.4 knots over land. Not too bad, considering I wasn't pushing.

"When I get on land there will be another hill to climb. There always is. I just know that getting to that island is the next step." I turned and smile at their two faces and sighed. I didn't want to say the word but it needed to be said.

"You guys don't have to go with me if you don't want to. I can leave you in the Marquesa. They aren't following you, they're really following me. If I leave you in the Marquesa with all of the passports, you could easily go anywhere you want. I could set it up with Zack and transfer some money to you. Whatever you guys want to do." My chest ached even as I said it. They weren't even 18 and I was setting them free.

Tristan and Issy shared a look, and Tristan tipped his head at Issy. She smiled.

"Mom, wherever you're going, then we are too. I want to take a shower, Tristan wants to see other faces, but you got like a life-changing call from above. And every fiber of your being says you gotta do this. We are with you. We just wanted to know what the first thing you would like to do when you hit dry land. I mean have a beer, or get a Piña Colada, something simple? Mom, life is about simple things." Her eyebrows lifted questioning me.

We all laugh.

"Okay, well when I get to the land I want to buy diesel, food and everything else that needs taking care of because I gotta be responsible. And of course...a Piña Colada," I smiled back at them.

Tristan clapped his hands together, "Okay, then it's decided. We get to the Marquesa. Mom goes to the bar to get a Piña Colada. I get diesel and Issy, you go get groceries. There, problem solved. Once you're done getting groceries on the boat and stowed away, then go take the longest shower you could possibly squeeze out of the stupid water tanks and I will turn on the water maker to refill them. And I'll go look at every pretty face I can find in the Marquesa. How does that sound?"

His eyes sparkled with mischief then he thrust his hand out. Issy put her hand on top of Tristan's and I covered them both, "Sounds like a plan."

After all the heavy we've been through, it was nice to laugh. My kids and I were a little too serious sometimes. Laughter is important. It helps take away the fear of death.

Darkness fell over the water and I stood my watch, then changed out with Tristan. I woke up when the sun was still low on the horizon. With the sunlight just out of reach, I noticed that one of the lights on the top of the main seemed to be crooked. We should have to take care of that before the sunset. That was Issy's job. She was the smallest and the easiest for Tristan to hoist.

"One of the lights on the top of the main mast is crooked. We need to straighten it out. You have to go up the mast."

She rolled over to face away from me. I rocked her again.

"You know I hate going up there. I really don't like being up that high," she huffed half asleep.

"Honey, this is the business of living on a boat. You can't get away from maintenance. It's always there. There is always something that needs to be done and it needs to be done right away. Crooked lights could give somebody the wrong idea about the placement of our boat. They could actually run into us. You want someone to run into our boat just because you didn't want to go and straighten the light?" I asked.

It was an old lecture that I'd used over and over again, but it wasn't as efficacious as it once was.

"No, of course not. You know I'll go do it. I just want to express my distaste for the work." She groaned and tossed the pillow to the side.

Tristan called from the other cabin. "What, do you think I want to hoist your ass up there? Whenever there is any heavy lifting to be done it's all me. I'm the man, it's a man's job, do the men's, blue work. I don't have a problem with doing blue work, but it doesn't mean I want to be used as a medieval motor." He said all this while flexing his arm muscles and posing like a bodybuilder and failing.

I laughed to myself. "Listen, Tristan, you know I don't believe in blue jobs and pink jobs. However, yes, the lifting is more of a blue job than a pink one. If it was up to me, it would be a lot more difficult for me to hoist your sister up there versus you. And yes, you are our medieval motor. I'm pretty sure that one of the motors could do it but I don't think it's a wise use of our machinery. Anyway, it's weightlifting and it builds bigger muscles," I said and shoved him.

"Yeah, yeah, yeah, I know, Mom," he smiled and winked at me.

Shaking my head I simply turned my back on the two, bunch of whiners.

CHAPTER 25

HERA

Log entry

The quaking of the ground never stopped. The land rose up underneath me. Using the forces of the wind, I raised my hand, pushing soil, sand, and coral away. I had to keep debris from battering my poor body. Lifting in the air, my agility increased tenfold allowing me to dodge the flying debris.

Zeus was on me in a heartbeat. The electrical charge tingled over my skin and through my hair. It made my teeth spark as my mouth opened and closed. He really did have a handle on the electricity of this planet. It didn't stop him from exercising it.

"So, Hera, you've left the land to join me in the sky." His laugh held no mirth and his eyes sparkled with distaste over having to behold me.

The wind pushed my hair into my face and mouth and I had to turn into it to even see Zeus.

"Don't be ridiculous. I haven't left the land to join you anywhere. I'm simply trying to avoid being buried alive by Poseidon's temper tantrum," I responded.

His perfect smile blazed back at me, never reaching his blue eyes. The moisture in the air clung to his chest, which raised and lowered as if he had walked from our hut to the dais and nothing more.

"He's without a conscience. You have ripped it all away from him. He will destroy all of the land and everyone on Alethea and he's going to bury it under the sea bed," Zeus boomed with laughter and thunder crashed in the background again, as big drops of rain fell. "Then, I'm going to bury them under water. I will rain down upon them day and night, unceasing until the entire planet is flooded."

He moved his arms straight out to his sides, opened his palms, and grasped two bolts of lightning, then thrust them at me in turn. I dodged in time to hear them hit the wet soil and sizzle.

He could do it. If he pulled all the water from the polar caps, he could flood this world.

My heart clenched at the thought of my children. They could not move as fast as I could. They might not be able to outrun the rising water. I had to finish this and I had to do it quickly. I pressed my lips into a firm line.

"And Poseidon, is he going to let the floodwaters flow back in for you? There's no way you could fight all these people without him." I moved my body out of reach.

"You really think I need Poseidon to drown all of humanity? I don't." His eyes flashed with irritation and a flicker of fear.

"You don't, do you? Why are you working together if you don't need him to crush me, Zeus?" I cocked my eyebrow, to mock him. His eyes narrowed as his brow clamped down, closing his face as a clam closes its shell.

That's when I saw it, my chance. My way in, to dominate him. Poseidon's ability, how he'd controlled the minds of the other Themian's. I was always a good student, even if the subject bored me.

Zeus, his emotions were all over the board, violent filled with rage, dripping with vitriol. Reaching inside myself, I built a small door in my mind then labeled it 'Zeus'. I dove into it like water, pouring in, eking it wider and wider, with every onslaught of my waves and slowly I forced his mind open. There he was - laid bare. I could see his every desire as a child, his arrogance, his power, his wants and his despair for approval. His mind was a broken world of needs.

Apollo appeared in front of Zeus, raising his sword and slamming it down on Zeus' outstretched arm. The metal of the bracer deflected the blow causing it to glance off, and Zeus raised his own sword for the battle dance.

I began my attack. Little pushes here and there just enough to knock him off balance.

"What are you doing, Hera? Get out of my mind!" He screamed.

He shook his head and his rage increased as did his fear. He blasted lighting at me while dodging Apollo's attacks.

"I'm doing exactly what humanity needs me to do," I calmly replied, while dodging to the right to avoid the electric bullets.

< Hera, pull him down! If you can dominate him, we can take him. > Athena whispered in the back of my mind.

I dashed back into Zeus' mind pushing harder this time, in any direction I could. I found his weaknesses. It was the fear of aging and becoming weak, the fear of losing his powers and all his ability to influence people.

I pressed into it. I wanted him to feel that fear. I tried to fill his entire being with it, to quake with it. I wanted the bile to pour from his mouth with it. I twisted the pain and anguish of that fear as if it were covered in salt, and I was the knife.

"You shall not overtake me, I shall push you out," his voice quaked, but he didn't sound sure of himself.

Apollo chose that moment to shoot an arrow at him. Zeus slipped in the sky and fell before regaining his power over the wind.

"Why do you sound strange, Zeus? Are you afraid of a woman?" I laughed at him but felt no mirth. "I've never known you to cower towards me. Now, I will teach why you should have feared me from the beginning." The words tasted sour and my chest quaked with their true meaning.

His roar echoed off the clouds. He threw fresh bolts of electricity at me, but I danced out of the way.

The deeper I pressed into his mind, the more I enveloped him with the vision of his withered aged flesh hanging from is weakened bones. Apollo moved in time with my mental blows crashing into Zeus' sword wearing him down. While in his mind, I paraded all his followers past him unseeing, and deaf to his pleas. His heart burst with the feeling of complete and utter terror. I couldn't allow him to continue his scourge on humanity. Tears poured from my eyes, but the rain covered my own pain. As I destroyed the one man I loved, my words came out hard and cold. I needed them to be this way.

The shaking of the planet's crust ceased, and dust from the sea bed settled.

Poseidon raised the waters up into the sky only to return them to the land with a vengeance. A giant tsunami was flowing back on the reformed ground. The wall was so high I was terrified it would hit me. I rose up, pulling out of the mental onslaught.

Looking back down, I saw Poseidon shaking his head. "You cannot dominate me so easily, Herathina." His voice was as deep as any ocean I'd ever seen.

I perched myself on the top of one of the local mountains. Zeus poised as if he was going to attack and I immediately laid open his mind one side and began to cut it apart, piece by piece. Apollo pounded from the outside while I shredded the inside, right up until I reached the small kernel where he held a little feeling of affection for me. Poseidon was coming, and I couldn't weep for the loss of the precious grain.

"So, Zeus, you did hold feelings for me." The jump of joy in my breast was brief before I crushed it.

I could hear him panting as his body slowly lowered to the ground. He fell onto his hands and knees before Apollo, and I waited off to the side.

"I have no feelings for you. You have always been a means to an end," he spat, bleeding from his many wounds. They didn't heal as fast a true Themian.

I took a shuddering breath. "You are right. I am an end for you."

The others descended upon him, turning his head to the side. He gazed up at me with his beautiful blue eyes through his black hair.

"Yes, indeed at one time, I did love you. Now, I curse you. I curse your entire line."

Humans were so simple. He didn't see how silly his superstitious curse was.

"My line is your line, Zeus. You would curse us all?" I hissed.

He coughed as Apollo lashed his hands behind his back with crystalline cuffs. They cut off his connection to the forces. He visibly shrunk with the loss. The air quieted and stilled, leaving nothing more than a human hybrid on the ground bleeding from many wounds.

"Yes, I would. If it has anything to do with you, I wish it dead."

My nostrils flared as the twist in my breast turned with pain. Even now he couldn't say he loved me even a little.

"Take that creature to Alethea and make sure he is encapsulated in a room where he can do no harm until the Council determines his fate," I croaked.

Fate, the word rang in my mind. Is that what this has always been? I shook my head. I didn't believe in Pythia's pronouncements.

Apollo took him away and Micah laid his hand on Apollo. With a swift nod of his head, he and Apollo along with Zeus disappeared. I had but a moment to think before the next maniac came at me.

I turned to Athena and she witnessed the disgust on my face.

"And now for Poseidon, we cannot let him get away."

"How many have you brought with you to overrun him?" I asked, with bated breath.

Her eyes sparkled. "Do we really need so many, Hera?" She spat my name out like the pit from a cherry. "There is no way I could've overtaken Zeus even with the three of us here. We don't have, whatever it is you have. Now, you will take Poseidon down the same way. I know you can." She leveled her dark eyes at me.

Even with my newfound ability, I was afraid. The last time I barely fought Poseidon off.

"Poseidon is mentally strong. Zeus is not Poseidon. If you really think I can take him, you've either not been paying attention, or you've underestimated your enemy." My bowels turned to water. What if Poseidon decided to use my life's water against me? He could pull the very fluid from my cells.

"No, Hera. You underestimate yourself. I see you — your emotions drive you to be greater. You are stronger with them than without. Just remember that if Poseidon should overrun you, it is guaranteed that he'll murder every one of your children. If we take him, I will spare them." She promised.

My breath caught in my throat. If I lose he will kill them and if I win they will live. But how could I win?

Looking out across the ocean, Poseidon headed towards us looking every inch the god of the ocean. The water that was carrying him on the high crest would break on a mountain near us soon. There were no choices left. Athena would win. She was a great tactician. She has outmaneuvered me at every turn. She outmaneuvered Poseidon before. She knew exactly how to play both sides.

Poseidon rode closer and closer. We would be overrun by the tsunami's wave if I remained where I stood. Using the forces, I rose up into the air. I didn't understand why she didn't use Micah to shift him to the Citadel, but perhaps Poseidon needed more than that. Maybe he was too strong for all of us.

"So you have beaten the little human pip-squeak? Thank you for getting rid of him for me, Hera. I see you brought your sidekick - the two-faced Athena. Shall I be battling both of you or do I get to take you on one at a time, in a more time-honored fashion?" He sneered at me, curling his nostril on one side.

He only wanted to toy with us. He was playing on our upbringing, hoping to cow us with the Themian need for respect and honor.

"No, Poseidon you will only be battling me. Apparently, I am the one you hate." The words were out of my mouth before I could bite them back.

"Oh, so Athena is going to stand off to the side for the action again? She's so well known for her warlike ways. I'm surprised." He sneered.

The bristling of Athena buffeted my mind. I pushed it back. I had no time for her petty feelings.

"Do not worry, Poseidon. She simply wishes to soften you up for me," she laughed.

< Now, Hera! Attack now! > Athena ordered and that was when I saw the sword and the helm appear. It was a single-handed sword with a glistening shield. She covered her head with the helm and immediately raised the blade to the sky before slashing down with all her might. Poseidon easily dodged her first blow with his triton knocking the sword out of the way, then pushed her back with the wind. He kicked out on her shield with the length of his leg.

I dashed into his mind looking for the cracks. They had built up little places of weakness over the years. I pushed at them wider and wider using the ocean of emotion that he rode.

Athena parried back and forth with him several times. Electricity bounced off of her sword. Physically, Poseidon was stronger, but Athena was not hitting him as hard as possible. She wasn't pulling her blows either. She played the long game to wear him down.

"You think to tire me out," Poseidon demanded. "Hera cannot win at mind games. It is like playing with a small child compared to me. You really think the High Council is going to sentence me to death? I dominated half of them for over a Millennium. You think the great Division and cleansing happened, and they got them all, silly girl? They never got me." The lie in his words were easily heard in his mind.

He swung the triton in a great circle to create an updraft before flinging it at Athena and calling it back to him.

"So, Poseidon, you claim you are the leader of the Great Division, the master dominator? I don't believe you, and there's no one here left to refute your claim. Maybe we didn't get them all. We will get the last one today." Athena raged at him.

He warred with anger and Athena reeled back. His mind attempted to attack hers, but Athena's sword wavered and sparked while sliding off the edge of Poseidon's Triton.

"Hera, do your work!" Athena called out to me blocking a blow with her shield.

I dove in deeper, cracking him open. It was difficult sifting through every little memory trying to find the one that would loosen him up and that would allow me the freedom to do my work. I dug with my hands sifting through the piles of memories. Everything here was a mess. He had been alive for so long it looked more like an ocean of information, floating like seaweed to be carried this way and that. Then the mind of a great leader and the Champion of the Great Division. Conquer of Tartarus. Killer of Anu.

"Poseidon, tell us exactly how did Cleito make you happy and brought fulfillment to your very sad world—with her body?" I laughed running my fingers through his memories.

His eyes narrowed, and his jaw set. I had ripped the words from his thoughts, a phrase he kept repeating to himself. Only I'd twisted them making them dirty and shameful.

"You will not speak of her that way, Hera. Cleito was twice the woman you are." He screamed.

I laughed at him, hoping he would lash out. He moved toward me, but Athena blocked him, forcing him to confront her. She roared with her war call.

I pushed, and his psyche filled with desperate loneliness, a deep desire to make an emotional connection with someone, to feel the love only a true mating could bring. His secret passion for it has made him insane, completely unhinged. There was no guarantee that even if he mated, it would save him. He has gone beyond the brink, and I was not sure anything could bring him back. But that was the linchpin. That was how I could weaken him enough for Athena to overpower him.

I started to press deeper into his psyche, pulling out the memories of Cleito and tossing them to the side. I wanted to make sure that any happiness she brought to him was gone. Anger makes one irrational. It also makes one dangerous, and I needed Poseidon to be irrational and dangerous. I needed him to jump without looking. I didn't want him making calculated decisions.

"What are you doing here, Athena?" He then turned his eyes on me. "Stop! Leave my mind. You cannot take her from me," his voice screamed with fear.

He tore back at me, flashing the death of my loved ones before me. I pushed it back and out of my mind. He would never be able to take all my children at once.

"Oh, don't worry, Poseidon, I won't take all of her. Just the good parts." I sneered.

His mind oozed with confusing emotions. It was cruel, I knew that, but my choice was clear. Him or my children and I would always choose my blood over anything else. They would always come first. All others must fall.

"No, please, I beg of you. Do not take her from me," he moaned and faltered.

I was not going to take it all. I left the painful memories. He could carry those around with him for the next Millennium, alone on Tartarus.

The vision in his mind of my children's death and his desire to kill them slowly spurred me on. He flashed their deaths at me in a strobing fashion, hoping to throw me off.

Pressing even deeper on his emotions, my gaze found Athena. She parried against him. He was visibly weakened. His shoulders were sagging and his breath ragged.

Micah appeared in the air.

"Take him now, Micah!"

Poseidon disappeared. His trident fell to the ground with a resounding thud and Athena was gone with him.

Feeling the ocean breeze on my face, I reached down and picked up the trident. Themia had created Poseidon and Zeus. There was no way we could right the wrongs he did or bring back all the people they drowned. You cannot un-rape a victim, or unmake a child. This world would never be the same.

Gazing out across the ocean, I saw them for the first time in thousands of years. They came forth from the deep and they were beautiful. A woman with flaming hair, the color of coral that grows near Grease, surfaced. I could see her tail and the watery blue eyes gazing up at me unblinking as a smile broke on her beautiful face. Her breasts were covered with green shells. She did not speak out loud.

* Greetings, Herathina, creator of the deep people, I am Ariella. I've come for the Trident. If you give it to us, we should take it away where no human will find it. We will keep it hidden. *

"And you, Ariella, what are you?" I asked in wonder remembering how all those centuries ago, I altered the bracelets for other Themian's.

* I guess you could say that I am one of your children, although I'm not genetically part of your family. I am Ariella of the Sea People. Some call me a mermaid. We do not surface often. Will you keep our secret? * she asked and placed a finger over her lips.

"I will. The fewer people know what happened to the trident, the better. I may come calling for it one day."

What was so important they need to hide it? Perhaps just the symbol of Poseidon's power. That was more than enough reason to protect it.

*As the mother of our people, we would answer your call. Goodbye, Herathina, safe tides! *

The beautiful woman disappeared under the waves. I watched as she reset coral and sand, smoothing the bottom and easing the fish from their hiding places.

CHAPTER 26

SYDNEY

We had only been at sea for 32 days and nobody's had a full night sleep in 30 days. We were all exhausted. I was thinking of pulling a double, so the kids could rest.

Everything inside me was churning. We were getting close. I could feel it every time I looked around. It was like I could feel my body being pulled towards the location that we needed to be.

The Voice stopped talking to me, the closer we got, the less he communicated. I remember hearing him in the background. No matter how many times I told the kids that we really needed to lock our minds down tight, I felt like I just couldn't close mine off quite that much. Tristan talked about going into his mind room and closing myself and Isolde out, but when I went into my mental room, my private sanctuary, I couldn't close the Voice out. His mind was filled with other voices that just kept filtering into me. I couldn't hear what they were saying, but I could feel everything. Shutting Isolde and Tristan off was actually a lot easier and frankly a relief sometimes because listening to the two of their minds wander around gave me a headache.

I always took the last shift just before sunrise when the world still believes in fairies and sheep leap over the moon to watch a dish run away with a spoon. The rosy glow that comes with it doesn't just brighten the sky but my life too. In all the years I'd been at sea I'd never seen the green flash, sailors spoke of. I had loyally watched as many sunrises and sets hoping for a glimpse.

This morning was no different, I wanted to see it with a desperation that filled my soul. Hoping for this sign, to show me that I wasn't crazy. That this wasn't just me running from Gabe's death. We were so close, and fear gripped me. The moment passed without the green flash, but something better was on the horizon - land. Unable to restrain myself, I screamed, "Land Ho!"

Both kids groaned and leaped up the steps and gained the deck, streaking with joy. We had been on this boat for more than 80 days, 30 plus without a break, and the sight of land moved me to tears.

I wished the voice would speak to me, but he never did.

Checking into the Marquesas ended up going quickly. Being a citizen of the EU made it easy. We didn't need to put up a bond as an American would. Our passport made us Spanish, but it didn't matter. They spoke French, English, Spanish and Italian, so we played our Spanish card and sighed with relief when they waved us on. It was early in the morning, so we were the only ones there. We arrived as soon as immigration opened and we were in and out in minutes. They were pretty surprised that a woman was the captain. I guess they were expecting I would have a husband or crew.

I moored the boat at the marina, and all three of us took the dinghy and immediately went to the nearest store. Tristan was in charge of diesel and I made sure to get enough cash to pay for whatever it was that we needed. I was sure Tristan would make several trips, but I had a feeling not as many trips as most people would make.

Issy was in charge of supplies and my job was information. Maps from the 'local-locals'. Polynesian language repeats most things. It's for good luck, so, local-local, Kau-Kau, k-k, stuff like that. When you want the low down, you talk to the locals at the bar. There was always a couple of old sea dogs sitting around, willing to tell a fish story. Everybody here speaks French, English, Spanish and some of them speak different forms of Polynesian. Luckily, I found a way to communicate with them.

I was told they were several atolls in the direction of the island. But not to sail too far South because bad storms live down there. They had no idea if we came from Australia or not so I just let them assume whatever they want. I told them we were heading to Panama, figured that way they would get the idea that we were heading that way.

It was a local British sea dog sitting at the pub and drinking an ale that told me that one of the best to atolls in the world was not far from here. He said that he'd be happy to take us out there. I knew he was really just looking for some extra beer to drink and a chance to get off the island, so I turned him down. Usually, I'd take him up on because it sounded like a lot of fun diving a wall and pulling up pearls, but we didn't have time for that.

Issy came back with a floral headdress on and another one on top of our pile of food. She was shining with her haul and immediately put the headdress on me.

"Awe, I wish we could stay. The people here are awesome!" She exclaimed. Her cart was filled with can goods and some fresh fruit. "There wasn't really a lot of meat that looked good, so we're stuck with some local fresh fish, a couple of tropical lobsters and a wahoo although, here they call it 'ono'," she shrugged then twirled around in the new sarong she sported.

I smiled quietly to myself, thinking how quickly Issy had taken to the culture here. Not even two hours on dry land and she already dressed the part.

The town was a quiet colonial Polynesian style with a French twist to it, but it was cute. There was a Polynesian flare everywhere. Lots of women wore a grass skirt and they danced off to the side of the walkways you passed by. All the children were excited to see us. I bought some chocolate at one of the stores and shared it with them. It didn't seem like something a lot of them ate, but who doesn't love chocolate?

< We're full, Mom. Do you and Issy a need a ride back? I'm at the dock now. > Tristan's thoughts always came through strong and in charge, manly.

I was proud and sad at the same time. Kids grow up, parents grow old.

< Yes, I'm heading to you, so be ready. >

I drug my feet a bit. This was a world outside all my troubles. Men carried banana bunches to the market, and women wove palm fronds. As I looked at them, Tristan responded.

< I am. There was a guy at the dock asking questions about our boat and wanted to know if I came alone. > Tristan remarked.

The dark undertone shook me. They couldn't have found us this fast.

< What did you tell him? > I asked

The magic spell of peace shattered. I picked up my pace, enough to get me there faster, but not enough to draw attention.

< I told him that I came with my sisters. > a joke laced his mental voice.

I smiled to myself. *< I don't look young enough to be your sister, Tristan. >*

< So what? He will still tell their buddies, you were my sister anyway. > He chuckled.

< What did he look like? > I bit my lip.

< Normal, local, tribal tattoos. > Tristan sent me a mental picture of a Polynesian man. He had a free and open smile, a tattoo circled around his left eye and down his cheek. There were a lot of Catamarans that make landfall here after the crossing, so why ask about ours?

It didn't matter, we were leaving, and the Marquesas don't have a navy that could stop me. The ground under my feet shifted with my resolve.

The weather report showed that we had clear skies for the next 3-6 days. That was a good enough window to hit an atoll and rest up. I figured it shouldn't take us more than 3 days to get to the coordinates on the map. After that, God knows what would happen. I had 150 miles to go. I figured if we didn't find anything, we could head back and melt away into the Asian world.

We sailed South to the atoll the Brit described. It wasn't much more than a sand bar with a couple of palm tree's sticking up from the mangrove bushes. We dropped anchor and swam. Everything here clung to their precious bit of life. One good cyclone and this would be gone. The trees had a few ripe coconuts, so I sent Tristan over in the dinghy to retrieve them.

That night we ate wahoo and coconut rice with fresh coconut water and papaya. It was island food, but for us, fresh was a feast.

We didn't talk during dinner, the conversation of what would happen next lingered in the air, sealing our mouths.

Issy broke the silence, "I'll take the first watch. Mom, you go to sleep because you need it more than I do. We need you frosty and something tells me we're going to need it real soon."

That was the first time Isolde ever expressed premonition. She still wore her flowered headdress, but she changed to another sarong. This was pink and covered with plumerias. She resembled an offering for King Kong more than a young woman with the ability to strip away all your secrets with a single touch.

"Okay, my jungle princess," I smiled and cupped her cheek. She leaned in and kissed me.

"Go to bed, Mom! We'll clean up," Tristan urged. He still wore his flower print board shorts without a shirt.

It hit me — in a few days it would be their birthday. They would both be 17 and Gabe had been dead for almost two years. The last year had flown by, and I'd miss both anniversaries. I moved the ring around my finger.

Time doesn't make easier, just less painful, in a dulling sort of way. They both moved to me in unison and I clung to them. My babies. We each carried our own wound from Gabe's loss. I kissed both of them several times. Then we parted, but Issy clung to my hand until our fingers parted.

I went to bed. The dream swept over me. There was a blonde woman with eyes like mine. Her voice began right from the start, "You're ready to come to us. Come to us! Don't wait any longer. Hurry!"

CHAPTER 27

SYDNEY

Blue, cobalt, indigo, midnight. To try and describe all the different shades of blue was like trying to grasp sand in your hand. It is impossible to hold it, nothing more than a perceived control. The way the blues met each other at the horizon, the ocean waves slapping against the sky creating salt spray foam it was magic, the perfect tranquility.

Of course, the island divided it all. The pyramid sprouts up from the water into the sky. I could see it clearly now for what it really was. After having seen the map, it looks like a version of the Vitruvian man. I love the site of all of the green vines hanging from everywhere but the white of the columns with its strange glistening stars trapped inside are blinding me.

The statue of Poseidon sits on the top of the temple with one arm thrusting up into the sky with his Triton. His muscles are sculpted to perfection, displaying the strength of a thousand battles. His other arm is reaching ahead of him, pointing to his enemies. It fills me with trepidation. He would strike anyone in his path down. The snarl on his face, the pinch in his brow, his gaze filled with malevolence, his chariot, and horses poised to leap right into the watery grave from the side of the falls. His stare engulfed the entire island and beyond. He could conquer the world in one blow.

The mist from the waterfall still made the temple look like it was floating. The architect's illusion worked on me even now.

And even though I know the island has to be real, the circles within circles boggle my mind at the sheer amount of work to dig them. Every time I look at the canals dividing the circles, I know that I am missing something. Something about this island tickles the back of my mind, just out of reach. It is not right.

Then the woman pulls me back like she would grasp the back of my body, pulling my soul back into the sky. My eyes tore away from the island, and the world turns sepia tone brown fading into a map just as the day I'd seen it in Spain.

Who would have known that it had lain in a catacomb in Barcelona all these years? Did Ponce de Leon find it? Is it Atlantis? The websites pointed to Atlantis as the location of the Fountain of Youth. The fountain on the map has the Infinity sign, so does that mean it's the Fountain of Youth?

Hopefully, I'll find the island and find out for myself. Looking at the map now, I can see how on every line, every word, every letter the edges crisp the ink dark looking fresh as if it had just been drawn. But no one alive today could possibly have been alive when this map was originally drawn.

The dream began to recede, the wind whipping around my face. My hair is lashing me in the eyes and filling my mouth. Finally, the wind blasts it back from my head and I hear her words booming in my mind.

"Come to me now! Don't wait any longer. You're ready for the truth."

****

Just as quickly, the dream ended. I was laying in the saloon awake hearing how the water was quietly lapping against the sides of the boat and a gentle breeze was blowing through the wind chimes.

I could hear the soft breathing of my children in their cabins. I felt like we couldn't wait any longer. I felt as if I'd slept for a week. I was energized and invigorated and I was ready to take on anything. The energy drove me to my feet. I made the bed back into the table.

I didn't want to wait for the sun to come up, so I pulled out all of our electronic devices and I turned on the SAT phone and picked up the Wi-Fi. With that done, I immediately began planning our course. I wasn't going to sleep here another night. The children could sleep all day if they wanted, but I was not going to sleep again until we found the island.

Her words pounded in my mind, like an energizing drug, urging me on, pushing me.

After plotting our course on the map, I figured we were probably only about maybe 75 miles away. We could possibly be there in a few hours. I went up on deck and turned on the windlass and pulled up the anchor just as the sun crested the edge of the horizon. The stars in the sky we're pushing off the various waves. The sky was crystalline blue without a cloud to be seen anywhere. It was a perfect day for sailing. Tristan must have heard the windlass as I reeled the anchor, but I didn't care.

I hosted the mainsail, and we immediately pulled away. I was going to make it to the island, or I was going to die trying.

The sky was blue and the wind was out of the Southeast. We were pulling 6 knots. It wasn't a great time but it was still a good. The wind pushed my hair back, so I moved to sit on the hard bimini and steered with my feet watching the horizon. My heart was beating through my chest in anticipation.

One moment the sky was pristine and the next, dark and ominous. The winds had grown to 30 knots, so I had to reef the mainsail. Our speed picked up almost dangerously. I moved in my mind to feel the water, but it refused to react to my commands.

Lightning and thunder dominated the sky in the direction we were heading, but we couldn't turn back. Tristan came out on deck running.

"What are we doing? What are you doing, Mom?" He demanded while gathering the gear and shoving it into the nearest locker or chucking it into the saloon.

"The sky was perfect a moment ago, Tristan. It came out of nowhere," I retorted.

What if I'm fucked in the head?

"Are we heading towards the island?" He yelled over the howling wind.

"Yes." My voice was calm.

Tristan immediately went out and made sure everything on the deck was lashed properly. The last thing in the world we needed was to lose one tank of diesel. We couldn't afford it. If we lost even one, we might not make it back. But we had come this far I wasn't going to turn around. I didn't care. I had to know. My whole life had come to this.

Issy came up on deck. Tristan yelled at her to make coffee or something. She put the electric kettle on. We moved all of the cushions inside to the saloon and Issy tossed my life vest and clipped in the lifelines.

"We are probably about 20 miles out," I shouted.

A loud crack filled the air lighting up the sky as bright as a nuclear bomb, and everything went dead.

"Fuck! No, no, no. Tristan, go check the electric. Issy, is there any power in there?" I screamed, tapping the tablet screen and turning knobs.

"No, Mom. It's all dead," Issy called from the saloon.

"Mom, even the Ipad is dead," Tristan held up the tablet pushing the buttons.

"God damn it! Can I please get a break?" I screamed into the wind.

Think Syd, think!

My thoughts came out of Issy's mouth.

"What just happened? Why is it all dead?" Issy asked.

I bolted for the mainsail and pulled it down, tucking it in its sleeve. We were adrift. There were reefs all over the place, and we were adrift. As quick as the storm hit, it was gone. And everything was dead. Not just our power, but the wind too.

We had no helm control and no motors. We'd lost the depth finder. The only thing we had left was our compass. As

I was trying to figure out what we could do, the Voice started talking.

< You have your minds. It is your most powerful tool. > he said.

< *Oh, now you show up. Thanks a lot, Johnny come lately!* > I yelled at him.

"Tristan go down to the workroom. Find that metal garbage can with the lid on it and bring it up here," I instructed.

"Were we struck by lightning, Mom?" Tristan asked.

"No. I don't know what it was. Check everything before you go. I want to know if there's even one electronic device working," I ordered.

Issy shot back "The only way we're boiling water is with the propane stove. The electronics are gone. I think they're fried, it smells a little funny in here."

The sound of breakers clicking from one position to the other and back came from the salon.

Tristan came back on deck and gave me the news. "No, Mom. It's all dead, everything, even the cell phone. Like somebody turned it all off." He shook his head and tossed the cell on the table. I watched it side across the top and slipped over the edge to the teak seat.

Was it a solar flare? It was all tied to the strange storm. I opened up the garbage can and immediately pulled out my spare tablet, I'd stored there, along with some emergency battery backups. Gabe always said my mini Faraday cage was a waste of space. I bit my lip. Being right isn't as sweet as you think.

The tablet booted up and I pulled out the emergency SAT phone.

"Alright, Tristan, pull out the hard maps. Isolde, grab the dry erase markers. Get your slide rule. I want the sextant, so pull it all out. Put it on the table here. We're going to plot our course the old fashioned way," I order, then scratched my head and bit my lip.

Issy huffed. "We can't even hoist the sails without the electric winch."

"Yes, we can. You don't need any of those devices or the motors to hoist the sails. You're just going to have to put your back into it." I urged.

"If you want, you can be captain, Isolde, while Mom and I work the sails," Tristan offered with a smile.

I nodded in agreement. "We can do this. It's not as hard as you think. We're not dead in the water, and I refuse to give up."

I glanced out over the ocean. Other than the waves, we were dead in the water - becalmed.

I booted up the tablet and the SAT phone just long enough to get ourselves a bearing. When the GPS marked on the map exactly where we were, I shut it all down. I didn't need a ping. If they are watching for us, they didn't need to see how close we were.

We were just far enough from the island that we couldn't see it, but close enough we could easily sail it in a couple of hours. We just had to stay the course.

"But, Mom, how are we going to know we're even on course?" Issy whined, but I threw her a sharp look.

"Stow that shit, Issy! There is no place on this boat for a whiner or a quitter. If we get the point where we think the destination is and we don't see the island, will boot up the tablet again." I put it back in the garbage can, then held out two solenoids to Tristan.

"We can't get even motor, Mom," Tristan said taking the solenoids in his left hand and looking up at me.

"Oh. Have a little faith or trust. You clearly don't understand how the world really works because of all these electronics and this technology that you're relying on. Sailors have sailed the seven seas for many Millennia without any of it. Most of them without even a compass. They simply followed the stars and dead reckoning. They made it from Norway to Greenland to Iceland to America. We can make it the little way we need to go," I said biting my lip.

CHAPTER 28

HERA

Log entry

Poseidon had been banished to Tartarus. He would be allowed back into our society, but he would never be allowed to leave any homeworld again. The last four members of Alethea who broke their oaths were also banished. They were returned to the homeworlds and none were allowed to leave for a Millenia.

Standing and looking around the devastation caused by Poseidon and Zeus, I could only imagine how many thousands of humans were murdered, drowned and killed simply by the sheer forced movement of the entire island. Actually, it was no longer an island. Now it was connected to the other continents by a land bridge. Poseidon pushed one end down raising the other.

The straits of Herakles were no more. It was nothing but wet sludge, muddy from the raising of the watery depths.

Atlantis was forever cut off from the Mediterranean. The plain of humans that fed Atlantis was covered in bodies as the water receded.

Floating above the devastation, I was filled with sadness. The scenery changed as I moved to Alethea. Standing outside the entrance of the citadel, I closed my eyes before facing the punishment I knew was mine.

Inside, two men were on their knees. My black-haired Zeus was on the right with his head held high, defiant to the end. On the left, there was the golden-haired Poseidon. Even now he held his body erect like the statue outside this citadel - proud and ready to conquer the world. The Council was already seated, with Athena proudly at its center.

"The High Council has already given the proclamation for you, Poseidon. Micah makes his punishment so. You will be exiled for the next fifty thousand years on Tartarus. At the end of your exile, should you find yourself able, you will be allowed to live out the rest of your existence on a homeworld never to be given a project or be part of one ever again." Athena stated.

She nodded to Micah and just before Poseidon disappeared he turned to stare me down.

Apollo and Artemis sat close by. Artemis had a gleam in her eye. I could feel the triumph flowing out from her. The hunt was over. She had won her prize.

"What are you going to do with me? Which woman is going to try to kill me?" Zeus let out a dry grinding laugh. "You can't kill me. I'm immortal. Many have tried, all failed. I always survive." His arrogant smile filled his face. He tossed his hair, tipping his chin up and his eyes flashed with glee.

Athena shook her head and her dark hair moved with her.

"Silly, simpleminded human. You think it is impossible for Themian's to die? You've obviously learned nothing from all your associations with us. Apollo, hold him!"

Apollo pulled both of his arms behind his back, placing his foot between both shoulder blades, forcing Zeus into a crouching position, but Zeus craned his neck back to keep his eyes on Athena.

"Artemis, remove this scourge from the planet!" Athena's arm extends, offering her a sword. My heart jumped into my throat as my hand covered my cry.

He must be stopped. It is the only way. His mind is twisted. There is no reason to show any mercy.

Artemis raised her sword and quickly lowered it. The crunch of bone rang in my ears. The sickening sound of a heavy thump on the cracked floor was followed by a fleshy squish as it rolled across the crystalline tiles and blood sprayed from the lifeless stump.

An awful cry reformed in my throat, pressing against my vocal cords. I placed a hand over my mouth, desperate to stifle the pain. Hands and arms covered me with tears and sorrow, only to be pulled away.

"Now that the human abomination is gone, let's talk about your offspring, Herathina," Athena turned to face me down.

I rose and took a stand on the main floor not far from Zeus dead body and the puddle of blood forming next to it.

"You helped with the capture of Poseidon and Zeus and for that I am grateful. I do not forget my promise, so we will spare your children. Have any of them reproduced?" Athena demanded.

I didn't know, but the denial didn't come quick enough.

"Did they have any children of their own?" She asked again.

I shook myself. This wasn't over, so I replied.

"No, my children are all pure." My eyes searched them out, only to light on all eight being held by guards. Their chins were raised in defiance and their eyes hard and determined.

"You will set them free?" I pleaded. "Will you allow them to live?" My hope sprung and died all at once.

Athena stared down with pity in her eyes.

"Of course not, Hera. We can't have them running around tainting the gene pool. That was Poseidon's folly. Now, they will be transported to a Themian homeworld. They can live out their existence amongst our people. I highly doubt they will reproduce. Your line dies here. Unless of course, you find yourself mated to someone. Then, you can pour your sorrow into those children." Her words burned.

My line dies here? And I am to be grateful?

"Thank you for sparing their lives," I swallow the bitterness back. Now wasn't the time.

Perseus contacted me < Mother, we reproduced. We all did. >

< Guard your mind, Perseus! > I pushed the knowledge down as hard as I could.

"As for you, Hera, you will stay here. You are never allowed to leave Alethea again. Your sentence is to stay until the end, whenever that may be. We may be here a long time and you are not to leave the ship. No matter where it is or what it looks like, you are never to stop touching Alethea. Your feet need to be constantly in contact with it. You're not even to use the forces to rise up into the air. Your bracelet has been altered, making it impossible for you to leave."

The weight of my punishment slammed down on me. To live such a small life. The project would never be over. Humanity would always be behind us, never catching up and I would always be here.

"I'm a prisoner? Even Poseidon will get a reprieve in 50,000 years. I will be punished for eternity." My voice broke, as tears pricked my eyes. I would never see my children again. My eyes devoured their faces. They had grown up so fast. The last twenty years had flown by in our search for Zeus. Hercules and Hebe were barely old enough to live on their own.

"Eternity, Hera? No, just until the project is complete. Your punishment is more severe because you were the one preaching noninterference and limited contact. You were the one telling everyone in every way how Poseidon had broken his oath. Yet, you yourself turned around and committed the same infraction. Not only are you an oathbreaker, but you are a liar and I don't know anything more detestable. 'Do as I say and not as I do'. You are a hypocrite. The Herathina I knew would have never behaved in such a fashion, or so I thought. Herathina is dead and only Hera is left. Your judgment is made. Accept it, or kill yourself. We're done here." She stood up, as the words burned in my ears.

I hung my head. There was nothing that Athena said that was untrue. I was a hypocrite. I turned my back on everything. At some point in time, I knew I'd have to pay the price for my actions. I didn't realize my punishment would be for all of eternity and that my children would live to be punished too, but at least they'll live.

The oracle's words rang in my mind. "The sins of the father visited on the children."

CHAPTER 29

SYDNEY

I took Tristan down in the starboard to sugar-scoop to the diesel engine housed there. I couldn't bring all of the electronics back on-line, and we didn't need to, but we weren't going to be able to start the engine without an electronic starter.

I took the starter housing off the block and pulled the old solenoid out, then popped in a new one. Unbeknownst to Tristan, I'd brought a can of whip-it with me.

"We're going to spark the engine," I shook the hell out of the can, angled the spray nozzle into the intake of the engine and filled it with the whip-it.

"Okay, fire it up!"

God, I hope I don't blow us up. Just to be sure I crossed my fingers on my left hand.

Tristan pulled the emergency start cord, and it roared to life. Isolde was able to control the throttle from captain's station. I handed him the can and the second solenoid.

"Go and handle the other engine," I instructed.

I climbed out of the engine hold, hoisting my butt up on to the deck. The cloud lingered over us.

"Bring the ship out of the shallows and into the deep water."

Issy maneuvered our floating box away from the reefs. I waved her out of the seat.

"Go forward and take the depth rope with you! You're the new depth finder. I don't want to run aground on a reef just because I misjudged my water," I pat her, pushing her forward.

She opened one of the watertight storage compartments and pulled out a rope covered in knots. Every knot was one foot apart with a lead weight at the end.

"I figured we sail around the shallows and reefs. There has to be a way through the coral. We may come to the island from the opposite side. None of our maps showed any reefs in this area. I don't know who drew these maps, but I think we have reached the point of 'here be dragons.'"

Tristan let out a mirthless laugh. After I was sure we were out of the shallows and could no longer see the reefs, I killed the motors. I wasn't going to waste the wind and the sun.

"Tristan, hoist the mainsail. Isolde, help him."

They were both sweating like pigs by the time they were done. Watching their muscles as they pulled each and every time hoisting the line, made me proud. They weren't quitters.

We sailed for about an hour. We would probably end up seeing the island soon.

"Mom, Mom!" Issy jumped up and down on one of the bow seats and ran back to me. "We're there. I can see it. Can you see it?" She demanded.

"What? I don't see anything."

She was pointing Northwest and Tristan pulled out the binoculars.

"I'll be damned, Mom. She's right. It's right out there. I can see the top of something, and it seems to be shining back at me like a mirror. There's something out there. It could just be another boat, but I don't think it's another boat, Mom."

I squinted to make out the point, and a flash of light reflected back at me. The figure began to form on the horizon. It started as a small bump, but it grew to epic proportions. The mountainous pyramid filled the startling sapphire blue of the sky. The wind bluffed my face pushing my hair away from my face. The glare from the sun caused my eyes to fill with tears that rolled back into my ears.

I altered the course so we could sail right at it. Tristan handed Isolde the binoculars and took the rope from her.

"I need you to give me depth," I called. The water felt shallow and tricky.

He threw it in and he said, "At least 20 foot of water here, Mom. No worries, just keep going." After ten minutes he gave me new updates. "30 foot of water, no worries. Keep going!"

We were getting too close for sailing. We had to be easily within 20 miles of the island. It was beginning to loom, and I could already see the pyramid peak. Tristan was right; there was something shiny. That's when the voice burst into my mind.

< Sydney, you're almost here. I've been here the whole time. > He laughed.

< *You could have told me sooner.* > I remarked.

< Would you have believed me? >

< *I don't know.* > I didn't know, not for sure.

I had the kids reef in the sail and batten it down. We weren't going to be needing it anymore. Tristan went and double sparked both engines and we began the tedious job of maneuvering through the reef ring around the island.

"23 feet. Move to your left, Mom." A few minutes later he spoke again, "Depth 17 feet. Move to your right. Back off and move to the left keep it coming." Tristan instructed.

We slowly pulled into the most beautiful cove and beach I had ever seen. Crystalline white sand and shooting stars glimmering back at us. The idyllic palm trees hung out into the water. Green-leaved plants and vines were clinging to the cliffs around the bay. It was a perfect crescent shape.

We pulled in just far enough to get out of the heavy winds. The sandy bottom was perfect. Once we made it through the barrier, the reef protected the entire island. It was a circular ring around the island.

We dropped the anchors just to help with a drift because the waves weren't high. I was worried. I stopped and looked up at the kids. It was three in the afternoon and we were exhausted but they were anxious to get on land. We lowered the dinghy into the water after locking everything down, and we headed to the beach.

CHAPTER 30

HERA

Log entry

I had not lived amongst my own kind for a long time, so to suddenly be thrust back into their company was a shock to my system. To never be able to float in the air again was painful. The only water I was allowed to swim in where the various channels formed between Alethea's rings.

Athena did not even allow me to return to my village to say goodbye. Soon, everyone who ever knew me in every village would be dead. I would become a memory, a story their children tell their children about the Gods and Goddesses. How we walked among them and living with them. The stories of Zeus had already begun. There were already stories of me and my jealousy against Zeus' sexual conquests. Humans claimed that I chased down his many lovers to wreak my revenge upon them, but none of this was true.

It was not why I visited any of those women, but it did not matter anymore. I would never see any of them again, and all their claims of Zeus seducing and fathering children will grow into history along with every story of all the other Demigod's, my children.

Yes, the women were visited by Zeus, and I was sure they gave themselves willingly, but they only claimed their children to be Zeus' to hide their infidelity and to justify having a child out of wedlock. At least this way they wouldn't be stoned. I could not blame their choices. A woman's life in the human world is ruled by men.

Alethea had become a place I did not recognize. I was out of step here. There were many Themian's I had never encountered before, most of them sent by the High Council to replace the fallen.

Log entry

Athena had called for a gathering in the citadel. I am required to attend her every whim.

"It is time Alethea is moved. She has sat here long enough. It is time that we vanished. Humanity thinks that with the flood, all of Atlantis disappeared. They can no longer reach us through the straits of Herakles and the city must disappear," Athena turned her head to stare at me.

With a quick swift nod, the pressure changed and the cold of the shift filled the air. With a pop, we found ourselves someplace else. I stepped out of the Citadel into the temple and looked down. We were several hundred miles away from a large landmass. Gazing over the side of the center ring, I noticed there were smaller islands as the ship slowly lowered itself down. I heard Athena's voice echoing from the Citadel.

"We have moved into the Northern hemisphere of this planet. We are now on the other side of a vast ocean. The indigenous peoples around here are simple and their technology is extremely low. They have no knowledge of Atlantis or anything to do with Atlantis. We'll be able to remain here for a long time since humanity's technology has not yet reached the level of crossing oceans, therefore, the knowledge of Atlantis is unlikely. We will study the humans here, then we shall move on."

The ship lowered, settling itself into its new home on the ocean floor. Athena's ideas rang of proclamation in the middle of the Citadel. I thought that her dream of keeping Alethea a secret was silly. For all her tactical maneuvering and her great warrior like prowess, she underestimated one thing. She underestimated the human mind. She didn't consider humans to be inquisitive and intelligent, but they were. They would figure out who we are and where we've gone. They would come for us, speak of us and they would pursue us across time and planet. All the while, I would be here watching unable to leave.

Log entry

The human people in this area were quite kind. Many of them had come with their boats out to our giant island looking vessel, bringing with them fish and all manner of fruits. They referred to their islands as Bimini.

I was not allowed to leave the ship, but I was allowed to greet each and every Homo sapiens that approached if I chose to. I did this because they were interesting and I enjoyed the ingenuity of the people. I liked how they were building small rafts and boats for themselves to row in between the islands. Many people here had dark skin. They were friendly, but I hadn't bothered to learn their language anymore.

My heart was too broken. I couldn't develop another relationship with any humans. They lived such short lives, and each time one of them died it was like a knife to my already damaged heart.

"You sit here staring out at the stars and the water. What are you hoping to find, Hera?" Athena's voice cut through my solitude to the quick of my pain.

"Peace, quiet, solitude, answers. Isn't that what everyone is looking for? What are you hoping to find out here, Athena? You plague my every move. You watch me as if you expect me to commit suicide or jump off the ship so you can torture me more," I respond with little joy.

"I'm afraid for you. You're so despondent. You take no pleasure whatsoever in your existence anymore," concern laced her voice, but I couldn't feel it. I didn't want to. I had built those walls around my mind and heart that none, except my children, may scale.

"What pleasure is there to take? I am not mated, so I have no love. My children have been taken from me and I'm forced to live here against my will. I cannot leave, so I must stay. Every time I see a human die, it breaks my heart. I cannot give them the Primordial waters. The world cannot have another Zeus. What would you have me do? I live to see my children and nothing more." I stated as plainly as I could.

The heat in my chest radiated out to my fingers. The water around me moved agitated, slapping back and forth. The wind picked up, but I could not rise with it. The wind buffed my face pushing my hair back and my pain away.

Athena was doing what I think Poseidon should have done all along. She moved the ship around the planet. So far, everywhere we had gone my medicine was my only diversion. It was a way to experiment with terrain plant life. Till now, we spent most of our time in the center regions of the planet, around the Equator.

Loge entry

Athena has moved the entire ship down to the Southern region of the planet. There were many curious creatures down here. We stayed just long enough for a cavity to form around the ship. I had a feeling every time Micha moved us we would leave behind a void under the ice.

She kept moving Alethea back to Bimini. I was not sure what her affinity with the area was. I created smaller drone like machines to go out and sweep the countryside collecting data, anything to stay busy.

My fellow shipmates looked at me with suspicion. The taste of anger and rage they direct to me, I could hear the echo in their minds, tainted. I didn't know if they thought I was tainted or that I tainted the human gene pool. Perhaps they thought that I corrupted the entire planet, which was funny because Poseidon did the very same thing I did, just long before me and in a fashion I never achieved, nor did I want to. Justification didn't justify my actions. I should never have allowed myself such weakness. I should never have given Zeus the Primordium. I should have let him die. I had brought nothing but death everywhere I turned.

Death, rebirth, hate.

The one bright light in my entire imprisonment was the dream of my children. It hadn't stopped me from visiting my children. I might have not been allowed to leave the ship, but I assumed she meant physically not mentally. I dreamwalked my children often. It was one bright place. I could dreamwalk Poseidon if I wanted, but I didn't.

Log entry

Athena was standing over me, obstructing the sun, "Do you intend to mope around the spaceship for the rest of your existence, Hera?"

"Am I moping? I was unaware," I replied, digging a new hole in the soil that had clung to the ship. I was planting seeds of flowers, to while away my time.

"You don't appear to be happy, and your zest for life and work is diminished." She sat on the ground next to me.

"I don't know why you trouble yourself with my mental status. If you truly wish to help me, allow me to leave Alethea and join my children on any world you wish," I said without looking at her and pouring water over the newly planted seeds.

"You know I cannot do that, even if I was inclined to. You are too dangerous, and your punishment is not done." She scoffed, digging a hole next to my previous one then picked a few seeds from my basket tossing them in. I covered them over and watered them.

"Poseidon's punishment is for 50,000 years, and mine is for an undetermined amount of time. I could be here forever. We have no idea how long my children will live, and you keep them unnecessarily." It was the only argument I had. I offered the same reasoning, and she returned with the same retort.

"Poseidon went into his sin, as the humans call it, with open eyes. He was tainted with human emotion and they overtook him. He wasn't capable of controlling. You, on the other hand, knew exactly what you were doing. You knew what he had done, you knew the cost, and yet you did it anyway. The only difference between you and Poseidon is that you aren't trying to dominate the world. But you did create a creature who did, Zeus. He was evil and you allowed yourself to be enticed by him. You believed all his wretched lies and then you gave him the Primordium. You made him an immortal. You made him like us, only his mind was warped. Do you have any idea what level of devastation he wreaked upon this planet, and that it is all your fault? So yes, what you did was worse than Poseidon. He kept Cleito alive for thousands of years by using Primordium. He did not turn her into an immortal. You did. You took everything one step further. And you knew the consequences you knew exactly what happened to Poseidon's children and you still gave birth. Not just once but many times. Hera, you deserve to suffer." She expressed an anger I didn't expect.

She jumped to her feet, angry. She wanted me to apologize, but I couldn't. I won't regret anything that brought my children to me.

"I do. I see my folly, and I have paid for my mistakes. There is no reason why my children should have to pay also. That is my real issue. Punish me all you will, Athena. I'm happy to take it. I will stay upon Alethea as long as you wish. Just give me back my children." My words came as mournful cries. I pleaded to deaf ears. She would never relent. I stared at the ground with hot, dry eyes. My tears were all gone, nothing could return my children to me.

"No, it's not up to me. The High Council has chosen. I must abide by their decision, and so must you. I cannot change it for you, even if I wish to." For once, her blue eyes burned with sadness.

Had I underestimated Athena? Was she following orders? If only I could force her hand, I could dominate her mind and get what I wanted. But then I really would be Poseidon, and that was the line I couldn't cross.

CHAPTER 31

SYDNEY

Reaching the sand of the windswept idyllic tropical beach was a balm to my soul. For some reason, deja vu filled me. Internally a light had turned on filling me with peace and contentment.

I needed to be here. I wanted desperately to be here. I just didn't understand how it was that I could have not known but still, I needed to be here. Every sense in my body tingled with the anticipation of new discoveries and I felt complete.

Isolde exclaimed. "This is where we should be. Why have we not been here the whole time?"

My smile froze. I turned my head to stare. She'd plucked the words from my mind. All three of our minds said 'home' and we exchanged smiles. Our eyes sparkled with joy. I lingered on their faces because I wanted to remember that day. It was the first happy day since Gabe died.

Tristan immediately started laughing, "We could go swimming, Isolde."

Cupping her elbows with her hands, she responded. "Or we could just sit still for 5 minutes. I'm so tired of constantly moving. I just want to feel my body without motion for 5 seconds. Please," tilting her head back, she smiled up at the sun.

I understood what she meant. When you're on a boat your body is in constant motion. You are never still because there's always the lashing of the waves, the gentle rolling of the sea and the wind movement. You're continuously compensating, re-adjust, balancing. Just a standstill on land it's a luxury, one we had not experienced in a long time.

Tristan pulled out the beach mats and laid them down. "Well, why don't we just catch some sun like normal beachgoers? We could lay here and be still."

Isolde's deep throaty laugh of pure joy filled the beach. My heart warmed at the thought of her and her happiness. If just being still was all it took to be this happy, I never wanted to move again.

"Alright, Tristan, how long can you lay still on the beach?" Issy giggled.

"At least as long as you, Issy," he flopped down on his mat like a dog and rolled on to his belly.

"Why don't we all stand still for just a little while? Then we can get up and go for some fresh fruit," I suggested.

Issy nodded her head, never opening her eyes. Her face was filled with bliss. Looking at her how happy she was, Tristan added, "You ladies take the first shift and I'll go to find fresh fruit. I'll be back in a couple of minutes," he leaped up trudging over to the dingy, reached into the seat storage, pulled out a machete and then proceeded into the bush.

Isolde looked at me, "You know he's perfectly safe here. There's nothing here but howler monkeys."

I hoped that was true. We were on an island that didn't exist on any map or Google Earth or anywhere. As a matter of fact, it was not supposed to exist at all. I tried to think of who here could possibly harm him. Maybe the people who'd been following us. I tried not to think of them, so I laid back on my mat, to relax.

Tristan can get away from anyone. He'll be okay.

I laid on the beach dozing, but I wasn't asleep. The hypnotic sounds of the waves lapped back and forth. Every now and again they were slapping and tickling my toes. I was between the dream world and being awake. There was a buzzing in the background like many minds were pressing in. They were all speaking and communicating, but they were just out of reach. I pushed it away. I wasn't ready to experience whatever was here just yet. I needed to recover. We had made it to the island. That was all I needed to know for the moment.

Tristan flopped down next to us, kicking the sand all over the place.

"Tristan, come on! I was almost asleep," Issy wined then toss some sand at him.

"I guess it's a good thing I came back, so you could turn over instead of burning."

Chuckling I remarked, "Thank you, Tristan, for saving us from ourselves."

His arms were bursting with booty. "Look, I found mangoes and papayas. Oh, and I think these are mangosteens. Anyway, there were some kiwis, nuts, bananas, and a mess of other things that looked edible. I grab whatever looked appetizing." He spread it all out on one of the beach mats.

We picked through an ate what we desired. Isolde picked up a particularly juicy looking purple egg-shaped thing. It was bigger than a grape and smaller than a lime. Her hand hung in midair. "What is this?"

Tristan shook his head and scrunched his shoulders. I smiled and grabbed it out of her hand.

"It's a jaboticaba. It's a Chinese plum. They make sauces and jam out of this. They're really yummy. Did you find them on the bark of the tree, Tristan?" I asked while popping it into my mouth.

"Yeah."

"Jobotacoba's popular all over the South Pacific. I hear they grow all over the place in Hawaii too." I never missed a chance to educate my children. They both snickered at me.

"Maybe when we're done here we can go to Hawaii and check them out. Mom, what do you think?" Issy sucked the flesh off of the pit and spit it out.

"Sounds like fun, Issy. We can find you a nice Hawaiian boyfriend," Tristan teased.

She curled her nose up to one side, shaking her head. "Thank you, but I am not interested."

"Why? Do you already have a boyfriend?" Tristan was wagging his finger at her and pointing laughingly.

"No, but I'm not interested in just any man. I want somebody truly amazing. I want something like Mom and Daddy had."

My eyes found the sand interesting and turned so she wouldn't see my face. What Gabriel and I had was special, but it wasn't what I had with Adrian. That was something that would withstand time and space for as long as I lived. I guess it was really the only word I could use for it. I would never be with anyone else. I did love Gabriel, but Adrian was more than that. And they were both gone.

We finished eating. I knew that if I laid back down, I would go to sleep. Judging by the heavy weight of the eyes of my children, I could tell they would too. I didn't want any of us to fall asleep on the beach. You never know what kind of animals come out at night. I stood up, pulling Isolde into standing position.

"Come on! Let's go explore."

They both groaned but didn't refuse.

CHAPTER 32

SYDNEY

Tristan pointed at the cliffs on the far side of the cove and we all headed over that way. The closer we got, the less natural they looked. Instead of having that sway back look of an unintentional wall they were perfectly vertical. Adding to that effect was the second level as if it was a terrace. The side was too flat and there appeared to be a break in the wall and steps cut into the rock.

The rock wall had the look of some of the monolithic rock walls I'd seen in Peru. The nubs that protruded from the sides were also common in Egypt, on the lower half of the Menkaure pyramid at Giza. It fascinated me to think that the type of monolithic building would be here too. Each of the stones fit together tightly in odd geometric shapes of six or more sides. Some of the shapes were regular and rectangular only to have a small curve at one corner or an angle from one side. It was intentional and straight in a way nature would never create.

"Why don't we go over there?" Issy asked and moved before I could reply, pointing to the recess in the wall.

"Okay, but I don't want to do anything too dangerous."

Twisting to look back at me, Issy raised her eyebrows lowering her lids. "Mom, don't be such a fuddy-duddy," she scoffed and I snorted at the turn of phrase.

"Yeah, Mom, after all, I think we will be just fine. Let's go climb some rocks."

We approached the cliff face and my feelings of encountering the unnatural grew. Gazing up at the sandstone, it looked like it had stood there for thousands of years. The rain and wind eroded it away. The cliff, however, wasn't high, but it was sheer.

Turning my head to the side, I hazard a glanced at Tristan. "Are you sure you saw a pathway up through these rocks or did just want to walk over here and look at them?" I teased, to push my own miss giving's away.

"I saw the pathway over there," he grabbed Issy's hand dragging her along. She was always the slowest, lagging behind, never wanting to put forth too much effort. We rounded a few large boulders. They looked as if they'd rolled off the side of the mountain. And low and behold, set into the recess, was a path just big enough for a man. It looked as though it was honed by human hands and then washed away by many hundreds of years of rain. There were steps cut into the side of the cliff.

"Is anybody game to go find out where this 'Stairway to Heaven' goes?" Tristan let go of Issy's hand and began his climb.

"I'm game, let's go! Comin, Mom?" She followed behind, lifting each foot a little higher than average to reach the next step.

"Of course. I wouldn't want to be left out. If you get hurt, Tristan's not the only one who can carry one of us down," I pushed the ominous misgivings away and embraced the joy of the day.

He laughed, and Issy replied giggling, "Of course. You're a big beast and a child in a man's body."

"Thank you, Isolde. I knew you would appreciate my finer manly qualities." Tristan chuckled and shoved her shoulder.

The playful banter between them was a relief after two years of stress and grief. Issy sighed, "Your manly qualities? You're a giant child stuck in a beast body. Don't try to twist my words around."

I laughed and jumped in, "Stop arguing or we'll never make it up to the side of the cliff before the sun goes down."

"Yes, Mom," they said in chorus then snickered.

Each step was cut a little high as if the people who had made them intentionally made them difficult or they were much taller than we were. There were handholds also, all properly placed as if by a human hand. I followed up the side of the cliff holding on, with Tristan in front and Isolde the middle. The further up we went, the more we zigzagged back and forth.

I trudged with every step to reach the pinnacle of the rock face. I was not used to stable ground, I strained to reach a hopefully flat surface. I still had my sea legs and found I was wobbling on the solid ground.

A cave opening formed yawning in front of us. It had an unnatural arch set back in the rock wall. It was smooth and yet rough around the edges, rugged enough that you might think it was a natural opening. It went straight back into the rock face and down.

"What are you rubbing your hands up and down the walls for Issy? Are they going to speak to you in Braille?" Tristan snickered then leaned back against the cool rock wall.

He had to be happy. I hadn't heard him tease his sister this much in a long time.

Cocking her hip to the side, Issy retorted. "No, Tristan, I'm checking to see if there are any symbols etched into the walls. Sometimes you can't see them with the naked eye, but you can feel the outlines with your fingers. You never know. I mean this is an island that's not supposed to exist." And with that, she went back to her explorations.

"Well, obviously somebody knew it existed or Ponce de Leon wouldn't have drawn a map of it." Tristan retorted.

I cut that off right away. "Actually, Tristan, Ponce de Leon map it, but he didn't know where it was. Why do you think he kept looking for it?"

"Yeah funny. How could you get here? Draw a map and then get back and forget how you got here?" Tristan laughed and ran his fingers down the walls too.

"Excellent question but I have no idea," I muttered, the map had the latitude and longitude on it, so why was he searching for it?

"Issy, look up! There's a symbol here," Tristan said, his fingers just reached the light etching there.

"Really?" Her head snapped back to stare at the ceiling, as did mine.

"I don't know. Give me a water bottle. I want to squirt a little water on it. Sometimes by doing that you can see what it really is." She squinted up at the ceiling.

Tristan looked at me hopefully. Neither of my children had thought to bring a bag or a bottle of water. I retrieved my squeeze bottle from my pack. Water jetted onto the side of the wall, and an infinity symbol appeared.

"Wasn't there one of those on the map, Mom?" They both asked.

"Yeah, but it was over the top of a fountain," I said scratching my head, then trailing my hand down the wall hoping to find more.

"Wasn't Ponce de Leon looking for the Fountain of Youth? Wouldn't you give it an infinity sign to suggest the everlasting life?" Issy asked, squirting more water on the wall and rubbing it around.

"I don't know, but I guess we're heading in the right direction. Tristan, break out our bug-out bags and let's check it out."

I took a glow stick and pulled out my LED flashlight. Tristan moved his and Issy's backpack over from the boat.

A long time ago, I learned that the best way to have light was to make sure you always had something that didn't need batteries. Our LED flashlight was one of those. You had to shake it for a long time to build up enough kinetic energy to run the light. As soon as it started to dim, all you had to do was to shake it again, and you were off to the races. It was my favorite light because it never went out. It was always there when I needed it, and it was waterproof.

Tristan pulled out glow sticks, snapped it and hooked one to his belt loop. Isolde hooked the other one around her bikini top, so it hung down over her belly. We headed into the dark. I was in the lead. The ground was relatively smooth with a gentle slope. Then the floor evened out and, in the distance, a bluish glow rimmed the end of the tunnel.

The walls suddenly transitioned from the yellowish-white of limestone to that brilliant reflective crystalline stars from my dream. I ran my finger along the surface and it sparkled back at me in an electrifying way.

"Mom, are you seeing this?" Issy whispered she splayed her hands across the new wall material.

"Yes." I whispered in disbelief.

"It's just like the temple from the dream," Tristan added as he was trailing both hands along the walls.

"Yes, but this is a cave. Maybe we're under the temple," Issy offered.

"I don't think so," I muttered as my eyes were too wide to talk.

The tunnel ended in an arched space. The walls were smooth and round and it felt like being in a stone shaped bubble. In the center, there was a perfectly circular pool. We stood on a ledge that once circled the space, adding to the sphere effect. Over it all, there was a bluish glow.

Everything here carried the feeling of déjà vu. I had never been here, but it still carried a familiar feeling.

"Mom, I think there are writings on the other side of the room."

As I was surveying the cavern, I realized there was no way to get there except through the pool and the water looked harmless enough.

"Do you think it's a mineral bath?" Issy inquired, thrusting a cupped hand in lifting it up.

The blue of the light was as indescribable as the dreams I had for most of my life. It clung to the walls and our skin.

"I don't know what it is."

Frozen, in fascination, I watched as the cold water reached her rosebud colored lips.

"It tastes just like normal water. It doesn't seem to be anything different, but it's nice and cool." She shrugged.

Tristan stripped his shirt off and dropped all of his gear. "Well, I'm going in cuz, I'm hot. I don't know about you, but a nice cool swim in a mineral pool is just what the doctor ordered."

"Tristan you're just looking for an excuse to go swimming–" Issy trailed off as he broke the surface and shook his hair out of his face.

"Just an excuse to go swimming? Look at it, it's ideal. Issy, it's a cave with a perfect round pool on an island that's not supposed to exist. A deserted island perhaps created by ancient man. Out of my mother's dreams. It's an insane story. I'm going for a swim. I mean after all, when we leave this place what are you going to tell people? *Look, I found this really cool pool. No, I didn't go in the water.*"

He made a pause to see the reactions, but when he didn't receive any he continued, "You drank the water, so what? Let's go swimming in it. What difference does it make now?"

All I could mutter was, "What if it's not safe? What if there's something in the water?" I dropped my gear on the ledge and knelt down poised to take a drink of the water.

Tristan laughed it off, "You can see to the bottom, Mom."

Before I could muster a good retort so the augment could continue, the slapping sound of flesh meeting water filled the room and two seconds later, frigid water splashed me in the face.

Issy charged in after him. Tristan whipped his head around as he breached, throwing droplets in every direction. Swiping his face and clearing his eyes and the hair. His low mocking laugh rebounded off the walls, then he splashed more water on me.

"Come on, it's not deep! It's perfect. I can stand up." Issy came up behind him, wrapping her arms around his neck. Her hair was blond as if the red coloring had never been. Her legs locked around her brother's waist to piggyback him.

I opened my mouth to speak, but at the same time, Tristan reached out with his mind and with a little push. It was enough to throw my balance off, and I plunged headfirst into the water.

His mouth turned into a large O, just before he flashed to the other side of the pool away from me, and on to the ledge before plunging back in.

My entire body sank down into the water engulfing me. I set down on the bottom, letting the air exit my lungs. I opened my eyes and looked around. It was crystal clear. I could see Isolde and Tristan splashing and kicking the water at each other. Issy climbed up to the ledge and jumped back in to try and push Tristan down as if she was going to dunk him. Not that she could do that because he was far too strong for her. When I finally broke the surface of the water and dragged in a deep breath, it was like I hadn't breathed in my whole life. Suddenly everything was clean and clear. I felt strong and energized.

I watched Tristan break the surface of the water. His hair turned from the dyed black to blond as he squeegeed the water down the back of his head. Looking over at Isolde, I realized her eyes weren't just green anymore they were now a blue-green with the dark ring just like mine, just like Tristan's.

"Issy, your eyes," I whispered.

"What about them, Mom?" She tilted her head to the side.

"They changed… changed color," I stuttered.

"Don't be silly! Come on. Tristan?" She looked from me to Tristan. His blue eyes were the size of saucers. He didn't say a word, but he nodded back to her.

"You and Mom are pulling my leg. They already changed color once in my life. I don't think they'd do it again." The dry laugh on her lips died.

"Mom, the dye in your hair it's gone. You're blonde again. You too Issy." Tristan pointed a shaking hand at us.

"How could this water change a hair color that was a permanent dye," Issy asked, looking into the depths of the pool, but the water remained clear and clean.

"I don't know. Everybody out!" I barked and scrambled to the ledge.

I climbed out on my belly before rolling over onto my back on the crystalline floor and I looked up at the ceiling of the dome. Every fleck up there seemed to glow blue and yet I could see little lines tracing and connecting. In my mind, I imagined they are all constellations in the night sky. I suppose I had been at sea so long navigating by stars, I'd reached the state where in my mind I saw them everywhere. The chamber was like a room filled with magic or energy. The water was perfect in every way, it was brisk and yet not cold. I realized how aching my hands and shoulders were from all the stress I had been carrying around, but that was gone.

That eerie clear blue glow the room had and the vibration that went with it, energized me. The buzzing of the voices in the back of my head ceased the moment we entered the sparkly walled area from this chamber.

I found myself drifting into a dream-like state. It was like the lull between being awake and asleep, and I heard her voice in my mind.

"Come to me! You're so close. Don't stop now!"

I realized I was being shaken. Tristan jumped out and bumped into me. I didn't know how long I had laid there. It felt like I'd slept for a year and just woke up ready to go and face the world. I sat up and looked around, and the blue glow intensified in the room, or maybe my eyes had become adjusted to it. I had no idea.

"Guys, I think we should head back down the rock cliff before the sun goes down," I said looking deep into the pool. I wanted to get away from the room and hide the fact we had ever been here.

On the other side of the room, there was the infinity symbol. I glanced back around the room and realized that they were everywhere. The walls glistened with glowing blue infinities. They ringed the pool in crystalline blues and grays.

The symbol was on the archway too and even the bottom of the pool had them.

"Let's go, now!" I said.

Isolde squeezed as much water she could out of her hair and threw on her beach cover. Both kids clipped their glow sticks on. I shook up my LED light and we headed towards the exit.

There was only one way out, so Tristan and Isolde ran ahead racing each other to see who could make it to the end first. When I finally saw the light at the end of the tunnel, it was later than I had anticipated. It was twilight and the sun was going down, so I stepped up my pace. I didn't want to be traversing anything in the dark.

Tristan stopped me at the top of the rock cliff, "Do you really want to climb down in the dark?" A smile scraped across his face and he moved us all to the dingy.

The sand under my feet was a reassuring relief. I looked at Tristan and it was like seeing somebody for the first time even though you've seen them a 1000 times. He was no longer a boy, but a man, tall and strong. My boy had grown up. Isolde wasn't much different. She carried all the marking of a woman, and the attitude to go with it.

The buzzing in my head returned and in the back of my mind, it was a pressure. I couldn't hear what they were saying. It was just a presence of all those minds somehow there, but just out of reach.

Something told me that I had to hide our trip here, so I took out my beach mat and draped it behind us so it could obscure steps all the way back to our dingy. We took all of the fresh fruits that were still on the beach and not covered with ants into the boat. We loaded up and immediately shoved off heading home, to Calypso.

Sleep came quickly and almost immediately my mind shut down. I didn't remember a thing. There were no dreams, no voices, no buzzing, nothing. It had all just turned off. Upon opening my eyes, the sun was relatively high in the sky. It was too high.

How long had I slept?

CHAPTER 33

HERA

Log Entry

How do you take your children back when someone is so determined to keep you from them? Even with all my abilities, I could not take what was mine.

I didn't really realize how powerful my children were until they were taken from me. I think that's the secret. Stress causes evolution. It causes you to change and become more, to reach a level where you are no longer what you were at birth, but something more. The stress is necessary to reach the full potential in our genes. They hold a secret encoding for evolution.

Humans have the potential to become more. My children were strong and healthy but they didn't necessarily have the capability of defending themselves at first, not against Themian control. Now was a different story. The full force of Themia was at their doorstep and they were not in a position to fight, but that didn't mean they couldn't.

With every passing year, I felt the changes in myself and my children. The stress of isolation and loneliness was speeding up our evolution.

I never believed I was capable of leading anyone. But after much contemplation, I realized there was only one way to be free. We had to carve it out and take it by force of will.

I dreamwalked my children. The eight faces gazed up at me for the answers that we all desire, but mostly our freedom.

"I have a way we may free ourselves from Themia," I paused and took a breath. but none of them ventured to guess the answer I carried, so I continued. "Breeding, we must breed our way out," I stopped and waited.

Ares scratched his chin. Hebe gripped Hercules' hand and Eros turned to Perseus. However, Hephaestus was the one to reply.

"Any chance at freedom is better than a life imprisoned in a world of strangers." He hung his head to hide his eyes, he had never been one to speak out. His always had a quiet way. The noise he made came from an anvil or a hammer. He let the work speak for him. Because of this, I was surprised he'd spoken first. His words carried a truth I dare not voice. In my case, the prison was a crumbling ship ruled by a woman I thought to be my friend.

"I can provide the means to dreamwalk anyone. You must tell me who," and with that I left them to discuss the plan, returning the next night.

Eros spoke for her siblings. "We have agreed. Your plan has merit and barring one of us becoming a shifter, there is no escaping the Themian's," she glanced around at all of us and continued, "I will play my part."

They all nodded their heads in agreement and I laid out the plan. I would bring my children the Primordial waters to keep them alive. Five generations ago, all my children had children of their own. They will keep reseeding their own bloodlines. Their hybrid children were still here. With every generation, the bloodlines grew weaker. Because of that, each of my sons agreed to crossbreed with their brothers' lines. The girls all decided to merge their lines together as well. I would help them dreamwalk.

My offspring were half Themian, making their children a quarter. Their offspring, in turn, would be 1/8th Themian. All we needed was to keep the bloodlines alive long enough for the genes to become dominant. The higher a level of Themian genes, the more likely a true mating would happen. It wasn't relevant whether it was between a Themian or another hybrid. Once a true mating happened it would alter everything my people believed about Themian's and this planet.

It was true that my people might decide to leave, taking me with them home to my children. Or they might decide to eject all of the hybrids from the Themian's culture. In which case I would still be able to leave with the hybrids.

The third and final option was for them to find the hybrids so disgusting they would kill them all. This was the only outcome that scared me more than life itself. I wouldn't be able to save any of my children. The fear of it tore at my belly and it was my constant companion.

Would I relax too much so Athena could see through me? Could I properly shield all their minds? Every question raised a new one.

This was why we needed a true mating. That would inject new life into my own people. Maybe I was selfish and my plan was crazy. I didn't care. They were my offspring, my children, blood of my blood. I didn't care who the High Council was or what Athena said. They would not keep me away from my children. I would find a way. Even if I had to break every bone in my body to do it.

I was not sure how my daughters would hide their pregnancies, but that was a hurdle to chance when the time came.

Log entry

Eris had lost much of her bravado, "Mother meeting in the dreamworld can be dangerous. I heard the ability to walk dreams is rare and difficult." She was probing. Most would bristle at her, but she knew no other way to be.

"Eris, that's the sort of thing that they tell children on the Themian's homeworlds to keep them in line, so you don't dreamwalk the wrong person and interfere in Themian's business." The floating construct of our dreamwalk had a cloud-like feel. "Do not let the fear of a few mean-spirited Themians stop you. I only wish to know how you will hide your pregnancies from the High Council."

Seeing her in the dreamworld was not the same as reality. It seemed real enough, but there were little differences. A fuzz at the edges, the tone of the voice was flat or hollow and body movements floated or appeared disjointed.

"We are social outcasts here, mother, barely above notice. I might as well run around wearing a sign saying 'hello, slightly different from you but not completely!!!' You know how it is on Themia. We have been given your living quarters and those of your parents. My brothers in one, us in another. Your parents hardly notice us and your brother has still not bothered to contact us. The truth is, I'm not even sure they would notice that I hadn't left our living quarters in months," she scoffed at being ignored. After the treatment on Earth, child of the Goddess worshiped as a Goddess herself, it chafed at her very being.

"Are you showing? Do the clothes hide you?" The dreamwalk didn't always show the reality. Most appeared as they see themselves and not as you see them.

"You know the fashions here never changes. They have been the same for thousands upon thousands of years, boring and repetitive. No, I think in their minds I've just gained weight and became sloppy. I won't be leaving the apartment or the living area again until my time has come. We all decided at the end of the fourth month to become a shut-in. Other than that, I'm fine." Her hands worked lacing together and pulling apart again. The agitation blazed in her.

"Are you giving birth in a dreamwalk?" I asked and the pain of separation from a newborn child blazed back to my mind. My arms still ached for my babes and the memory of handing them over to Jorhan.

"I will go to the child's father, give birth there and leave. That is the only way, Mother. We cannot let our bloodline die out simply because we're not a man and can't leave our genetic material behind so easily. We all agreed and the choice is ours. I will miss my child but I'll be able to visit him. We can all be together even if it is generations from now. I only wish that all my children will be able to live as long as I," her lip trembled, but she bit it to keep it still. Eris was not prone to emotions and seeing the pain of her decision sliced me to the core.

"You know I cannot give the Primordium to them, no matter how much I desire to do so. It would be noticed, things like that always are. The humans would think them an abomination. They will live longer than most humans to begin with. I will not watch Athena kill another person I love." My throat closed, as my eyes welled up with tears.

I knew Zeus didn't love me, but that didn't change the fact that I loved him. However, I loved the human Zeus, not the evil thing he became.

"Do not worry, Mother, I will not force you. I would not ask you to risk exposing all of us, no matter how painful my desire is. We must stay the course," she said, putting on a brave smile while her beautiful blue eyes with the dark ring stared up at me.

For a moment she showed me what she really looked like and I ran my hand along her full belly. I could already feel the life inside of her. A bright light in an otherwise dark and dull world. She embraced me and I clung to her. The scent of motherhood lingered on her. I wanted to drink it in. She was still so innocent.

"By the way, Mother, every time I give birth, my abilities change and I look forward to it." She smiled again, her eyes taking on the mischievous look I knew so well.

"I only wish one of you was strong enough to shift you all back. Then none of this would be necessary," I whispered.

"No, Mother, it would just bring up a whole new wealth of problems, a new mountain to climb, a new hill to level. Although, I do miss the fields and the animals and the quiet of the mountain village. Everything here is so orderly and clean. No one ever seems dirty. I guess that's why you all wear white."

I kissed her on her cheek and she embraced me. Feeling the wetness of her tears, she let me go, "Go back, Mother! I will see you again soon." She did not have to tell me she loved me, but I knew that she did. I unequivocally loved her.

I was however frightened if we were to be discovered. I had to push that fear aside because it was the time to train the mind and the body.

CHAPTER 34

SYDNEY

My nostrils filled with the scent of freshly ground coffee brewing and bacon. Someone must have dug deep into the freezer to find that bacon. I heard the crackling sound of something frying in a pan combined with the scent of butter. My mouth watered to the idea of coffee and it seemed like forever since we've eaten anything not freeze-dried.

I headed to the salon bypassing the head. Tristan's wide shoulders stood at the stove, with a spatula in his big hand. Over his shoulder, he said, "Well, good morning, sleepyhead!"

Issy smiled at me and shoveled some eggs in her mouth.

"You look like you got enough sleep and you look great. Not that you didn't before now, Mom, but you were looking a little tired." Tristan's ears turned pink as he stumbled over the compliment he was trying to make. Sauvé was not Tristan's strong point.

"Thank you, Tristan. That's very nice," I smiled and patted his shoulder to reassure him.

"Wow, Tristan. That's what every woman wants to hear. You'll be some heart breaker someday," Issy said and rolled her blue-green eyes.

"Oh, Issy, don't worry. He'll find some silly girl to fall in love with him. He'll win her over with his sweet talk," I snickered.

"No really, Mom. You look great. Like–."

"Hold back on all the compliments superstar," Issy shushed him snickering.

"Well, I'm just...I'm just trying to say how great Mom looks and you guys are mocking me," Tristan huffed and shoveled an egg onto a plate before thrusting it at me with a few strips of bacon.

"Sorry, Tristan, yes, I did sleep well and thank you." I took the offered plate and sat down at the table. The sun was high up in the sky. This was the latest I'd slept since St. Croix.

"I love you and I'm sorry. I'll try and hold back," Issy giggled then rearranged her sarong.

"Thank you!" Tristan quipped.

"So, who dug into the freezer for bacon?" I asked over a bite of the gooey egg yolk.

"I hid that one," Tristan said with a sly smile and a wink.

"Really? Were you hiding it under the ice? Or did you chip out the bottom of the freezer to see what was there?" I laughed, hoping he'd done it so I wouldn't have to.

"Actually, I put ice on top of this when we got to the Marquesas. I hid it until we had something to celebrate." He flipped an egg using the pan. Then grinned in triumph.

"Are we celebrating?" I quirked an eyebrow over my coffee cup.

"Yeah, Mom, we're celebrating finding this island. Does there needs to be another reason?" Issy tossed a corner of her toast at me.

I swatted it away from me. "You will pick that up later, right?"

She smiled while chewing and nodded her head.

Eating fresh food was like heaven.

"I was thinking that today we should pull the anchor and sail around the island to see what else is here," I threw it out over a bite of bacon, then rolled my eyes into the back of my head as the delicious flavor of pork and syrup met my taste buds.

Tristan raised his hand "I vote that we stay here for a month. Right here in this spot," he smacked the table with his hand as he sat down.

Isolde swallowed her last bite of toast, "I vote that we stay here for a week and then start exploring more of the island."

"We don't have enough stores to stay anywhere for that long." With my words, Tristan's shoulders dropped. "We have enough maybe for a week, then we have to head back to the Marquises. Unless we want to live off fish and fruit otherwise, we'll run out of food," I stared past the two of them at the coconut lined beach.

Tristan replied, "Then, Mom wins. We sail around the island today and if we don't find anything, we head back to the Marquesas, stock up for a months' worth the food and then come back." He popped and extra crispy piece of break-in bacon in his mouth.

Issy set her cup down, pulled her legs up and crossed them under the table. "What if we do find something? We head back for food, get our electronics fixed and then turn around. All in favor of Tristan's idea?"

Issy and I raised our hands.

"It is unanimous, the motion is carried," Tristan gave the table a single hammer with his fist. We all giggled.

We finished breakfast, lashed everything down and turned on the windlass to pull the anchor, then we tossed a coin. Heads meant North and tails meant South of the island, heads won. It really didn't matter because the island was perfectly round and eventually, we would make it back here anyway.

The feeling of wind blowing my hair back invigorates me every time. Forty minutes later, a cape jutted out from the gentle curve of the island and I adjusted my course to motor around it. The jungle fell away and the island opened on to the vista of a city. It was right there, on the side of the mountain, as large as life and it was real.

"Oh my God!" A gasped issued from my mouth.

"Mom, are you seeing what we're seeing?" Issy demanded.

< Yes, beautiful girl. It is real. > The Voice confirmed.

"Yes, I see it," I said.

"It's the temple, Mom." Issy pulled at my arm jumping up and down and squeaking.

"Yes, it is, Issy. You didn't think it was real?" I replied, my own doubt has always been in the background.

"I didn't know what to think, Mom," she giggled nervously.

I spied a dock off to the side of the inlet. "We're heading over there to see if we can pull up and maybe meet the residence," I said.

The closer we pulled up to the dock, the more I realized it was like going back in time. Everything here seemed to be made of that white starlit material, yet it resembled marble. Certain areas resembled pink granite. The pier appeared to be black granite and yet it had that same reflective quality like it was filled with black stars. The dock didn't look like it was made of wood. There was a lining of gold like material at the water's edge, but I had no idea what kind of material it was made of. The closer we got, the more people began to swarm to the edge of the city.

Keeping my mind on maneuvering the boat was probably the hardest thing I'd ever done.

"Mom, do you see all of the buildings?" Tristan demanded.

"Yes, what about them?" I asked without looking away from the edge of the dock.

"They weren't on the map," he stated flatly.

"I know that Tristan but, what's the big deal?" I turned the helm so the bow thrusters could ease us into the place.

"Stop gawking and throw the bumper over the side for fuck sake," I knew we hadn't docked in a long time, but….

"Mom, look over there!" Tristan pointed to a narrow roadway, then threw a bumper over the side after securing it.

I looked in the pointed direction and I saw that in the center of the roadway as if you were heading straight for the Temple, was a beautiful dry fountain with the infinity symbol all around the bottom. On top of the fountain was the statue of a woman. I couldn't make out who she was, but there were fish surrounding the base of the fountain. The water should have tripped down the three tiers to splash into the shallow basin.

Dragging my eyes away, I refocused on the dock and the three people standing there. My first instinct told me to defend and protect, but I swallowed that back.

< Issy, go below and hide anything that needs to be hidden. Tristan, go get our immigration paperwork. Everybody put on shoes and put the money in your shoes. Use our standard bags and pack a weapon. > I instructed them.

The kids disappeared. I knew we only had a couple of minutes. The closer I got to the dock, the louder the buzzing became. Minds pressed in on mine. Finally, one broke through. It was her, the woman from the dream.

She said < Close your mind down. Shut us all out. Do it as quickly as possible. > Then she was gone.

The Voice whispered. < Don't stop now! You're almost here. >

I had to keep my eyes on the ball or I was going to crash this boat right into that dock and I had no idea how much give there would be.

Maneuvering my engines, we eased into the edge of the dock. Tristan threw out the bow rope and one of the islands residents grabbed it.

Now for the big moment of truth.

I hadn't thought about the fact that we were all still in swimsuits and t-shirts. I didn't even have my shoes on. Issy handed me a bag with my shoes and our immigration documents. I was grateful.

I turned the boat off and thrust the engine key into my bag. The man standing on the dock looked vaguely familiar, but I couldn't quite place him. He had salt and pepper black hair and chocolate brown eyes, the kind of eyes that beat into you, ripping you apart thread by thread. His smile was similar to a predator. I almost expected his teeth to be sharp like an animal's. He gave me the creeps and my skin crawled as my hair stood on end, but I shook my head to try and throw off the feelings.

A vision slammed into my mind, it was of us and it was disgusting.

Why can't people just keep their thoughts to themselves, for God's sake?

Isolde grabbed my hand. I didn't have to tell Isolde not to touch anyone here, nor did I need to tell Tristan not to let anybody touch her. I had the feeling if that happen, it would go very badly for all of us.

The man introduced himself, with a smarmy smile and an extended hand.

"My name is Travis." His toothy smile irritated me.

"Good morning," I replied without thinking or taking his hand.

"Sorry, here it's afternoon. Your time clock must be off." His smile never wavered.

"Oh, okay, thank you. Tuff to keep your time zones correct sometimes when you're at sea," I remarked.

"Don't worry about it. We don't get many travelers. We're always happy to see new faces." He stepped back and motioned for us to get off the boat.

Travis did not introduce his fellow cohorts. I thought that was strange. All the women lingered back. None of them was the least bit interested in speaking to us. Many of the people moved out of the way. But they all appeared to be completely normal. There were young and old, male and female, all healthy. No one was least bit infirm and they all had perfect teeth.

Travis led me to a 5-story building made out of the same white shimmering materials. The moment we entered the building, the buzzing in the back of my head died. I couldn't hear the kids either.

We walked down several corridors, twisting and winding.

Are we lost yet?

Finally, we entered one of the lower offices. We followed him into the cubical area and a back office with one window in the room. I arrange myself spatially.

"Well, you made it here. We don't get a lot of visitors," he repeated.

"Yes, I don't even know we're 'here' is. We got lost in a storm and lost all our electronics. We were heading towards the Marquesas, but I think we might have gotten turned around. What island is this?" I tried to sound interested, but unconcerned.

His deep chuckle rippled over me. The eerie feeling from before filled me again. He walked like a man in power and liked it too much.

"This island has gone by many names in the past, but none of which really matter. You can call it Paradise." He smiled and waved at a seat.

That's a stupid answer.

"Can you tell me where we are? I mean what country is this?"

Dipshit.

"The island isn't affiliated with any countries."

The first words came out of Tristan's mouth. "That's not possible. Everybody's affiliated with some country. Whether it be their own or another."

"We're not. People here don't call themselves anything. We're just people," he said.

The nagging in the back of my mind about him wouldn't let go. I'd seen him somewhere before but couldn't put my finger on it.

"You look familiar. Do I know you?" I inquired.

"Yes, I was waiting to see if you would recognize me." Travis smiled but didn't answer the question. This pattern of unanswered questions grated on me.

"Who are you?" I demanded.

"The great Sydney O'Dear doesn't recognize me? Well, I recognized your face. I was one of Tobias' friends. Travis, Travis Helmsly?" he supplied with a wide grin.

Relief washed over me. Travis was a weaselly little fuck, but a harmless one. However, it did explain the red-line on the creep-o-meter.

"How did you end up in the South Pacific on an island with a stupid name?" I threw out casually.

"My family and I went on a cruise. One of those private charters out of Tahiti. There was a big storm and my wife and I got washed overboard, but my kids didn't. They had their lifelines and jackets on and they were down below. We got washed overboard and the two of us ended up here."

The idea of being separated from my kids like that terrified me.

"Why don't you leave and go back to your kids?" I asked fingering the arm rest of a chair.

I looked down at Issy who'd sat in the offered chair, but I preferred to stand.

"That's a little difficult. Why don't we catch up later? Right now, we need to go through the immigration process. Okay? I need to see all your documents and we need to take a blood sample." His smile was locked in place.

Ugh!

"What are you taking a blood sample for?" I demanded staring at his frozen smile.

"We run a few tests to make sure that you don't have any diseases," he replied.

"We don't have any diseases," I replied with a fake smile of my own.

"Are your vaccinations up to date?" he shot back.

"No." I crossed my arms. This was going downhill fast and my belly fluttered with coiled power.

"Okay, so we just need to test to see if you're carrying anything." He was trying to comfort me, so I would comply.

I looked at Tristan and his eyes reflected my own thoughts. I didn't trust Travis but it sounded like we didn't have much of a choice. If I wanted to find out more about this place, we had to be willing to give up some blood. I had a sneaking suspicion there was more to this place than meets the eye, but suspicion wasn't enough.

Nothing that Travis had said allayed my fears. I had to play along. Travis reached across the desk and pricked our fingers one drop per container.

"Is that really enough blood?" I asked and took in the unusual shape of the container. It was a teardrop.

"We only need one drop," he said with the cement locked smile on his face as I watched a drop of my blood was sliding down into the small plastic vial. He placed the vials in a small box and slipped it into what appeared to be an old fashion mail shoot. I watched the vacuum of the shoot suck the samples away.

"If you go to the hospital anywhere else, they want like several CC's. What can you learn from one drop?" Issy asked while fidgeting in her seat.

His reply came instantly. "Everything. I can learn anything I want, from one drop. How many vaccines you've had, if you're low on vitamin C."

"Are you a scientist?" Tristan jumped in.

"No, but we have scientist working here." Travis should have worked for the CIA with the amount of information he didn't give.

His simplistic answers bothered me.

"Is this a research facility?" Tristan continued while staying close to one of the two doors in the room.

"You could say that." His obfuscation was annoying. I needed to find someone else, because I wasn't going to get anywhere with Travis.

"Now that we have that out of the way, all of your immigration paperwork seems to be in order. There are some forms to fill out. If your kids want, they can go and investigate the resort. Lots of stuff to do here. They can go to swimming pools or meet other kids." He sat on the edge of his desk keeping one leg on the floor and the other one hiked up. In a casual fashion.

"Resort? If this is an island with no name, how can it have a resort?" Issy asked and quirked an eyebrow at him.

"We don't really refer to the welcoming center as the municipality building. It's kind of a resort. You can stay there. It's temporary housing but a lot of people come here and they socialize. There are restaurants and bars and it's just a place where you can have a good time." His pearly whites flashed with every word.

I looked at Tristan and Isolde, nodding to them. "You guys know how to behave correctly?"

"Yes, Mom," they chimed.

"Don't be crazy and don't go anywhere alone. Stick together as much as possible," I gave them my old orders.

Isolde smirked. "Well, I'll do my best to keep my eyes on Tristan. I'm sure he's going to find some girl to talk to."

Tristan elbowed her. "What about you? Boys always flocked you," he returned, then his eyes searched my face.

"I have no interest in boys anymore, Tristan. I'm just here to babysit you." She growled.

Travis handed them both bracelets. they had several shells on them and small white shimmery beads.

"What are these?" I asked.

"They're bracelets, but they also allow you to get food, drinks, and entrance for two different parts of the island."

"We can pay for our own food and drinks, but thank you," I replied crossing my arms.

"You don't understand. Mainland money doesn't work here. Your credit card won't work here either." Travis supplied with his plastic smile.

Great! Creepy island with their own monetary system.

"Oh, okay. How do we pay it back?"

"Don't worry. It's not a big deal. Money or credit is really just an idea. I'll explain everything later." Travis continued.

As if I needed a bureaucrat to explain the concept of a fiat monetary system to me. However, Tristan and Isolde put the bracelets on and Tristan immediately checked to see if he could take it off, which he could, so he put his in his pocket.

"You're supposed to wear it. People need to see it." Travis raised his eyebrows.

"Why? If this is to pay for food, supplies or whatever, then why do I need to wear it? What is it, to let them know I'm new? I'm pretty sure everybody on the island knows everybody else. They will be able to tell we aren't from around here." Tristan retorted without pulling the bracelet from his pocket.

Well, Tristan certainly pointed out the obvious. However, Travis' smile plastered back into place and he simply said, "You need to wear the bracelet."

"You said I only need it to pay for things and for the entrance to different parts of the island. I don't need to wear it. I just need to present it when I'm at a store. It's in my pocket. If it uses scanning technology, then I should be able to scan me whether it's on my wrist or in my pocket." Tristan was purposely pushing Travis's buttons and Travis's patience was beginning to crack.

I looked over at Tristan. < Stop giving poor Travis a hard time. Just put the bracelet on. >

Tristan smiled sticky sweet out loud, "Yes, Mom!", but then he looked away and added without speaking:

< As soon as I leave this room, I'm taking it off. >

< *I know. All we need is the appearance of compliance.* > I replied.

Isolde stepped in the mental conversation. < He's always causing trouble. >

< Oh, yes. I'm the big trouble maker. > Tristan couldn't have his sister have the final word.

Both of them smiled as if nothing had happened and said they would probably be at whatever the largest pool was. I watched the door slip shut and the mental murmur of my children ended with it.

"I waited a long time to talk to one of you O'Dear's again. How's your brother Tobias?" Travis asked and stood up.

"Tobias is good. He's married and has two kids. He seemed pretty happy the last time I spoke to him." My answer was quick and to the point.

"Yeah. What's he doing for a living these days?" I didn't want the small talk and had never had time for Travis even as a teen.

"He's working construction. He likes working with his hands and wood."

"Yeah, Tobias always did like working with his hands." As the conversation progressed, I noticed that Travis had taken several steps closer to me. I casually moved back a step towards the door. He was now practically standing over to me.

"So, Sydney, I see you're wearing a ring. Are you married?" He licked his lips.

"No. My husband died 2 years ago." My weirdo meter was beginning to rise.

"That's so sad" He looked down my body, then slowly traveled back up to meet my eyes.

"Yes, it seems like yesterday. I think about him all the time," I remarked.

His move was lightning fast and his hands latched around my wrist slamming them against the wall. He pushed himself against me with his breath in my face. His nostrils flared as he inhaled my scent and his bad breath mixed with spearmint overwhelmed my oratory factors.

I was staring into his beady brown eyes when he said, "Do you know how long I've waited to get you somewhere where your brother wasn't around? He was always guarding you, scaring everyone away, threatening to beat them up. Everybody wanted you." He smiled.

He licked the side of my face. Panic rose in my belly but the earth movement that usually came with it didn't. I tried to pull the air to me, but the air around us remained stagnate.

"Don't be ridiculous. Nobody was interested in me," I muttered and turned my face to the side to gauge my distance from the door.

"No, they were not really interested in you. They were interested in something else that you have," he said looking at me like a rabid animal.

He pulled my arms down to my sides, then lashed his arms around me. Both of his hands were planted on either side of my ass, squeezing and pulling me towards his pelvis. I could feel his erection through his pants.

I squirmed to get away, "Let me go!"

Focusing on just what was in the room, I attempted to move a chair into his back, but it only inched forward.

"Don't be ridiculous! I'm going to finally get what I've been looking for." He locked his lips over mine with his tongue pushing to enter my mouth. He stopped to then nibble on my neck.

"No, Travis, you're not. You will be sorry." Bile rose up my neck poisoning my throat. I wanted to push him away, but with my hands trapped I couldn't.

"Why? What's little Sydney going to do? Always scared, always in the shadows, always letting your brother fight your battles for you." He mocked with every bite.

"Travis, the girl you're thinking of died many years ago. She doesn't exist anymore, so stop living in the past. You've clearly been on this island too long. What about your wife? Travis, don't you care about what your wife thinks?" I was playing for time. I tried again to move the chair in the room, but couldn't.

"I couldn't care less about what my wife thinks. My wife is boring. I only married her because she was pregnant. After living on this island, seeing her face every day for the last 10 years and being forced to live with her and only her, I'd do anything to see a fresh piece of ass next to me in bed, sucking my cock."

Ugh!

"You're disgusting. That will never happen. You're dreaming." I hissed.

The chair near us inched again. Adrenaline raced through my body, energizing my muscles.

"Oh, I've been dreaming about you, doing all of those things, for a long time. What do you think kept me going through high school and made me want to be Tobias' friend even though he was an asshole?" Travis smiled.

My stomach clenched. He was bigger than me. My eyes darted left and right.

Breath dumb ass! If he sees you looking desperate, he'll win. Work the problem. Talk, keep him talking, buy time as much as you can!

"Tobias is a lot of things, an asshole maybe one of them, but he never really thought you were one of his good friends. He knew you were good-time Charlie," I retorted, pulling at the edges in my mind. Moving my body as much as possible, I was trying to free my arms.

< Voice, if you are fucking here, I need help! > I screamed in my head.

His forehead crashed into mine and pain exploded over my eyes, shooting into my brain. Stars entered my line of vision. My head rolled to the side as I slipped to the floor. I couldn't move as the pain crashed through me.

As soon as my body laid down, he was on top of me, pawing at me, groping and ripping my shirt. I heard the popping sound of buttons as they flew off the fabric ricocheting off the office furniture. He tugged at my shorts and a renting sound filled my ears. His grubby hand reached down into my pantie and touched me.

My eyes opened and shut several times attempting to shake away the fog in my mind. All I could think was to cry out to the Voice.

< Make him stop! Get him off of me! > I screamed.

He had my arms pinned to my side. But my legs were free. I tried moving things with force, but I couldn't focus enough to do anything. The stapler flew off the desk and hit him in the back, he flinched but didn't stop.

Think! What else was on that desk?

I closed my eyes. There wasn't a computer. A few papers and paper clips, but none of them big or strong enough to do anything. I imagined stopping him with a pencil, but I couldn't focus enough to control it.

Wiggle, what had the self-defense instructor said?

'Keep moving anything you can. Even if it was just your mind. Movement is life, it's the only way you will survive anything.'

I was good at survival and running. It was all I knew how to do.

His face moved closer. His eyes closed as his lips puckered up to plant a kiss on my lips. I turned my head to the side as his slimy lips made contact with my cheek. He slid to the side and it threw his body to the side enough for me to manage to free one of my arms. The space was too tight to get a good pull back, but I managed to punch him.

However, it didn't faze him. He shook his head. It shocked him enough to leverage my body to one side forcing him off me.

I kept the momentum going and rolled over to my side facing the wall. My shoulder hit the wall bringing me to a stop. I was desperate to de-tangle an elbow from underneath me. I needed to get up.

Get up, Sydney! Get up, for fuck sake!

I grabbed the door handle pulling with my right hand and pressing down with my left arm to get up off the floor. I levered a knee under me and stood up.

Surveying the room, my mind mapped every item on every surface. They finally answered to me and rose into the air. His hand flashed out and lock around my ankle. I lifted my other foot, then smashed it down on his hand to release me.

"You fucking bitch!" he yelled.

His grip was like iron. There was no way he was going to let me get away from him. He took to his feet and gripped my arm as he pulled himself up and pulling me off balance. In one move he was standing next to me. I kicked my foot to the side of his knee to drop him. I missed as he dipped. He just laughed at me and whipped my body around to face the wall.

"That one never works on me, you stupid bitch." He growled.

I willed the office equipment at him. At the same time, he pressed his body to mine. I could feel his breath on the back of my neck as he laughed to himself and push me down onto the floor. Everything on the desk hit him at once.

"What the hell is that?"

I rolled over to get up, again, but he was on me before I could go anywhere. He pinned my arms down to the floor with the weight of his body. I began wiggling my hips back and forth, kicking him as best I could with my legs. Something in me snapped.

This isn't how I'm going out.

I heard the sound of the door being bashed.

"You think it'll be that easy to get away from me? The only reason why I didn't bother you before was because of your brother. Nothings stopping me this time. He's not getting in my way. No one even knows you're here." His heavy breath filled my nostrils again.

"That's not true. I know everyone saw my boat pulling in." I retort.

"They don't know who you are and they don't care. All they know is that another straggler wandered in from the ocean lost, looking for a place to stay."

I could hear both the children yelling in my mind and outside the door, desperate to get in, their hands beating against the surface.

He laughed. "They'll never get through that door. You've no idea what this place is made of. It's never going to break." He pulled at the fabric of my swimsuit and the sound of seams popping followed.

I was struggling and desperate to get out from underneath him. He had me pinned and I was incapable of causing enough damage to get away.

The air pressure in the room changed and my head pressed to the inside of my skull painfully. I felt the weight of his body lifted. With the sudden release, I took a deep breath and jumped up, heading towards the closest door.

The sound of meat slamming against a wall filled my ears, as I desperately pulled at the door handle. It wouldn't open. I turned it left and right all the while putting every ounce of my weight behind it. I heard a groan and then a body hitting the floor behind me.

Just as quickly, two hands locked around my arms. They slid around me locking my back against the broad chest. I couldn't break out of the two arms. I lifted my feet off the ground, but he lurched forward slightly before leaning back to compensate. It was just enough, so I planted my feet against the wall and pushed with all my might. The feeling of free fall filled my belly.

The air in the room changed squeezing me and pressing into my ears as everything went black. We reappeared in the room. The new arms were still locked around me and blues eyes dominated the face that filled my vision.

The Voice filled my mind

< Stop fighting me! >

The familiar smile curved his lips and I froze.

"It can't be... You're dead!" My voice was barely a whisper over my heavy breathing. My head was tilted back and I was staring into the clear blue eyes. His blond hair fell over his eyes. Unconsciously I smiled and stilled my squirming.

CHAPTER 35

HERA

Log entry Earth 1954 AD

It happened. I should have known it would be the girls' line that would do it. They were always methodical. A set of twins have been born. They both received the gene but the daughter is stronger than her brother. I walked through their minds. There is something wrong with the boy, but I can't quite put my finger on it, but somehow, he's broken inside.

Log entry Earth 1970 AD

The girl, Mary, she started talking to someone and it's not her brother. However, I can only hear her side of the conversation. Whoever it is she's talking to, has heavily shielded themselves. She doesn't have a name to reveal. The other person hasn't told her who he is or where he is.

Her brother knows she's talking to someone. He's jealous, irrational and angry. He feels that it's a betrayal of their relationship that she can communicate with someone other than just him. She's frightened, her brother scares her. He hasn't physically lashed out at her, yet.

I can see that he has it barely under control. Under the surface, he is a rolling boiling mass of putrid rot. I tried to nudge him in the right direction to fix what's broken in his mind. The only cure may be Primordium, but after my experience with the Zeus, I worry that could just send him over the edge. He may not have enough of the gene to maintain himself and it might just amplify all of the broken parts of him.

Athena ruled a long time ago - no Primordium was allowed for humans. The Universe could not have another Zeus. I shudder to think what would have happened if he had been a shifter and had access to a space vehicle.

Log entry Earth 1972 AD

Edward is insane. There is no way to stop him. If I could shift out to her, I would. I can't dreamwalk her. She's clearly become mated to someone, but whoever that is, is blocking her. I can tiptoe through her mind but that is it.

Mary finally admitted to Edward that she was communicating with someone else. He flew into a rage, breaking her nose and arm. When he finally got control of himself and took her to the hospital where she lied for him and said she fell down the stairs, which was ridiculous, because their house is a one-story.

He had her committed. If it's up to Edward, he'll never let her out of that facility. Edward has power of attorney and Mary has been declared mentally incapable. There is a doctor at this hospital that agrees with Edward. Not because he thinks Mary's insane, because he doesn't. He thinks she's fascinating. He's infatuated with her. He sees it as an excuse to keep her to woo her.

I should have dream-walked Edward. I should have given him the Primordium. I should have changed him.

Mary accepts her fate. She didn't even cry, almost as if she was expecting it. Most of her mind is locked from me. There's a great deal in there she's hiding.

*****

Edward married his high school sweetheart right away. Mary told him to. I don't understand the dynamic between the two of them. He's physically dominant, angry and controlling, yet at the mere suggestion he hops to do whatever it is she tells him. Mary didn't suggest that he get married, she told him he needed to marry Carol. Her choice of words has me baffled and intrigued. Why would she need him to marry someone?

Log entry Earth 1972.6 AD

There's need and then there's need. Somehow Mary knew Carol was pregnant, five months along. Edward must be the thickest man on planet Earth. How could your girlfriend be 5 months pregnant and you not notice? She gave birth to a baby boy and they named him Tobias. Edward has not shown any violent tendencies to his wife or child. His irrational jealousy and violent behavior are only directed at his sister.

Log entry Earth 1974 AD

Mary has the ability to either shift or unlock doors. The staff keeps finding her in the garden when she should have been locked in. They remove her from the gardens and put her back in her room but the doctor is so baffled he wants to put her on 24-hour watch.

*****

Mary got out again last night and no one is sure how she did it. The orderly swears she was in her room awake the whole time. Dr. Rappaport flipped a lid and put her in a padded room with a straight jacket. He also drugged her. It took almost three days to come out of the stupor.

Dr. Rappaport is an evil man. He left her in restraints for almost 45 days. In solitary confinement, the only time she saw someone was when they came in to force-feed her or clean feces off her body.

She only saw one of the female orderlies, but that's not what I find the most intriguing. After 45 days of having contact only with women, being restrained in a locked room, somehow, she became pregnant.

Dr. Rappaport demanded that she tell him who impregnated her and she simply smiled at him and with her calm demeanor and told him, he could "go to hell."

The entire time that she's been in this facility, her brother has only visited her once.

Log entry Earth 1975 AD

I thought for sure Mary would have twins. Fewer and fewer of the bloodlines are having twins these days and not all twins are carriers of the gene. Some of the carriers are individual births, but I felt sure Mary would give birth to twins. She had a baby girl named Sydney. Her brother came and took possession of the child immediately. Mary did not exhibit the emotion I would have expected from a new mother relinquishing her child.

Her reply chilled me. "Do what you must."

Hera

~ 475 ~

Killing Gods III

https://amzn.to/36c3DdO

If you've enjoyed what you've read here please give it a little

love and leave a review or feel free to follow me on Amazon

Or send me an email slmason1889@gmail.com or follow me

on Instagram @s.l.mason_author

For the most up to date information on the Killing Gods

Universe or These Hallowed Hills visit:

Quickquillpublishing.com